ROSE CITY RENEGADE

DL Barbur

ISBN:9781983210341

Thanks to:

Dr. Mindy, for explaining what happens when somebody gets shot, and how to chill somebody out with Ativan.

Dan, for being the guy who actually ran down the tunnel in real life.

Indy, for the awesome beta-read.

CHAPTER ONE

I was trying to figure out what it would take to get two gangsters to pick a fight with me.

They were parked on the street. The black BMW stuck out in this neighborhood full of minivans and pickup trucks. I didn't think they were trying to be subtle. Two guys sitting in a car for hours, blatantly watching a house, was a great way to attract attention, regardless of the type of car.

We were in a lower middle-class neighborhood in suburban Vancouver, Washington, right across the river from Portland, Oregon. The house was an older two-story, set well back from the street. It looked like all the other houses on the block until you noticed the security cameras on the porch, and even that wasn't too unusual these days. The place was a safe house for New Hope International, a group that provided shelter for people who had been victims of human trafficking. Most of them were girls and young women, but there were plenty of boys too. The group had been started by a woman named Linda. In her twenties and thirties, Linda had made millions at a software company, then in her forties put her fortune to work helping victims of human trafficking.

Six months ago, I'd rescued some young women from a trafficking ring. In the process, I'd lost my job as a police detective, and damn near my life. They'd needed a place to stay, and that's when I found Linda. She took the survivors, and I helped her out whenever I could. Linda had a very short list of people who dealt with the survivors directly, and they were all women. I helped out with light carpentry and maintenance at the various safe houses. She kept my company, Dent Miller Security And Investigations, on retainer. I hated to bill her, she did such good work. When she spotted the BMW she called me right away.

I parked a couple of blocks away and walked past them on foot. They were both big guys, blond with short hair and dark clothes. Their clothes and their bone structures made me think they were from Eastern Europe.

As I walked past, I looked them both in the eye, hard. The guy behind the wheel was younger, maybe his early twenties. He visibly bristled, unconsciously puffing himself up a little. The guy on the passenger side just looked at me placidly, with heavy-lidded eyes that put me in mind of a snake.

I listened for the sound of a door opening as I kept walking down the street. I was a big guy, 6'3", and very proudly down to 230 pounds with my new exercise regimen, but the kid behind the driver's seat looked like he would be willing to have a go at me. In some ways that would have made things easier.

Nobody got out, but they didn't leave either.

"Did you get the plate?" I said under my breath.

I wasn't just talking to myself. I had one of those phone headsets I hated so much stuck in my ear. I was also wearing a wireless camera clipped to the lapel of my jacket.

"Got it, Dent," Casey said in my ear. After the events of six months ago, she was one of my few remaining friends, not that I'd had that many to start with. She'd been a computer forensics and security consultant for the Portland Police Bureau. I'd rescued her from the back of a van before she could be loaded on an airplane and tossed out over the Pacific Ocean. These days we were strictly platonic roommates and business partners.

"I'm running it now," Casey continued. "I got some good frames of their faces too. In a few more minutes, it's going to be too dark for that camera to be much good. It's too small to have much night vision capability."

I'd memorized the plate number, just in case, a habit as natural as breathing for somebody who'd been a cop as long as I had. As I walked back to my SUV, I thought about what I'd seen.

During my brief walk, I'd learned a couple of things about the guys in the car. Human trafficking victims in the Portland metro area were pretty evenly split between people who had been born in the US, and people born in other countries. Most of the latter came from Eastern Europe, Asia, and Central America. I was reasonably sure the guys in the BMW were from Eastern Europe, and I was absolutely convinced they weren't professional operatives.

The trafficking ring I'd broken up last fall had been run by rogue American intelligence contractors. They were professionals. They would have never staked out a house in plain view, in a car that didn't fit the neighborhood. And if an obviously switched on guy walked by and gave them the stink eye, they would have calmly started up their vehicle and driven away.

Nope. These guys were thugs. They probably worked for one of the many Eastern European organized crime outfits that had been setting up shop in the Pacific Northwest since 9/11, when we started ignoring everything but Middle Eastern terrorists. When I'd been in law enforcement, the European gangs had been incredibly opaque to us. We had zero informants on the inside, and very little insight into how they worked.

In some ways, I was relieved. Last fall's adventures had ended with my best friend dead, me injured and unemployed, and lots of unfinished business left hanging. I'd been looking over my shoulder for six months, waiting for my enemies to make a play for me. Every day that it didn't happen, my paranoia grew a little stronger.

I was carrying a hot little ball of anger in my belly, and every day that got a little bigger. I'd been a good cop. I'd worked long hours, never had a family, and had damn near died on a couple of occasions, all in the name of protecting innocent people. All that had been taken from me.

I knew the guys in the BMW likely didn't have anything to do with the events of six months ago, but they still represented something I had hated since my first fight in grade school: people with power that bullied and abused those weaker and smaller than them.

I stopped at the front and rear bumpers of my SUV so I could pop the license plates off. They were held on by powerful rare earth magnets. They held the plates on but made it quick to take them off if I wanted.

I knew what I was about to do was probably stupid, but I didn't particularly care.

"The car is registered to a car lot on 82nd Avenue in Portland," Casey's voice said in my ear. "The lot is owned by a guy named Zakarova? Sounds Russian to me. Maybe Ukrainian? I'll do some checking. I'm still running the faces through recognition software."

"That's awesome, Case. Thanks," I said as I slid behind the wheel. I disconnected the wireless camera from my lapel and put it in the glove compartment.

"Hey. I just lost the video feed. Everything ok?"

"I turned it off," I said as I started the SUV.

"You want to let me in on the plan here, Dent?" Casey was starting to sound a little irritated.

"I'm going to go have a little chat with them," I said, and killed the connection. I put the phone and the headset in the passenger seat. I didn't want the audio of what was about to happen to broadcast over a cell phone line. I'd learned to be very paranoid about cell phones these last few months.

I drove the couple blocks pretty much on auto-pilot, not really thinking about much. The BMW was still there.

It was late spring and the sunset later every day. Right now it was taking a brilliant red plunge into the west, right into the eyes of the two guys in the BMW. Poor planning on their part. Maybe it would work to my advantage.

I slowed down and pulled way over to the right as I passed the BMW, leaving only a fraction of an inch between my passenger side mirror and the side of their car. Then I cut over in front of them, rolled forward until I was parallel to the curb, and backed up, so close you could have maybe fit a sheet of paper between the two bumpers, but maybe not. I thought about actually bumping into them, just to spice things up a little bit, but I didn't want any paint transfer from their car to mine.

I threw the SUV into park and was out of it before it even rocked back into a complete stop. As I got out I slid two items out of my pockets. Neither of them was a gun. I hoped I wasn't about to regret that. I left the SUV running and the door open.

There was a reason I'd parked so close, other than to violate the unconscious space bubble that men tended to project around their cars. To run me over, the driver would have to back up quite a ways, leaving me more time to react. I didn't need to worry though, the engine wasn't even running. Amateurs.

I trotted forward, stopped just before the crease where the driver's door met the front fender. I could see everyone's hands this way. I gave the younger guy a hard look through the windshield and he couldn't get the window down fast enough. The smell of harsh tobacco and the sound of some kind of Euro-pop music wafted out.

"Get the fuck away from my car," he said. English was clearly his second language. He sounded like the villain from a bad 80's action movie. Apparently, Casey had been right.

"You need to leave the girls alone."

He smirked. "The girls are our property. We will take back what is ours."

Well, that confirmed my guess that they weren't in the neighborhood looking at real estate.

"Your property?" I jerked my chin at the older guy in the passenger seat. "Are you his property? Does he pay you to suck his dick, or do you do it for free?"

I was standing far enough forward that the door didn't quite smack me in the knees when he flung it open. I was in the pocket of space forward of the door, so he had to get out, step around the door, and then step back in towards me. He was yelling in some other language as he came. I guessed he wasn't saying nice things.

Behind my right thigh, I was holding an 8" flat sap. It was made of a piece of spring steel and a lead weight, all covered with four layers of leather. I'd bought two, one to practice with, and one to carry. I liked to burn off steam in the garage by cracking two by four pieces of lumber with the practice sap.

He came at me and I stepped a little to his left, and brought the sap up and round, pivoting my hips and driving with my knees and ankles. It connected right with a dull sounding crack, above his jawline, just below his cheekbone. He dropped instantly. Fat droplets of blood hit the side window of the open car door and I saw a tooth fragment ping off the windshield.

I was curious about what the other guy would do. He could get out and run, slide over into the driver's seat, pull out a gun and shoot me, or join in the fist fight. I thought the gun was a low probability choice. Most of these guys didn't pack iron except when they were out hunting somebody.

He opened the passenger door and was pulling himself out of the low slung little car when I turned to meet his gaze. He snarled something to me in a language I didn't understand.

I brought up my left hand. I was holding a small, but powerful flashlight. You could get on the internet and read all about lumens, candelas, color spectrum, and battery discharge rates, but what I really understood was the thing was ridiculously bright. I'd shined it into the bathroom mirror once, and had a big purple blotch in my vision for an hour like I'd looked at the sun.

I mashed down the button with my thumb and managed to get him right in the eyes.

"Gah!" he said and flung his left arm up to cover his face. Perfect. Now I could see both hands. His left was over his face and the right was hanging onto the door frame. If there was a gun in play, it was either still tucked away on his body, or in the car.

The first guy was on the ground making snoring, gasping noises. I jumped up on the hood of the BMW, hopefully denting the hell out of it, and ran across it. I dropped down in the grass on the other side and brought the thin edge of the sap down on the older guy's right hand, smashing it between the sap and the door frame. He gave a surprisingly high-pitched yelp, then I backhanded him with the sap where his neck met his shoulder and he dropped onto all fours in the space between the open car door and the car.

Now it was my turn to run around an open car door, only I pushed on it, trying to slam it shut with the guy in between. He gave a grunt.

He was down on both knees and his left hand. His right was a bloody, gnarled mess. I soccer kicked him square in the ass, driving his head forward into the door. That seemed to stun him for a second, so I took a pause to pocket the flashlight and sap, then looked around. The street was quiet. Like most American neighborhoods, everybody was inside, probably looking at one screen or another.

The guy was making sputtering sounds. His hand was surprisingly deformed. I looked at the shifter in the car. Good. It was an automatic. It would be good if one of them could drive the car away. I kicked him in the ass again, maybe this time getting a little bit of his testicles. He retched and a little vomit hit the pavement in front of him.

I stepped on the back of his leg, right above his heel, with my weight on his Achilles tendon.

"Hold still or you'll walk funny for life," I said. I wasn't exaggerating. 230 pounds coming down on that spot could do some things even a skilled orthopedic surgeon couldn't fix.

"You are a dead man," he said through clenched teeth. This guy was my age, mid-forties, maybe a little younger. The gangster lifestyle tended to age people. He was smart enough to know that if I planned to kill him, I would have done it already, so for the moment he was compliant. The younger guy would have kept fighting, which was why I'd knocked him out first.

"Stay away from the girls," I said.

He spat out some bile. "They are whores. I will turn you into a whore. You will beg me to kill you." He sounded like an 80's movie villain's older brother. They were quite a pair.

The conversation didn't seem to be going anywhere. I let off the pressure on his ankle, then teed off again with another soccer kick. There was a rule of thumb in fighting that said you should never do the same thing more than twice in a row, but this really didn't count as a fight. This time I made sure to angle my foot a little and blast him good in the balls. He gave a moan and collapsed.

I thought about slamming the door on him again as I walked away, but like I said, one of them needed to be able to drive.

I got behind the wheel of my SUV and drove away. It used to be after a fight, I'd feel shaky and a little wired from the adrenaline dump. Now, I didn't feel anything. I would have bet good money I had a normal pulse rate. I wasn't sure what that meant.

After a few random turns, I got on a major arterial road, keeping my eyes open for cops. I thought about what I needed to do. I'd probably left a good sized boot print on the hood of the BMW, so my boots were destined for the dumpster. I didn't think there was any blood on me, but my jeans and my shirt were dark colored, so it would probably be safest to ditch them too.

It occurred to me, not for the first time, that I'd gotten quite good at covering up my crimes.

I pulled over to dial Linda's number. I hadn't thought to replace the phone headset and it was illegal to drive and dial a cell phone in Oregon and Washington now.

"Hello, Dent," Linda answered. "That wasn't much of a fair fight. There were only two of them."

Shit.

"You saw that? Did your cameras record it?" I was instantly on guard.

"I watched out the window. The cameras didn't see it, and if they had, they would have had a memory malfunction just after."

I was relieved. I trusted Linda not to lie to me. I realized we were talking on unsecured cell phones, so I changed the nature of the conversation quickly.

"I told the two uhhhh... vacuum cleaner salesmen that you had hardwood floors, and not to come back, but they are pretty persistent and will probably come to see you again."

"Yes!" she said, apparently realizing we shouldn't be too specific about what she'd just witnessed over the phone. "I'm going to move anyway, to a safer neighborhood."

"That's a good idea," I said, glad she was catching on. "Let me know if you need any help, uh, moving the furniture, or you know, with more salesmen."

"I'll do that. Thank you, Dent. You're a good man."

With that, she hung up. I was thinking about how she'd called me a good man when, I saw the spot of blood, about the size of a quarter, on the knee of my jeans.

CHAPTER TWO

The next day I subjected myself to a couple of different forms of torture. I woke up, forced myself into a pair of sneakers, and ran. Even while jogging, I was armed. I slid a little compact 9mm into a Hill People Gear Runner's Kit Bag before setting out. The little bag kept the gun accessible on my chest, where I didn't have to worry about it falling out or pulling my pants down.

I was probably most vulnerable during my morning run. It would be a simple matter for somebody to pull up in a car, or even on a motorcycle, and shoot me. For that matter, they could just get a big truck and run me over. But I ran anyway. The constant, grinding paranoia was getting to me. I was tired of waiting for the attack that never came. Making myself vulnerable was my way of defiantly giving a metaphorical middle finger to my circumstances. You want me? Here I am. Come try me.

During last year's unpleasantness, my old house had been burned to the ground, courtesy of a firebomb. After the remains had been carted away, I sold the empty lot to a nice couple who had just gotten married. Steve was an architect and Rick was a construction contractor, so they were excited at the possibility of building their own home. I was excited to pocket their check, along with my insurance settlement and get rid of a bad memory.

My new neighborhood was one of the last vestiges of what I considered "Old Portland." It was solidly working class, something that was going away in Portland, as housing prices rose and working families fled to the suburbs. Compared to my old neighborhood, which was rapidly gentrifying, the cars were older and had fewer bumper stickers. There were more than a few work trucks with ladders and tool boxes attached. I liked it.

Every week, I found that I had to do one more lap around the neighborhood before the burn really kicked in. I'd gotten out of shape and complacent working as a detective. I spent too much time sitting at a desk, writing reports, or sitting in a car, drinking cold coffee and surveilling a suspect. In the last six months, I shed fat and gained muscle. The last time I'd been this fit, I was a 21-year-old Army Ranger. There were quite a few things that hurt now, that hadn't hurt twenty years ago. My knees, my ankles, and my back kept telling me this wasn't a good idea. I tuned them out, and just kept running.

I pounded my way around the last corner, pausing to make sure Mrs. Lee saw me as she pulled her minivan into the street. Up the road Jorge and his brothers were piling into their crew cab pickup truck, heading out for another backbreaking day of hanging drywall. One of the many things I liked about this neighborhood was there was no through traffic. I'd quickly learned the vehicles that belonged here, and any newcomers stuck out like a sore thumb.

The house was nothing special, a rambling two-story bungalow that needed paint and a new roof, but I'd bought it cheap, with cash, which made obscuring the purchase through a shell company LLC and a real estate trust easier. It wasn't bulletproof security, but I wasn't going to make it easy for people to find me with a property records search.

I scanned the house before walking in. Everything looked good. Doors, windows, and curtains were as I'd left them. The unobtrusive security cameras didn't look like they'd been tampered with. The only thing different was Casey's bike was no longer locked to the front porch rail.

I let myself in, passed through the kitchen for a drink of water on my way to a shower and sighed. One of the kitchen cabinets was left open, and there was a dirty spoon sitting in the sink. I maintained a level of cleanliness and orderliness in the house that even I admitted bordered on the obsessive. My roommate, Casey, wasn't quite so fastidious, and it grated on me even though I knew it shouldn't.

After a shower, I checked email on my laptop. I was hoping for work. I was spending much more money than I was taking in. What I got instead made my heart stop.

It was an email from Alex.

Dent. I've been thinking and it's time for me to come home to Portland. I'm finishing things up here and will fly home soon. I'll let you know when I arrive. Alex.

I sat there for a minute at my desk, still dripping from the shower and watching the blinking cursor on the screen. I'd wanted this for months, but now that it was happening I was apprehensive. Alex and I had connected during the tumultuous events of last fall, become lovers, but she'd watched her father shot down right in front us and had withdrawn. Before I'd known it, she was on a plane to Hawaii. She'd ping-ponged back and forth all over the Pacific and Asia, Japan, Indonesia, back to Hawaii, then to Nepal for a month, then back to Hawaii.

She had been constantly in my thoughts, and frequently in my dreams. I'd worried about her safety. The people we'd fought had a global reach. But she'd made it clear she wanted me to leave her alone. Her emails were infrequent and brief.

I shook myself, made myself get up and get ready. It was out of my control. Whatever would happen would happen. I resolved to go about my day and shove it out of my mind.

My next form of torture was physical therapy. Last fall I'd taken a nasty knife slash across my left forearm, from my elbow to my wrist. Alex had patched me up, kept me from bleeding to death. But I had lasting damage to muscles, nerves, and tendons. I could move my hand, and it didn't hurt most of the time, but occasionally I would twist my wrist the wrong way, and my pinky and ring fingers would go numb. I still frequently dropped things when I tried to pick them up with my left hand, and my grip was weak.

My physical therapist was fifteen years younger than me and looked like Eddie Vedder's little brother, but he knew his business. Once he figured out that I would actually go do the exercises he prescribed, he threw himself into my case. I'd made quite a bit of progress.

I left my forty-five-minute session the way I always did, with a sore arm and a new sheet of exercises to do at home. In the parking lot, I did my usual routine, looking for signs of surveillance, then checking the car for any signs that it had been tampered with. After finding no signs of a GPS tracker or a bomb, I could finally be on my way.

I spent hours out of every day on things like this. Every time the car left my sight, I had to check it. A vehicle that stayed in my rearview mirror too long could trigger the need for half an hour of aimless driving around through side streets, checking for a tail. Once a cable TV crew had parked out front of the house, and I'd watched them carefully with binoculars, making sure they were legit.

It got old. But I wanted to keep breathing.

The smart money would have been to get the hell out of Portland, go somewhere else entirely, but I was stubborn. Portland was my home. I'd worked countless hours, bled, and nearly died protecting it. One way or another, this was where I was going to make my stand.

In some ways, I wanted them to come for me. We had unfinished business.

I spent a few hours at home, in front of the computer. I told myself I was working, but really I was just passing time. I checked messages, made sure my company website was up and running, it was all busy work. Clients weren't exactly beating down my door. I'd had a few fraud investigations for local businesses, some security surveys, that sort of thing. I'd resisted doing divorce work, but soon I might have to do.

Then I did my usual round of web searches, checking up on a company named Cascade Aviation. They were a shadowy outfit, a contractor to intelligence agencies. Some of their employees and the owner's son had been involved in a human trafficking ring. I'd discovered it and it had kicked off the festivities last fall, which had left me with no job, a nasty scar on my arm and my best friend dead.

There was nothing new. I don't know why I expected there to be. There never was.

Finally, it was time for Krav Maga class. I headed farther east, and south, to Milwaukee, Oregon and spent the next hour in constant motion, sweating my ass off. I'd tried and rejected various martial arts half a dozen times over the years. They were too intricate, too flowery and I'd find myself in the middle of class thinking "there's no way in hell this would work," and I'd quit.

Krav Maga was different. The Israelis had taken the best, simplest and most brutal techniques from all over the world and blended them together. Every time I went to class, I found myself nodding my head because everything I was learning jibed with my experience dozens of fights on the street.

Today was kick day. Steve, my favorite workout partner, was as big as me, and a glutton for punishment. We gave each other a high knuckle and wasted no time, taking turns holding a kick shield and blasting full power kicks into each other. We worked round kicks, side kicks, and front kicks for an hour, and by the time we were done there was a puddle of sweat on the mat around us and my hips and hamstrings were screaming.

I had just enough time to gulp a bottle of water, and out of deference to my next partner, change into a shirt that wasn't soaked with sweat, then it was time for Brazilian Jiu-Jitsu class. Brazilian Jiu-Jitsu had a complicated history, starting in Japan, but coming to the US via a family in Brazil. Most of the time was spent fighting on the ground, maneuvering for dominance and trying to apply joint locks and submission holds.

I wasn't very good at it. I took to the striking in Krav Maga like I was born to it. I like to hit things. Jiu-Jitsu was like a chess game. You defeated your opponent using sensitivity and technique, not brute strength. When I first started, I found myself routinely getting folded up like a pretzel by people half my size. It was frustrating but I stuck with it and I was making slow progress.

Most of the class was tough going. I struggled with applying new techniques, and barely held my own. At the end of the class though, I surprised myself by applying a sneaky little weight shift and rolling my opponent into an armbar. I think Ron, my opponent, was actually happy for me, despite the pressure I was applying on his elbow. He'd displayed a tremendous amount of patience with my newbie clumsiness.

After class, I had nothing to do. That was the biggest adjustment to life after police work. Before, I worked non-stop, chasing criminals, slept whenever I could, and then got up to do it again. I'd managed to squeeze in some time here and there with a girlfriend, but had no other life than that. Now I had hours of free time, time to sit and stew, rehash old memories and worry about the future.

Casey wasn't home when I got back. She ran her own computer security consulting business. I'd told myself I'd taken her on as a roommate because I needed the money. That was partially true, but the real reason was she had gone through the events of last year with me. It all seemed so surreal that I think I wanted to keep her close. I wanted somebody around me who had seen the same things, just for reassurance that I wasn't crazy, that it hadn't all been a delusion.

I'd finished my second shower of the day when one of my cell phones rang. It was the one I used for my business. I got excited at the prospect of work, both for the money and for something to do.

"Miller Investigations and Security," I answered on the third ring, still holding a towel around my waist.

"Dent?" It was a woman's voice. I recognized her, but I couldn't quite place it. I wanted it to be Alex, but I knew it wasn't.

"Yes, this is Dent," I said, refusing to play the whole "who is this?" game.

"Dent, it's Gina."

Finally, the voice clicked. Gina. Al Pace's widow, and Alex's stepmother.

"Gina. How can I help you?"

"Dent, I need help with something. Can I meet you?"

I blinked. Frankly, I hadn't thought much about Gina since Al's death. I'd never liked her, and had never expected to see her again. But she was Al's wife. Even if I didn't care for her, I cared for Al and his memory.

"What's going on, Gina?"

"I can't tell you. Not on the phone. I need to see you." Her voice trembled like she was on the verge of crying.

"Ok," I said. "I'll try to help you. Let's meet somewhere. Downtown? Say in a couple of hours?"

She paused for a long moment, and I thought the call had dropped when she finally said, "I can't... I'm not able to travel right now. Can you come to me?"

A warning bell went off in my head. If I let her set the meeting place, I was letting her control the situation. I was giving up all control. I could be walking into anything.

I rationalized it. It was Al's widow for crying out loud. My paranoia had to stop somewhere.

"Ok," I said. "Tell me where."

She rattled off an address in East Portland, the Hazelwood neighborhood. It wasn't really all that far away from me. I was surprised. Gina's usual haunts were over in the northwest corner of town, where the rich people lived.

I looked at the clock. "Ok, Gina. I'll be over in a little while. I've got some things to finish up."

"That's fine, Dent." She sniffed. "Thank you."

"You're welcome, Gina. See you soon."

I put the phone down, wondering what I was about to get myself into.

CHAPTER THREE

I'd lied to Gina. I didn't really have anything to do, but I wanted to keep my arrival time vague. I wanted to get there as soon as possible.

One of my old sergeants in the Army had a saying: "make haste slowly." I don't think he invented it, but he used it often enough it stuck in my head. So I hurried, but I did it deliberately. I dressed in khaki pants, a t-shirt, and a button-down shirt with a square bottom that would cover my gun. Then I took a few minutes to look up the address Gina had given me.

It was a rental house in a neighborhood between Glisan and Halsey streets. The lots were small and the streets were narrow. There were no unpredictable ways in or out. If I tried to drive by and reconnoiter the neighborhood ahead of time, I'd be spotted.

I tried to figure out what was bugging me as I strapped on my equipment. The Wilson Combat 10mm went in a holster on my right hip, inside my waistband. I slid a little five-shot .38 revolver in my front right pocket. I clipped a funny looking little fixed blade knife, called a Clinch Pick, to my belt, just to the left of the buckle. The sap in my back pocket completed the ensemble. That was how I dressed when there might be trouble. If I was certain there would be trouble, there was body armor, a rifle, and a shotgun in the back of my SUV.

It was nine o'clock, but just starting to get dark as I drove. I'd splurged for the satellite radio when I leased the Ford Explorer I was driving. Jimi Hendrix's version of "Killing Floor" was coming through the speakers as I made my way through Portland traffic. I hoped it wasn't an omen.

Al's first wife committed suicide when Alex was twelve years old. He raised Alex himself, juggling the demands of being a beat cop, then a detective, then a lieutenant, with the demands of a single dad until

Alex was safely off to college. Gina appeared out of nowhere. Before any of us knew it, the two were married. I'd seen much less of my old mentor after the marriage. Gina didn't seem to approve of his old cop buddies.

Al had gone to work for the federal government. He'd teamed up with a shadowy FBI agent named Bolle, who ran a Department of Justice anti-corruption task force that had been investigating Cascade Aviation. When I arrested the son of Cascade Aviation's owner for murder, all those worlds collided, and Al wound up dead, shot by a sniper only an arm's length away from me.

I wondered what Gina had gotten herself into. I wondered if it had something to do with a man. It probably did. She'd cut quite the swath through Portland before Al. I was a little fuzzy on how many ex-husbands she had.

I told myself I would be polite and respectful to Gina. She was Al's widow. But if she wanted me to spy on her latest husband or boyfriend to see if he was cheating, I would draw the line.

The route I took was nonsensical, with plenty of doubling back, lane changes and last minute turns. I was certain nobody was following me. I had my phone turned off, and inside a special pouch that blocked signals. The car was clean, it had sat in the garage the whole time it had been out of my sight.

Fairly certain I wasn't being followed, I turned off Halsey and headed towards the address Gina had given me. The neighborhood was quiet. Most of the houses were old enough not to have driveways, so there were many vehicles parked on the street. They all looked like they belonged there, though. They were older, bunches of mini-vans, little commuter cars, and beater sedans. I was keeping my eyes open for bland looking, late model sedans, SUVs and vans, particularly ones with lots of antennas, but I didn't see any.

I drove past the address and parked. The house looked vacant. There were no curtains and there was no furniture on the porch. A single light burned inside. The porch light wasn't on. There was a Volvo parked out front. I recognized it as Gina's car.

There was a satchel hanging from the headrest of the passenger seat. I reached over and found what I wanted by feel, a night vision monocular. It was just dark enough for the monocular. I gave the street and the area around the house a look.

Nothing.

I still felt like something was wrong.

I pulled my phone out of its signal blocking wallet and sent Casey a quick text message, letting her know what was going on. I waited a minute or two for a reply, but the phone stayed silent.

I got out of the car and pulled a tan windbreaker out of the back seat. It wasn't really cool enough to need it, but I put it on anyway. I fished my little revolver out of my pants pocket and slid it into the pocket of the windbreaker. Somebody watching would have been hard-pressed to see what I'd done. The gun was small and I did it quick.

Hand in pocket, on the grip of the little revolver, I walked toward the house. It was a nice night. A gentle breeze blew from the west, carrying the scent of flowers from the yard of the house next door. The traffic from busy Halsey and Glisan streets was a barely heard murmur. Many folks had their windows open and I could hear the clank of dishes being washed, the murmur of conversations, the laugh of a child.

In my pocket, I felt my cell phone vibrating with an incoming text message. Unlike most people, I was able to ignore an incoming message. I was busy right now. I'd get back to it later.

The porch was still dark. I knocked with my left hand, my right was still on the grip of the gun. I stood off to the side, in case somebody decided to cut loose with a shotgun.

Gina popped the door open so quick she must have been standing right on the other side waiting for me. As soon as I saw her I knew something was wrong. Her makeup was streaked and her eyes were red. There was a smudge of dirt on her blouse. Something was very wrong. Even if she had a new husband and she thought he was cheating, even if she'd killed her husband and had asked me over to help hide the body, the Gina I knew, would have fixed her makeup and put on a clean shirt.

She stepped back, pulled the door wide open.

"Good evening, Dent, please do come in," she said. She always talked like that. It was affected like she was trying to mimic Jackie Kennedy from watching 1950's newsreels, but this time her voice broke and went up a notch. Her hands were shaking and her eyes kept looking over to her right.

The smart thing to do would have been to turn around and run away. Maybe I could grab Gina and pull her with me.

Part of me was scared. Part of me felt an immense feeling of relief. The moment I'd been waiting for was finally here.

When I'd been a young, and drunk, Ranger, I'd gotten a tattoo on the center of my chest. It said "Front Towards Enemy," taken from the instructions molded on a Claymore anti-personnel mine, it summed up my attitude towards life. I tended to meet things head on, and charge, determined to obliterate my enemies or die trying.

So that's what I did.

I took two long steps through the doorway, shouldering Gina out of the way, and pivoted to my left, the way Gina's eyes had been darting.

All I had was a fraction of a second to take in the surroundings. I stepped into a large, empty foyer with a door and a set of stairs dead ahead, and an open archway to either side. I got just enough of an impression to realize the house was dark and empty of furniture, when a bald guy appeared out of the archway in front of me, holding a pistol at eye level.

I sidestepped and brought my hand up, still in the pocket of the jacket, and still holding the revolver, up to the level of my pectoral muscle and triggered two fast shots. The range was close, and they both hit him. Gina screamed. He dropped to the floor and the weapon discharged with a clacking, buzzing sound. I realized it wasn't a gun, but rather a Taser.

There was no time to ponder that. I pivoted a 180 to cover the other entrance way just in time to get out of the way of a bullet. I heard a boom and felt the wind of a bullet passing right by my ear as I turned to see another scrawny guy with a big shiny revolver in his hand. He'd cranked his shot off one-handed and the muzzle had risen nearly to the ceiling.

He fought to bring the gun to bear on me, and I had just enough time to register that he had really bad teeth before I fired another round from the revolver in my coat pocket. I rushed the shot and I didn't think I hit him, but he ducked behind the wall. My stress level was rising and my vision narrowed like I was looking through a soda straw. I was vaguely aware of Gina screaming something, but she sounded like she was far away. Time had slowed down, and my movements felt slow and sluggish like I was underwater.

I pulled my right hand out of the jacket pocket, and transferred the little revolver over to my left hand, grateful I'd practiced this exact move at the shooting range. As I started to draw the big 10mm off my right hip, the guy behind the wall stuck the gun out and pegged a shot at me. It was a dumb move. He didn't even look, just stuck the gun out and pulled the trigger. People do funny things in gunfights. Plaster dust rained down, so he must have hit the ceiling.

It was a bad way to hit anything, but it helped me figure out where he was standing on the other side of the wall. The 10mm came up to eye level and I fired several shots. The big 200 grain slugs didn't even slow down as they passed through the plaster and lathe walls. The guy came into view as he hit the deck, twitching.

I stared at him for a second. He looked young and was covered in bad tattoos. I made out a swastika and the dual lighting bolts of the Nazi SS symbol. Part of my mind wondered what was going on. I'd been expecting hardened, trained contract killers, but not this.

One of the things you learn in police firearms training is to make yourself look around after you've dealt with a threat. People get tunnel vision and focus on one threat, to the exclusion of everything else. They also got something called "auditory exclusion," where your brain just edits out sounds, doesn't process them, because all its computing power is used up by whatever threat you're looking at.

Belatedly, I realized I'd been standing there, mouth agape, with a gun in each hand. I took a step forward at about the same time I realized Gina was screaming something about "the stairs." Then she shoved me out of the way. She was half my size, but she did a credible job, burying her shoulder into my ribs just as the guy standing at the top of the stairs opened up on us with a rifle. My little step had brought me into his field of view.

Apparently, my auditory exclusion was over. The rifle shots were excruciatingly loud. Big splinters flew out of hardwood floor where we'd been standing, and the muzzle flashes lit up the stairwell. Gina freaked out totally, and ran for the front door, taking her right through the line of fire. I couldn't see the shooter from the angle I had, but I pegged a couple of shots in the direction of the stairwell.

Somehow Gina made it through the front door. I could hear her screaming, but I didn't think she'd been hit. I didn't dare follow her though. We had a stalemate. If the guy at the top of the stairs tried to come down, I could shoot him before he saw me, but if I made a break for the front door, he could cut me in half.

It was time to leave. I'd managed to John Wayne my way through this so far, with a combination of luck and balls, but I'd already pushed things too far. I turned and ran through the archway to the left of the front door. The guy I'd shot first was gasping and tugging at something in his waistband, so I shot him with the revolver in my left hand as I walked by. The gun went off once, then clicked on the second pull. Empty. It did the job though because the guy stopped squirming.

I ran through what would have been a big dining room if the house had any furniture. I realized why all the lights had been off. There were no curtains, and I'd have easily seen a bunch of armed assholes inside waiting for me. I made a right turn, towards the back of the house, and through another archway into the kitchen.

There was a guy there, on the other side of a kitchen counter, his face lit up by the glow of a cell phone he was frantically typing on. Good grief. Texting and driving was bad enough, but texting in the middle of a gunfight?

I covered him, with the glowing night sights of the 10mm on his chest.

"Don't..." was all I had to say before he dropped the phone and went for the pistol on the counter. I shot him twice, center of mass, then paused to line up the sights on his face, but by then he'd already dropped and hit the floor.

I ran around behind the counter. His pistol had gone flying and I couldn't see it. The guy was lying there curled up in a ball, making the wheezing and gurgling noises from when somebody has holes in their chest that aren't supposed to be there. I thought about shooting him again, but he wasn't bothering anybody at the moment, so I decided to let him take his chances.

I took a deep breath, held it for a couple of seconds, then blew it out slowly, keeping an eye on the entrance way. Out front, I could hear Gina screaming, and male voices yelling. I needed a plan.

First I tended to my weapons. I was running around with a pistol in each hand, like a character from a John Woo movie. It had worked so far, but now one was empty, and the other nearly so. It was time for some juggling. I shoved the empty revolver in my waistband to free up my left hand, then swapped the mostly depleted magazine in the 10mm for a fresh one out of the pouch on my belt. I holstered the 10mm long enough to shove the .38 back into my right front pocket. I'd reload it later. I drew the 10mm again, and with my left hand, pulled a flashlight out of a pocket.

Gun juggling over, I took stock. There was more screaming and yelling from out front. I heard the creek of a footfall in the dining room and dropped to the floor, just as the guy with the rifle opened up. He'd followed me, slow and careful, and now was shooting blind through the doorway. Pieces of wood from the kitchen cabinets fell all around me. The sound of the rifle going off in such close quarters was deafening. I felt like my eardrums were being pushed inward and were sure to pop at any second. Shards of glass from the sliding glass door behind me peppered my hair and the back of my neck. A few inches from my right cheek, a bullet ripped through the front of the dishwasher, leaving a jagged curl of metal sticking out.

Then he was out of ammo, and there was silence. Despite the ringing in my years, I heard a curse and the hollow, metallic thunk of an empty rifle magazine hitting the floor.

I stood, turned on the flashlight with my left thumb, and there he was, yet another bald guy with tattoos, trying to stuff a new magazine into his AK-47. He squinted when the light came on and I shot him in the face. He dropped like a puppet with the strings cut.

It was time to leave. I had a notion to fetch the guy's rifle, but I didn't want to take the time. I did grab the cell phone from the counter and shoved it in a pocket. Maybe it would provide some useful information.

I struggled to get the sliding door open for a few seconds until I saw the piece of broomstick in the track. I slid it open and the rest of the glass fell out. Luckily none of it cut me.

I ran into the backyard and turned left. I hoped to double back and get back out to the street. I wanted to reach my SUV. I had a rifle, body armor, trauma kit, all sorts of goodies in there. Plus, I could just get in and drive away.

A black Suburban was parked in the middle of the street, all four doors open. Two more rough-looking guys were standing there, one with a pistol, the other with a rifle. Both were bald, with tattoos. What was it with these guys? The young guy with the pistol had a hold of Gina's arm, and as I watched he smacked her in the jaw with it and started dragging her towards the Suburban.

The guy with the rifle was older. Right about the time I realized I was silhouetted by the lights of the house behind me, he saw me. He jerked the rifle up just as I pulled my head back around the corner. A pair of rifle rounds hissed through the place where I'd been a second before.

I'd already shot four men. It was time to stop pressing my luck. It felt wrong to abandon Gina, but I wasn't going to commit suicide trying to save her. I turned and ran, expecting a bullet between the shoulder blades as I went. There was a low fence separating the backyards and I was over it in a flash, grateful for all the work I'd been doing in the gym.

I ran pell-mell through the backyard, dodging kid's toys and vaulting over a rake somebody had left in the middle of the grass. As I hurried through the narrow space between houses, I saw a woman's face at a window. Her mouth was an "o" of surprise. I hoped none of the bullets that had been flying around the neighborhood had hit anybody sitting down to dinner.

Off in the distance, I could hear dozens of sirens. I ran to a street corner and oriented myself by the signs. I was on Multnomah Street. Grateful for the few minutes I'd spent looking at a map myself earlier, I turned to the east and jogged until the street dead-ended into East Holladay Park.

When I hit the park, I slowed to a walk. The green space was deserted. I heard the squeal of tires and the roar of a big V-8 engine over by the house where I'd had the gunfight. The sirens were getting closer. I breathed deep, trying to slow my heart rate.

I checked myself for injuries. I brushed some fragments of glass out of my hair, but somehow I'd come through the whole thing unscathed. I realized the front of the windbreaker was scorched and insulation was leaking out from the fist-sized hole blown out by the revolver's muzzle blast.

I took my phone, and the one I'd taken off the dead man out of the jacket. I made sure they were both turned off. They both barely fit in the signal blocking pouch, which I stuffed into my back pocket. Then I wadded up the jacket and stuffed it under a bench. I made sure my untucked shirt covered my holstered pistol and walked north, skirting an electrical substation, and wound up on Halsey street. I went farther east to cross at a crosswalk. Instead of jaywalking, I forced myself to maintain an unhurried pace as two more police cars screamed down the street, lights and sirens going.

Then I went north and started winding my way through the neighborhood. I'd just shot four men. I couldn't get back to my car without being arrested. Todd's people would kill me the second they saw me. I was on foot, alone, and low on ammo.

There was only one thing to do, go get coffee and pie.

CHAPTER FOUR

I worked my way north through a neighborhood, then back west towards 122nd Avenue. I forced myself to maintain an unhurried pace, to look like a guy out for a stroll. After being shut up the whole cold, rainy winter, Portlanders seemed to be reveling in having their windows open. I heard snatches of conversations, laughter, and the occasional argument coming from inside the houses. I felt like some sort of spirit from another plane of existence, full of loneliness, violence, and death, intruding here in the land of the ordinary. Not for the first time, I wondered what it was like to have a normal life that didn't involve carrying a gun. I wondered if I'd be happy living like that, or if the boring normalcy of a minivan and soccer practice would begin to chafe, and I'd find myself wishing for a life of gunfights and dead bodies.

Portland was home to a chain of 24-hour diners named Shari's. They had uninspiring food, decent coffee, and good pie. I'd eaten there more times than I'd care to admit when I was a cop, not because I particularly liked it, but because they were open 24 hours and guaranteed a certain level of mediocrity. I was fortunate enough to have been ambushed about half a mile from one.

There were only a few cars in the lot at the 122nd Avenue Shari's. I knew from experience there would be a lull around this time. Most normal folks had already eaten dinner. People like cops, tow truck drivers and the like weren't ready for a break yet, and the bars were still open, so the crowds of hungry drunks hadn't made their way here.

I double checked my reflection in the cars as I walked past. No blood, no scrapes, no cuts, and most importantly no bullet holes. I was still having trouble believing it. I found myself grinning with a certain sick exhilaration. I'd just been ambushed by four guys with guns and come out on top, without even a mark on me.

I didn't feel particularly bad about the men I'd shot. For one thing, I'd killed people before. Most importantly, they'd been lying in wait for me, clearly intending to do me harm. Big boy games, big boy rules.

At one point in my life, I'd wondered if there was something wrong with me. I could hurt somebody, even kill them in a fight, and not feel the slightest bit of remorse. After a few years of being a detective, I realized there was nothing wrong with me. The sick people were the ones who hurt people for fun, went out of their way to cause pain and suffering. It was the job of people like me to put a roadblock up for their plans. I'd be perfectly happy if I could go through life without ever hurting a fly, but given my choices, that wasn't likely to happen.

The sign just inside the front door of Shari's said "Seat Yourself," so I did, picking a booth in back near the restroom, where I could see the front door. The place was pretty empty. There was a couple in their 50's eating silently, each engrossed in something on their respective phones, and a lone guy in his 30's shoveling food down like it was going out of style and looking at his watch. I guessed he was gobbling down a quick meal before working that late shift somewhere.

The waitress sized me up as she walked over, probably trying to decide if I was drunk, an asshole, likely to run off without paying, or some combination of all three. I gave her a smile, trying to look harmless. I kept my hands under the table. They'd developed a tremor in the last few minutes. It was like that for me sometimes. I'd be fine during the fight, then half an hour later, the shakes would start.

"Coffee?" she asked.

I nodded. "And I'll just have a piece of that strawberry rhubarb pie tonight. I need to get back out on the road before my boss gets mad."

She gave a little nod. She probably wasn't even conscious of it. I'd just been categorized as another working stiff just like her, unlikely to be a problem. She filled my mug and went back behind the counter for the pie.

I went to the men's room. My real interest in Shari's wasn't the pie or the coffee. It was the fact they were open 24-hours and had a dropped ceiling in the men's room.

The men's room was made for a single occupant, which was a bonus. I locked the door and lifted up one of the ceiling panels. Inside the dead space between the dropped ceiling and the roof was a nylon satchel. I pulled it out and replaced the ceiling tile. I sat on the toilet and unzipped the bag.

My weapons were the first priority. Inside were a couple of spare magazines for the 10mm, and some plastic strips of ammo for the .38. I got both guns topped off and put away. Then I zipped up the bag. I remembered to flush and wash my hands before going back to my booth.

The pie was waiting for me. I took a bite and my stomach rebelled at the cloying sweetness. I was jittery, still coming down off the adrenaline high. I gave my stomach a few minutes to settle before I tried to eat or drink any more.

The satchel held all sorts of useful stuff: ammo, knives, flashlights, medical supplies, but what I wanted now was one of the pre-paid cell phones inside. I turned it on, pleased to see that the battery was still good. I dialed a number from memory.

A man's voice answered on the third ring.

"Send it."

"Prairie fire," I said.

"Copy," he answered.

"One," I said.

"Copy," he said again and hung up.

I looked at the call log. Sixteen seconds. Perfect. Then I started doing math in my head. On a ranch just east of Redmond, Oregon, a man would be getting ready to head out the door of his house. Say ten minutes, fifteen tops to wake up, get dressed and grab his car keys. It would then take a good three hours to drive here.

"Prairie fire" meant I was in a jam and I needed to be picked up. "One" meant I was in the northeast quadrant of the city.

Last year, my former partner Mandy had been badly beaten. She would likely never work again. The man coming to get me would be one of her brothers. He wouldn't waste any time getting here, but he wouldn't attract attention by going too fast either. Once he got here he'd make a circuit of northeast Portland, driving around four pre-arranged pickup locations, until he either found me, or four hours had gone by.

I tried another bite of the pie. It went down a little easier this time, but I wished I had time for a real meal.

Laboriously, I started typing a message out on the phone, to another number I'd memorized.

Soylent green is people. Casey had picked the phrases for our emergency communications plan. I didn't know what the hell half of them meant, but at least we weren't likely to use them by accident.

I sat there for a few minutes, slowly eating my pie and sipping coffee, trying hard not to stare at the phone like I could force it to spit out a reply. I was worried about Casey. If they had tried for me, they would try for her. She was a smart woman, and very tough in her own way, but gunfights weren't her forte.

Finally, the phone buzzed.

I read her reply. **Open the pod bay doors HAL.** She was on the run and taking precautions, good.

One. I typed on the screen. If I'd used the numeral one, instead of spelling it out, she'd know I was under duress.

One. Her reply came back almost instantly this time. Perfect. She could make a pickup in northeast Portland.

I wiped the phone down carefully, removed the battery and dropped it on the floor under my table. Then I used my foot to scoot it back under the booth. With luck, it would be there for years before somebody found it.

I left cash on the table for my pie and coffee, making sure the waitress saw me doing it. I gave her a nod and a wink on my way out.

"Bossman wants me to go look at a pipe leak, gotta run," I said.

She gave me a friendly nod, in working-class solidarity as I walked out the door. Hopefully, if word got around about an armed suspect running around Portland, I wouldn't be the first person she thought of.

There was something I was thinking about doing, something rash, and maybe even suicidal. I'd reached this point in my life where I just wanted something to change. I was tired of waiting.

As I walked south, I pulled a ball cap and a dark gray sweatshirt from the bag. The only person who had seen me at the shootout, other than Gina and the shooters, had been the woman in the window. Her description wasn't likely to be very good, but I thought it was prudent to don a hat and something other than a tan windbreaker.

Two people were waiting at the bus stop at 122nd and Halsey, a young guy oblivious to anything other than the music playing in his headphones, and an elderly woman who looked sort of nervous to be at a bus stop at 11 pm. I gave her a smile and tried to look harmless.

I stood there and waited, just like any other Portlander who had someplace to go.

Since I had some time to kill, I thought I'd go see my old boss.

27

CHAPTER FIVE

I'd been unfortunate enough to know a few cops who should have never been handed a badge. Steve Lubbock was one of them. Up until last November he'd been my boss. It was hard to say which one of us had hated that arrangement the most.

I strongly suspected Lubbock had been complicit in setting me up last year. I didn't have hard proof, but there were too many coincidences. I'd thought often about confronting him over the last six months. To be honest, I'd thought more than once about kicking the shit out of him and then sticking my 10mm in his ear until he told me what I wanted to know. He was still a Portland Police Lieutenant, so I'd restrained myself.

Tonight I seemed possessed by a certain reckless energy that I'd never felt before. I'd never been a stranger to taking chances, but over the last six months, I'd been dealing with two competing urges. On the one hand, I spent hours every day guarding my life. I watched out for surveillance, car bombs and potential attackers. I spent hours working out, training in martial arts, and busting caps at the shooting range. I was in better shape than I'd been in decades. I could run and barely break a sweat, hit harder and shoot better than I'd ever been able to, all so I could live another day.

On the other hand, sometimes I just didn't give a damn whether I lived or died. I'd been dating a woman named Audrey last fall. She left me when things went bad. Then I lost my job and the sense of purpose that came with putting bad people in prison. Finally, for a few brief days, I'd had Alex in my life, and that had made everything seem ok, then her dad, my only friend, was dead, and she was gone.

In my darker moments, I sat in my office, with nothing to do, surrounded by guns, and wondered which one of them would end it all the quickest. When those thoughts would seize me, I'd go work out. I'd run or hit the heavy bag until my muscles were reduced to a quivering mass, then I'd finally be able to sleep.

Putting away the people who had ruined my life was a mission to accomplish. That was something I'd had my whole life, and I very much needed it now.

Riding the bus was a calculated risk. There was a chance the police were circulating a description of a shooting suspect among bus drivers. I knew from experience it could take hours for Tri-Met, the local bus company, to get the word out though, and even then the bus drivers had plenty of things to do besides play junior policeman. I doubted the cops had a good description of me anyway.

Lubbock lived over by Mt. Tabor Park. I got off the bus and started walking. I'd been to his house once when he first took over the major crimes unit. I talked about it later with some of the other detectives and we all agreed it had been one of the most uncomfortable experiences of our lives. Cop parties tended to be relaxed affairs, with plenty of beer and grilled meat. Lubbock had greeted us wearing a tie. He'd served cocktails and had the affair catered. I think the food was French.

On sleepless nights when I had nothing to do, I'd often take long meandering drives. Sometimes I'd wind up driving past places where I'd investigated crimes or found bodies. Once I drove as if in a fugue, down Interstate 5, to a highway rest stop, and found myself standing in the bathroom where I'd shot a man to death, with no clear memory of how I'd gotten there.

A few times I'd found myself driving by Lubbock's house. He hadn't been the main actor in my downfall, but he'd been a part, and he was accessible. The rest, Rickson Todd, Henderson Marshall, they were out of reach.

It was after midnight when I walked up Lubbock's driveway. The front of the house was dark, but it looked like there was a light on in the back. I cut through the side yard and walked around to the back door. There was a little titanium pry bar in my shoulder bag, but it turned out I didn't need it. The back door was unlocked.

I stepped into the kitchen, which was half lit by the light coming from a lamp in the living room. Lubbock had a nice place. The countertops were all granite, and the appliances all stainless steel. The cardboard box from a microwave dinner sat on the counter, next to a single dirty plate and fork. Five empty bottles of Heineken were lined up next to it, like soldiers standing by for inspection.

The soles of my Danner boots made little noise as I crept into the living room. Things were missing. Most noticeable was the couch. There were still divots in the carpet where once a couch had sat, but now it was gone. There were gaps in the pictures on the walls. The only shoes in the rack beside the front door clearly belonged to a man.

I heard a door open from farther into the house, then the soft murmur of a television. Next came the sound of a pair of feet on the carpet. Lubbock walked out of the hallway, carrying a bottle of Heineken. He was barefoot, wearing a robe, and looked like he hadn't shaved in several days.

He dropped the bottle when he saw me.

"Hello, Steve. Why did your wife leave you?"

His eyes darted back towards the way he'd come from. I wondered if he had a gun back there.

"What are you doing here?"

"I just wanted to talk to you, Ell Tee." Back when Lubbock had been in charge of the detectives unit, he always wanted his guys to call him Ell Tee. Most guys didn't do it. The ones that did were either sucking up or subtly mocking him.

"Are you going to talk to me, or shoot me?" he asked, gesturing at the 10mm I hadn't even realized was in my hand.

"I guess it depends on what you have to say," I said. I realized then, that I wasn't completely averse to shooting him. Maybe it had been in the back of my mind the whole time and I just hadn't let myself think about it too much.

"I'm not sure I really care," he said. He walked over to a chair and sat down, elbows on knees. It had only been six months since I'd seen him, but Lubbock looked like he'd aged years. His face looked puffy, like a man who had been drinking a six pack of Heineken every night for a while.

"She left me..." he trailed off for a minute. "She left me because they made me retire, Dent. After I fired you they gave me a choice, I could be investigated, or I could retire. She just didn't want to live with the stink of it."

I realized he was more than a little drunk.

"The Bureau made you retire?" I asked.

He nodded his head. "Yes. The assistant chiefs. Those assholes. They just wanted the whole thing gone. You, Williams, me, all of it. I think Cindy had been looking for a reason to leave me for a long time, and my little scandal was what she needed."

"I lost my woman too, Steve. When you fired me."

He stared off into space for a minute.

"I didn't know what I was getting into," he said. It was almost like he was talking to himself like I wasn't in the room. "I really wanted to make Captain before I retired. They didn't ask for much, just some copies of your reports, updates on the investigation, that sort of thing."

"Who was it?" I asked. "Todd? Big bald guy? Former Army?"

Lubbock hung his head and nodded, like a kid that had been caught doing something he wasn't supposed to.

"Who else, Steve? Who else in the bureau was in on this?"

He looked at me and blinked. "I think just Bloem. It seemed awfully convenient that he was right there when you had that wreck. I found out later he'd traded shifts with somebody that day."

When I'd been framed for beating up Mandy, Bloem, a patrol cop had been right around the corner. He'd kicked the shit out of me for no good reason too. It fit. Bloem. Maybe I should go talk to him too.

I looked at Lubbock sitting there with his hangdog expression. I actually found myself starting to feel sorry for the guy.

"What aren't you telling me, Steve?"

That was an old cop trick. I'd sprung that question on more than one suspect and gotten some good information.

Lubbock was either too drunk, or too unaware, to realize what I was doing to him. He looked puzzled for a moment.

"That's it, Dent," he said. "I just wanted to make Captain before I retired. I thought it would help me find a job after. Cindy had expensive tastes."

Somehow all my anger had left. Lubbock looked so pitiful sitting there that the idea of shooting him had lost its luster. I slid the 10mm back in the holster.

"Well, Steve, you sure fucked things up. They probably let you keep your badge when you retired, but you really ought to give it back. You were a shitty cop."

I turned and walked away from him, feeling drained and spent. There were a million questions I could ask him, but right now I felt soiled just being in the same room with him.

As I walked into the kitchen I heard him say, "I'm sorry."

I stopped and looked back. He was still sitting there in his bathrobe.

"Yeah, you sure are," I agreed.

31

CHAPTER SIX

Like most of the United States these days, Portland didn't have any big factories running three shifts. So by midnight on a weekday, Portland became a whole different city. While most of the hipsters were donning their artisan silk pajamas and brushing their teeth with vegan toothpaste, there was another, grittier reality out on the streets.

This was when many of Portland's homeless people came out of hiding. Many of them holed up during the day, either catching a few winks at libraries, community centers or a similar place where they couldn't be bothered, or in tents set up along the freeways and other wastelands of the city. They came out at night, to pick trash, socialize, and I often thought, to enjoy the freedom darkness provided. Being looked at like you were a human version of a rat got old.

After midnight, most of the cars out on the street were older. There were few Subarus and Volvos, and nary a Lexus to be found. They were American cars, most of them on their third or fourth owner, often with dings and dents, the occasional mismatched fender or bumper. The people out right now were on their way to work, to jobs cleaning office buildings, guarding construction sites and working at convenience stores.

I enjoyed my forty-five-minute walk through east Portland. The night was cool, but not cold. The sky was clear and the stars were out. Not for the first time in my life, I was enjoying the euphoria and sense of enhanced perception that frequently comes after almost dying. I felt wholly alive, and in an odd way even cheerful. I had never been an adrenaline junkie, but I could see how people could get addicted to skydiving, and driving motorcycles too fast.

I walked down 82nd Avenue, rebuffing offers for various goods and services. As I walked, right hand in the pocket of my new jacket, wrapped around the butt of my Smith and Wesson, I was sized up by two hard cases standing on a corner. I smiled at them, showing some teeth and they stepped back a little.

In many ways, I preferred this Portland, the Portland of hustlers, prostitutes, dope dealers, and thugs, to the Portland of lattes, yoga and all the latest fads. It was more honest and straightforward. It wasn't trying to pretend to be something it wasn't.

There was a Winco grocery store at the corner of 82nd and Powell. Open 24 hours, the store would have been fertile ground for a lifetime of study by a team of sociologists. The late-night shoppers were broken into two camps: people who looked really tired, and people who looked like they were expecting sniper fire at any moment. The latter walked around with their head on a swivel, avoiding aisles that were occupied and doubling back when they were clear. I imagined most of those folks had PTSD or agoraphobia, or something similar. For them, grocery shopping was more tolerable in the middle of the night when stores were less crowded.

The bathroom was empty. I took a stall and sorted through all the cell phones in my shoulder bag. I had the one I usually carried, along with the one I'd taken off the dead skinhead back at the ambush safely secreted in the radio signal blocking bag. Now I pulled out a third phone, yet another anonymous pre-paid. I hated cell phones, but lately, I'd been juggling close to a dozen of the damn things, hidden in my little caches all over the city.

The keyboards were always too small for my big fingers. I fought the urge to curse under my breath. I navigated to the Internet, and found the Yelp! review page for this store. I laboriously tapped out a review.

I love the coffee here, but the sushi is squamous and rugose!

That was another one of Casey's references. I had to Google it.

I sat there for a while, continuously refreshing the review page.

Finally, a new one showed up.

I shop here all the time. I can be in by 1 pm and out by 1:15.

I checked the clock on the phone and was surprised to see it was almost one in the morning. It was over four hours since the fight at the house. My ride was fifteen minutes out. I bought some random stuff, cold medicine, a bottle of aspirin. To walk out of the store without buying anything, particularly while carrying a big shoulder bag, was bound to tickle the radar of the loss prevention folks. Then I headed out to a corner of the parking lot.

It was perfect timing. A crew cab pickup pulled into the lot, and I gave a little wave. The truck parked next to me and I climbed in the passenger side. The driver was a big man, wearing triple denim. I sometimes had trouble telling Mandy's four brothers apart, but I could recognize Robert the easiest because he was the oldest. He'd done a few tours in Iraq and Afghanistan, before settling down to work on the family cattle ranch in eastern Oregon.

"Dent," he said, sticking out a hand.

I shook it. "Thanks, Robert."

He just nodded.

"Hey Dent," a voice said from the back. I turned and there was Casey. She looked a little out of place, sitting in the back seat of a farm pickup with her black leather jacket and recently dyed blue hair. Her right hand was inside a tennis racket case on her lap. I was willing to bet what was inside wasn't a tennis racket.

"Case," I said. "Good to see you."

We gave each other a fist bump, a goofy little ritual we'd fallen into.

"There's coffee and donuts. Guns are in the back," Robert said. Casey handed up a thermos and a paper bag. On the seat beside her were several black nylon cases.

We were silent for a few minutes as Robert drove a zigzagging route through southeast Portland. I drank some of the coffee and ate a donut as I watched in the mirrors for a set of headlights that stuck with us. The donut was welcome, but I was going to have to find some real food soon.

"I believe we're clear," Robert said. Casey and I agreed. He turned us east on US 26, headed out of town and towards eastern Oregon.

"You have any trouble?" I asked Casey.

She shook her head. "I got Bolle's warning about an hour and a half before you."

"Bolle?" I asked, surprised.

She nodded, handed me a cell phone. I could tell by the little icon at the top it was in "airplane" mode, so we wouldn't give ourselves away. On the screen was a text message.

Casey you and Dent are in danger. Take precautions. Bolle sends.

There was a phone number after that.

"Huh," I said. "I wonder if it's for real."

I remembered something from earlier.

"I got a text message right as I walked in the door back there," I said, pulling the phone pouch out of my shoulder bag. "I wonder if it was from him. Can we check without giving ourselves away?"

Wordlessly, Casey held out a hand. When it came to technology, I had learned to defer to her.

"There are two phones in here," she said. "Yours is the Samsung. What's the other one?"

"I pulled it off one of the guys who ambushed me."

She grunted, her attention focused on manipulating the phone inside the bag. After a minute she handed it to me.

There was a message on the screen.

Dent you and Casey are in danger. Take precautions. Bolle Sends.

The same phone number was attached.

Interesting. After the events of last year, Bolle and his crew from the Justice Department had all but disappeared. They had blown town, leaving me and Casey behind like discarded cigarette butts. We'd tried to make contact discreetly a couple of times with no results.

Casey had used her skills to look into Bolle. The man was an enigma. He'd been in Army intelligence for a few years after 9/11, then he'd joined the FBI. She could find evidence of him being assigned to the New York field office for a couple of years, and then it was like he had disappeared until he showed up in our lives last year.

"So what exactly happened back there?" Casey asked.

I took a deep breath and recounted the ambush. Then, I went ahead and told them both about my visit to Lubbock. In many ways, it had been a stupid thing to do, but I was trusting Casey and Robert with my life. I needed to be honest with them.

"Huh," Robert said. "The guys that tried to smoke you at the house don't sound like what we've been expecting."

He was right. Cascade Aviation employed mostly former military special operators, with a smattering of spooks from the CIA. They had started out just doing logistics and transport but had evolved into a full-fledged private military company. They had plenty of job openings for former Army Special Forces, Navy SEALS, and Air Force combat controllers and the like.

Even though I hadn't had time to fully examine them, it was clear to me that the men back at the house didn't fit that description. They looked like common criminals. Tattoos weren't uncommon in special operations, but Nazi stuff was still forbidden. The second guy I shot had been toting a big magnum revolver, something I wouldn't expect from a special operations guy.

They just hadn't looked the part. Even out of uniform, you could pick a special forces guy out from across the room.

More importantly, they hadn't acted the part. If I'd walked into a room full of trained operators, I'd be dead right now, or at least handcuffed, hooded and drugged as I took my last ride to a quiet spot in the national forest. My survival back in that house had been a close thing. I remembered the feeling of a bullet whizzing past my cheek and shuddered.

"When we stop, I can crack the phone you took," Casey said.

"That would be good," I said. Maybe that would give us a lead.

We rode in silence for a while. We were gaining elevation as we headed up and over Mount Hood. Soon it grew cool enough that Robert turned the heater on, and I sat there, lulled by the heat and the drone of the tires on pavement. I was tired. I'd woken up at dawn for my run, had trained hard and then capped my evening off with a gunfight. Robert turned on his satellite radio and started listening to a talk show related to farming. Most of it was incomprehensible to me, except the part where it was getting tougher to make a living running a farm.

I woke up when the tires of the truck went from pavement to gravel. The first bare hint of pink was showing in the eastern sky as we drove under a sign that said "Williams Ranch." Where the west side of the cascade mountains was wet and lush and reminded me of something out of one of those Hobbit movies, the east side was dry and open. It looked like you could expect to see John Wayne or Clint Eastwood ride up on a horse at any minute.

I didn't know much about ranching, but I'd read enough Max Brand and Louis L'Amour novels as a kid to know it was impolite to ask a man how many acres he owned, so I looked it up on the Internet. The Williams family had started out with a 160-acre homestead in the late 1800s. As their neighbors had either gone broke or just gave up, the family had expanded their holdings to over 300 acres. Dale Williams, the current family patriarch was keeping everyone's head above water courtesy of the market for grass-fed, organic beef.

We drove for several minutes down a long dusty gravel road. Cows stared at us mutely as we rolled past in the half-light.

The main ranch house was dark, except for a light in the living room. Robert stopped the truck and we all stepped out. I was grateful for the chance to stand, and shook all the kinks out of my back and legs. A man in a long coat came around the corner of the house, with a rifle in his hands, very carefully not pointed at us. It was Mandy's father.

"Good to see you, Dent," he said as he shook my hand.

"I appreciate you taking us in."

He nodded and shook Casey's hand. She'd been out here a couple of times with me. Given that he was an old school eastern Oregon cattle rancher, I thought he'd done an admirable job of warming up to Casey with her blue-dyed androgynous haircut and penchant for black leather jackets and a nose ring. I think Dale Williams recognized serious people when he saw them, and that trumped appearances.

It was cold out here, and I was grateful to step inside the warm house. It smelled of brewing coffee and baking bread. As we stood in the foyer, Mandy appeared from around the corner, wiping her hands on a towel.

She stood there for a second, with that vacant, flat expression that I'd had to get used to. I could tell that she knew she should recognize Casey and me, but couldn't. This happened more often than not when I came, and I could tell it frustrated her.

"Hey Mandy, good to see you," I said softly.

She gave a little start and smiled. "Dent!"

Then she gave me a hug. It seemed like once I spoke to her, she recognized me. In the last few months, I'd had plenty of time to read about traumatic brain injuries. While the areas of the brain weren't as neatly divided up into particular functions as some people would have you believe, damage to some areas affected some functions more than others. In Mandy's case, there seemed to be a disconnect between her visual processing and her memory. Her auditory processing seemed less affected.

She pulled back and I looked at her. Her front teeth implants looked good, they were hardly noticeable. When she'd been attacked last year, they'd both been broken in half. Between me, her dad, and her brothers, we'd managed to send her to one of the best dental surgeons in the Northwest, making up the difference between what workman's comp would pay, and the surgeon's astronomical fees. Her face still looked a little lopsided, thanks to a crushed cheekbone. It was probably always going to be that way. I'd flown with her to Los Angles, to consult with two of the country's best plastic surgeons, and they'd concluded that it would take a quarter of a million dollars to make it a little bit better, and the surgery would be horribly invasive, with months of recovery.

"We're getting ready for breakfast," she said.

"That sounds good."

She gave me a smile, and I watched as she disappeared back into the kitchen.

"She still has good days and bad days," her father said. "But lately the good have been outnumbering the bad."

That was probably the best we could hope for. Mandy seemed to have resigned herself to the fact that she wasn't going back to work as a police officer. In her more lucid moments following the attack, all she had talked about was how she was going to get better and go back to work. Perversely, as her cognitive abilities improved, she seemed better able to understand how impaired she was. Back in April, she'd almost burned the house down with a kitchen fire. After that, I hadn't heard her mention going back to work.

People started filtering in for breakfast. Days started early here on the ranch, and it was their custom to gather for breakfast to hash out a plan for the day's work. Mandy's two youngest brothers were still in high school and lived here in the main house. They were on summer break and would be working on the ranch from sunrise to sunset. Robert lived with his wife and two kids in another house here on the ranch. Daniel, freshly back from a tour in Iraq, lived in a line shack farther up on the ranch. The quiet of the open plains and the fourteen-hour days of back-breaking labor were exactly what he needed after a year in the Land Of Bad Things, something his father, who had done some tours in Vietnam, understood all too well.

You didn't leave a Williams family breakfast hungry. I consumed embarrassing quantities of coffee, bacon, eggs, and biscuits in silence, content to listen to the conversation around me. It was interesting to watch a functional family at work. My own family meals had been full of tense silence with the occasional outburst of screaming. In some ways, I felt uncomfortable, like an interloper that shouldn't be there, but I also found sitting at the table, surrounded by Dale, his kids, Robert's wife Anna, and their two toddlers comforting in a way that felt both foreign and comforting at the same time.

I was savoring a last cup of coffee, and contemplating another biscuit when Dale cocked his head towards the door and said, "Dent, you want to join me for a smoke?"

I didn't smoke, but I was interested in whatever Dale had to say. The sun was up over the ridge, and it was already noticeably warmer outside. Dale shook a Marlboro out of a pack and lit it with a Zippo lighter with the Marine Corps globe and anchor engraved on the side.

"Sounds like things have kicked off," he said as he breathed out a cloud of smoke.

I nodded.

"Feels good to finally get some licks in, doesn't it?"

I almost laughed. One of the things I liked about Dale Williams was that I could admit that finally getting into a gunfight after waiting for six months was a form of relief, and he wouldn't think I was crazy.

"I'm looking forward to bringing this to an end, one way or another."

Dale took another drag on his cigarette. "I want in this time."

I stared off towards the corral. The horses were milling around, knowing their day was about to start.

"You sure about that?" I asked. I thought about the peace I'd felt sitting around the breakfast table. "You've got a fine family here, Dale. You've got a lot to lose. Besides, you've already helped me out a bunch."

He took a drag on his cigarette, then laughed. "I've fed you a few times and gave you a rental car. It was hell explaining the bloodstains on the upholstery, I admit, but I've got some more direct action in mind."

Dale snubbed out his smoke, threw it in the coffee can by the porch rail. "I'm down to three of those things a day, and I only smoke 'em halfway down. Seems like I ought to be able to quit."

He turned to face me.

"What you're forgetting, Dent is that my daughter got her head caved in by these assholes. I don't really need a by your leave to go after them. I'm politely expressing a desire to work with you, but what I'm really saying is that I'm determined to put some blood on the walls, whether you agree with it or not."

My mouth dropped, and I realized I was being an asshole. Dale's family was his own lookout, and I needed to stay in my lane. Behind me, the screen door creaked open and Casey stepped out onto the porch.

Dale gave a little blink when he saw her.

"My apologies, Casey. I should have invited you out here for this little palaver as well."

She gave him a little half smile.

"Thanks."

She'd accepted, with wry amusement, the fact that most of the Williams men didn't know what to make of her. Beneath the sardonic hipster exterior, Casey was pretty down to earth.

"Dent and I were just discussing how it's a kind of a relief to finally have the conflict out in the open again," Dale said.

She nodded. "I prefer a straight up fight to all this sneaking around."

That sounded vaguely familiar, but I couldn't place it. Casey was found of movie quotes.

Dale gestured at me. "Dent and I were just trying to figure out how we might best work together."

Casey looked back and forth at the two of us.

"I think we need to reach out to Bolle. I don't entirely trust him, but he wants what we want. If we can take out Todd, Marshall, and Cascade Aviation we can walk away from this mess and get on with our lives."

I opened my mouth to talk, then realized that a noise had been building in the background. It was the beat of helicopter blades. I saw a black dot moving towards us, a couple of hundred feet above the Williams' ranch road. It quickly resolved into a helicopter, an MD-500. It was a small, little bulbous helo that could turn on a dime and land in a space barely bigger than a parking spot. I was intimately familiar with the military version, the MH-6, from my time in the Army.

It slowed to a hover about a hundred yards from the front porch of the house, scattering cows in all directions. Robert stepped out with a pair of rifles. Wordlessly, he handed one to his dad.

The helicopter settled onto the grass. The pitch of the engine changed as the pilot throttled down to idle and one of the doors popped open. I recognized the man that stepped out immediately.

"Don't shoot him," I said.

"Friend of yours?" Dale asked.

"Yeah. Also, he's a big, mean son of a bitch. You'd need a bigger rifle than that."

I stepped off the porch and started walking towards the helicopter.

CHAPTER SEVEN

Big Eddie was from the Pacific Islands. Hawaii, Samoa, Guam, someplace like that. He'd been pretty vague and I never pressed him. I was a big guy. Next to Eddie, I felt small.

He ducked under the helicopter rotor arc and strode toward me. He wore aviator sunglasses, khaki pants, and an untucked shirt that no doubt was hiding a gun. He looked perfectly comfortable out here on the high prairie, picking his way around cow pies in the morning desert sun.

My relationship with Eddie was complicated. He'd proved himself a good man to have around in a tight spot. He'd stood by me during a particularly hairy gunfight that ended in a transport plane exploding in a giant fireball, but he worked for Bolle.

Most importantly, last year I'd shot a man down in cold blood. My only defense to a jury would be "he deserved it." Some of them probably would agree, but they'd have no choice but to send me to prison anyway. Eddie knew where the body was buried, or in this case, which stretch of the river it was lying in.

Once he got close enough that I could hear over the sound of the helicopter, he yelled, "Morning, Dent! You're a hard guy to find."

Despite my other misgivings, I shook his hand.

"I'm kind of curious how you found us."

His grin got bigger. "I can't reveal my sources and methods, my friend. Introduce me to your hosts?"

We walked towards the house. The rifles had been put away, probably just inside the door, and Casey, Dale, and Robert stood there watching.

"Want to fill me in?" Eddie asked.

"I might ask the same of you," I said. "Let's wait until we get up on the porch so we don't have to tell it twice."

He nodded and we walked the rest of the way up.

Casey surprised me by running up to Eddie and giving him a big hug. She was closed off and reserved, except when she wasn't. I introduced Eddie to Dale and Robert.

"You know anything about four skinheads having a bad night last night?" Eddie asked me.

"I heard it was some kind of firearms accident. Unsafe gun handling," I said.

He laughed. "That's out of sight, man. Four on one?"

"I got lucky. They've got Gina though. I don't think she was with them by her own choice."

His grin faded. "I know and I think you're right. We've got a bigger problem though. Alex is on her way here from Hawaii. She'll land in a couple of hours. I've got people headed to the airport. If we leave right now in the bird, we'll get there in time. I'm worried Todd will make a play for her too."

I looked at Casey. She looked tired, just like I probably did.

"I'm in," she said. "I need to grab my bag." She headed inside.

"Me too," I said. I looked at Eddie. "I'll be right back."

He nodded, and just like I'd hoped, Eddie stayed outside, and Dale followed me in. I collected my shoulder bag from where it had been sitting next to my chair and turned to him.

"Look, you're right. You want in on this? You're in. But let me run out front. I'll keep you posted. You and your boys can be our little secret. I trust Bolle, but only to a point."

He gave a slow nod. "That works. You stay in touch. You need some overhead cover, give a holler. Portland ain't that far away. We'll use that commo plan we cooked up?"

I nodded and shook his hand. Mandy walked in from the kitchen and gave me a hug.

"I wish I could come," she said.

"I wish you could do."

She turned quickly away. I guess she walked off so I wouldn't see the tear in her eye, but I did anyway. I walked out of the house and Casey and I trotted to the helicopter. Ducking under spinning helicopter blades always made the hair on the back of my neck stand up and the top of my head tingle. No matter how low I got, I was afraid the damn thing was going to take my head off. It was horrendously loud.

Eddie opened the back door, and Casey scrambled in. As she did, I noticed something interesting. There was a pair of brackets welded to the bottom of the fuselage. The work looked fresh. The welds and brackets were still bare metal. Back in the bad old days, the Army used helicopters almost identical to this one to insert special operations troops into various hot spots, urban areas in particular. In a matter of minutes, a metal mesh bench could be mounted on the brackets for three operators to ride on each side of the helicopter. The little helicopter could squeeze into tight spots at high speed and troops could jump off the benches and be on their objective in a matter of seconds.

There was also a gyroscopically stabilized infrared camera mounted on the front of the right skid. Interesting. The little bird was painted a nondescript white and gray, but there was more to it than met the eye.

The back of the helicopter was cramped and spartan. I slid in next to Casey. Between the two of us and the gun cases, there wasn't much extra room. The pilot, a guy with a goatee and close-cropped salt and pepper hair, cocked his thumb at a pair of headsets hanging on brackets. Casey and I each put one on as Eddie climbed into the front seat.

The sound-dampening headphones killed the skull-busting roar of the engine and blades, but my ears were still ringing. Eddie put on his own headset.

"This is Jack. He used to fly these things in the Army. We're about an hour and a half from Portland. We should set down and meet Bolle just in time to meet Alex at the airport."

Casey and I gave him a thumbs up, and then we were off. The helicopter gave a lurch and the ground fell away like we had been catapulted upwards. I could see the instrument panel over Jack's shoulder. We leveled off at a thousand feet above ground level and he pointed the nose down and gathered speed. We headed north. I figured Jack was planning on following US 26 over the mountains, then dropping down into Portland.

It had been years since I'd flown in a helicopter. It brought back not very pleasant memories of cruising over Mogadishu, Somalia, inhaling dust and the stink of cooking fires and burning tires while waiting for somebody to fling a rocket-propelled grenade at me. I had a million questions for Eddie but didn't want to try to communicate over the scratchy headsets. Plus he would probably give me an inscrutable smile and tell me to wait until we could talk to Bolle.

I looked over at Casey. She was staring out the window, but her eyelids were drooping. I was bone tired myself. As a young Ranger, I'd spent weeks at a time living on a couple of hours of sleep a night, but I'd been in my twenties then.

I leaned my head back and fell into a restless, troubled sleep. I dreamed about death. I couldn't tell you how many dead people I'd seen in my life. During the seventeen-hour gun battle in Mogadishu, there had been bodies in the street two and three deep, courtesy of the gun runs from helicopters just like this one. My time as a police patrol officer and detective had been punctuated by dead people. I'd literally hurdled dead bodies responding to a shooting rampage at a shopping mall. I'd found dead bodies dumped in parks, stuffed in car trunks, and laying in the middle of the street. Sometimes when I slept, they played through my head like a slide show.

From that, I went to a replay of the shootout back in Portland. Only this time, the men trying to kill me didn't fall. I lined up my pistol sights, squeezed the trigger perfectly, and they just laughed at me.

I jerked awake, surprised to see that we were near the Columbia River. I guessed I'd been out for maybe an hour or so. I didn't feel particularly rested. My eyes burned like they were full of sand. I needed to shower and brush my teeth. Casey was leaning against me, with her head resting on my shoulder. She was drooling on my shirt.

From the view out the front windows of the helicopter, I could tell we were approaching Troutdale Airport. We were just east of Portland. We were headed for a helicopter landing pad with two black SUVs parked nearby. Jack set us down, light as a feather. It was hard to tell the exact moment when the skids touched the earth. There was only a gradual feeling of settling as the chopper's weight transferred to the skids. He had the touch.

I shook Casey awake and we both doffed our headsets. I climbed out, and again the roar of the helo assaulted my ears.

Bolle got out of one of the Suburbans. He was tall, taller than me, but cadaverously lean. He wore an old-fashioned buzz cut, like somebody from the fifties, and a charcoal suit that probably cost more than some of the cars I'd owned.

"I'm glad the two of you are here," he yelled over the sound of the helicopter's engine. "Let's get inside and we can talk on the way to the airport."

We both nodded and got in the back of the Suburban. The door was unusually heavy, and the glass was thick and tinted green. The

Suburban was armored. The heavy doors thunked shut, and it suddenly became much quieter. Bolle sat in the front passenger seat. The driver was a guy in his early thirties wearing a rugby shirt and jeans. The trim beard and hairstyle made him look like any other young Portland professional, but in the rearview mirror, I could see that he had an older man's eyes.

Bolle turned in his seat to talk to us.

"This is Dalton. It's ok to speak in front of him," Bolle said.

Dalton gave us a nod and dropped the Suburban into gear.

"We'll make it to the airport in time to meet Dr. Pace," Bolle said.

I blinked. I wasn't used to thinking of Alex as "Dr. Pace." She was an MD, had worked as a pathologist for Multnomah county before getting wrapped up in last year's madness.

"I know you have many questions," Bolle continued. "I wish I had more answers. I want to start off by showing you this."

He handed me a tablet. A video was paused on the screen, showing an empty lectern with a microphone.

"This was filmed three nights ago at a fundraising event for the Oregon Faith and Justice Alliance."

I'd heard of the Oregon Faith and Justice Alliance. They were an activist group that seemed stuck on one message: the country was going to hell in a handbasket, and only white heterosexual men could save it. I wasn't the most liberal of people, but these guys struck me as a bunch of assholes. They spent quite a bit of time protesting one thing or another in downtown Portland and seemed to be surprisingly well funded when it came time to suing the police after we broke up some of their demonstrations.

I pressed play on the screen. A man in a suit walked up. I recognized him immediately: Henderson Marshall, owner of Cascade Aviation, father of the late Gibson Marshall. Decades ago, Marshall had served a brief stint in the Army, then his history became murky. After a decade or so of working overseas for various government contractors, he somehow came up with the cash to start Cascade Aviation, which was widely known to be a CIA front company. They provided discrete transport to all sorts of garden spots like Afghanistan and Iraq. It was Marshall's son, Gibson, who had been kidnapping young women in the United States and selling them overseas, with the help of Cascade Aviation employees. It was hard for me to believe Marshall had been ignorant of their little scheme.

"Good evening ladies and gentlemen," he said, and the crowd

hushed. Marshall had a hell of a speaking voice, I had to give him that. He had that distinguished guy in his 60's thing going for him. Dressed in a tailored suit, lean and fit, he exuded authority and experience.

"I come to you tonight to ask for your help. All of my life I've dedicated myself to the service of this great country. I've sweated and sacrificed for decades, only to watch the principles upon which this country was founded slowly fade away. We've traded law and order, and rewarding old-fashioned hard work for political correctness and special interest politics. My family blazed a trail to settle in Oregon generations ago, and now we find ourselves surrounded by people who mock those pioneer values."

He paused for a second, his eyes darting around. A smattering of applause started in the room, then quickly it grew to a crescendo. Marshall needed to work on his act. His body language told me the applause had been planned. The crowd had probably been seeded with a couple of people to get it started.

It died out pretty quick and he continued. "Even though I'm at an age where I should be sitting by the fire, enjoying a good Louis L'Amour book and a good whiskey, I feel a responsibility to continue serving this country. I come before you today to announce my candidacy for the United States Senate."

Again, a pause and the room erupted into applause. It sounded more natural this time.

"I will affiliate myself with no party, and I will take money from no one. I care enough about this that I'm going to pay for it out of my own pocket. That means I can say the things that need to be said, without worrying about making big donors happy. The first thing I have to say will make some people angry, but I'm going to say it anyway."

He stopped and looked around the room again. This time it was quiet. The guy did know how to work a crowd.

"Over the last few generations, we've allowed our country to become corrupted by degenerate influences. This nation was founded by white, Christian people. It was based on white, Christian values. It is time for us to struggle for the very soul of our democracy. We need to fight! And I aim to lead that fight!"

The applause sounded very real this time. It overwhelmed the microphone with white noise. Then the video ended.

"Wow," Casey said. "What an asshole."

I handed the tablet back to Bolle.

"What the hell?" I asked.

Bolle cocked an eyebrow at me. "You're a loose end, Dent. You, Casey, Alex. Me. We're all loose ends that could derail Marshall's political ambitions. That's why there were four men in that house waiting to kill you the other night."

"This is crazy," I said.

Bolle shrugged. "Crazier than being framed for trying to kill your partner?"

My mouth clicked shut.

Beside me, Casey muttered something about "taking our first steps into a larger world."

"Why is he doing this?" I asked. "What's his angle?"

"Hubris," Bolle said. "Simple ego. A desire for the world to be exactly as he wills it. If you're interested, I have a fifty-page psych profile you can read, but I think it's pretty simple."

"What are you doing about this?" Casey asked.

Bolle didn't hesitate. "I'm going to make sure he doesn't get elected the US Senate."

My first impulse at hearing that was to agree. It was still murky whether Marshall knew about the human trafficking ring, or if it had been a scheme cooked up by his employees. Even if he'd been innocent of that, he was the kind of person who I intuitively didn't trust: rich, powerful and involved in some shadowy government contracts overseas.

But the more I thought about it, the more uncomfortable Bolle's declaration made me. Cops were supposed to be impartial, to not try to influence the political landscape. During my time in the Army, I'd visited countries in both Africa and Central America where the cops were loyal to one political faction or another, not the law. I hadn't liked what I'd seen.

"What do you have on him?" I asked.

Bolle turned and fixed me with that gaze that made me wonder if he really could read my mind.

"I could indict every single executive in his company right now, except him. Rickson Todd, his operations manager? I've got a trail of illicit money leading from Dubai to Todd's offshore bank accounts in the Cayman Islands. I've got similar evidence on his head of logistics, his chief pilot, and his foreign military sales director. But Marshall himself? I've got suspicions and guilt by association. Not enough to indict him. Yet."

"Yet?" I asked.

"It's there, Dent. I refuse to believe this man is an innocent dupe. He's directly involved in the day to day operations of that company. Do you really think he didn't know his employees were trafficking American women to other countries? Or that they were smuggling foreign nationals with terrorist ties into the country?"

Last fall, we'd disrupted Rickson Todd's human trafficking ring, terminally. In the process of rescuing a shipment of young women going out of the country, we'd discovered Todd's people bringing a group of men into the country. They'd perished when the transport plane went up in a giant fireball, and a very convenient narrative had been created that blamed them for a terrorist attack on Cascade Aviation.

"Who were those guys anyway?" I asked, remembering a group of faces lit by muzzle flashes and the flames from the burning aircraft.

"They were all young men captured in either Iraq or Afghanistan by US forces. They were all suspected of being low-level foot soldiers."

"Where were they taking them? Some kind of secret prison?" That didn't make sense. The US had been warehousing prisoners overseas for over a decade, but they'd worked very hard to avoid bringing them to US soil.

"I suspect they were here to commit a terrorist attack," Bolle said.

I blinked at that. I'd pondered why those guys had been on that plane for months, but that hadn't ever occurred to me.

"What? But Cascade Aviation was flying them into the country."

Bolle gave me the kind of grin you gave little kids who were missing the point.

"Yes. And if your agenda is making people afraid, so you can make them feel safe, terrorist attacks are pretty useful."

I chewed on that for a minute. Like most Americans, these days I got my news from the Internet. I'd learned long ago to ignore the "comments" section because it was usually full of the kind of conspiracy theory bullshit Bolle was spilling.

Out the windshield, I could see that we were approaching the terminal at Portland International Airport. Bolle's phone buzzed. He listened for a few seconds then nodded.

"Ok. We're right outside," he said.

He put the phone away and turned to me.

"Alex's plane has landed. I've got a man inside the airport already, but we've arranged for some delays with de-planing until we can all get inside."

We pulled up to the curb. I pulled my revolver out of my pocket and dropped it in my bag. I slung the bag over my shoulder, then opened the door and got out. I was turning around to tell Casey we'd be back soon when I saw her getting out behind me.

I opened my mouth to ask her to stay behind, but she cocked her head and gave me a look.

I shut my mouth. Now wasn't the time to argue, plus, Casey had as much right to be here as anybody. She was the one that had almost gone for a long swim in the Pacific Ocean, after being thrown out of a plane.

My desire for her to stay was partially driven by a desire to protect her, but also an uneasiness with her abilities. Casey was a tough, resourceful, smart person who excelled at her job, but she'd also never been in a gunfight. She was carrying a handgun. Driven by her fascination with all things mechanical and complex, she was toting a Heckler and Koch P7 pistol. It was finely made but would have been one of my last choices due to its complicated nature.

In the last six months, Casey had burned thousands of rounds of ammunition through her growing collection of eclectic firearms. She had acquired skills but wasn't tested. I tended to group people into two categories: people I would trust around me in a gunfight and people I wouldn't. It didn't have anything to do with whether I liked them or not. There were people I liked that I wouldn't want around me when the bullets flew, and people I didn't like I'd trust to cover my back.

This was why I always had trouble working in teams. I really did prefer to be alone.

Eddie, Casey, and I followed Bolle into the terminal. Traffic in the airport was light. I started scanning the crowd, looking for threats. I didn't care if I stuck out while I did it. Todd's people were likely to have photographs of all of us.

I stood right outside the area where incoming passengers exited the secure area. As usual, the TSA agents were making sure nobody brought in too much hair gel or a knitting needle and were oblivious to the four armed people standing right outside the barriers. At least the TSA folks here in Portland tended to be nice and polite.

There was a guy across the concourse who caught my interest. White, 30's, and athletic looking with a baggy shirt and jeans. He was watching the exit for arriving passengers, but he was also watching us. I caught him giving me the odd extra glance out of the corner of my eye.

I looked sidelong at Bolle and he gave me a little head shake. Not one of his men then.

There was a burble of voices, then people started coming out of the gate. Most of them were older folks, coming back from a vacation in the islands. There were a smattering of Hawaiian natives and folks who were probably flying on business.

Then there was Alex. I could see her in the middle of the crowd. She was tall, nearly six feet, and for some reason, there was a little bubble of space around her in the crush of people. She was wearing a t-shirt, jeans and a pair of sneakers. There was a backpack slung over one of her shoulders. Her face looked thinner than the last time I'd seen her, and her hair was shorter, barely below her shoulders.

She recognized me from a dozen feet away. She looked surprised to see me. I walked towards her smiling and spreading my arms.

"Dent?"

I grabbed her in a hug, hoping she wouldn't knee me in the balls. We'd parted on somewhat ambiguous terms.

I whispered in her ear. "There are people here that might try to either snatch you or kill you. Will you please just come with me?"

She stiffened. Then hugged me back.

"OK."

"I'm going to hand you a bag. There's a five-shot .38 in the outside pocket."

"OK," she said again. I let go, stepped back, and handed her the bag.

She gave a smile to Eddie and Casey, and a nod to Bolle, then we were headed for the door. Alex put her hand in the bag, no doubt around the grip of the .38. Even though I was trying to scan the crowd, I couldn't help but glance at her. She was different somehow. There was something about how she carried herself, head upright, with her weight on the balls of her feet.

Across the concourse, polo shirt boy wasn't even trying to be discreet. He was staring at us and talking into a cell phone.

"It might be best if we made arrangements for somebody to come for your luggage later," I said.

She gave a little laugh. "Everything I own is in this backpack."

Dalton was discreetly trying to show one of the airport parking enforcement guys his credentials. Across the lanes of traffic, over where the shuttle buses picked up arrivals, there was a plain white van. A man got out of the van and stared at us.

It was Todd. He was a little older than me, maybe his early fifties. He was still lean and fit looking. He was wearing jeans, a button-down shirt and a sport coat just right for concealing a gun.

My hand twitched. From behind me, Eddie said, "You know, there are all sorts of surveillance cameras out here. It's not like it's a highway rest stop or anything."

"Is that him?" Alex asked.

"Yeah," I said. "That's him."

Todd smirked. I wanted to shoot him then. I could wait for an opening in traffic, draw, get a sight picture and drill him in the chest. But Eddie had a point, there were too many witnesses, too many cameras. So I got in the Suburban.

It was only later that it would occur to me that the only thing that kept me from shooting a guy to the ground was the witnesses.

Casey climbed into the third row. I slid into the second beside Alex and we were off.

Alex looked at Bolle.

"I want in," she said. "They killed my dad."

He looked at her for a few seconds, as if sizing her up.

"You're in," he said.

CHAPTER EIGHT

We drove a long, looping surveillance detection route. Nobody said much. Alex seemed perfectly content to remain silent. There was much I wanted to say to her, but I'd be happier saying it without an audience. It felt good to be sitting next to her again. I'd missed her, and wanted to reach out and touch her, but she seemed so self-contained right now, I wasn't sure how she'd take it.

After a second loop through southeast Portland, we wound up not far from where we started, in a light industrial area maybe a quarter of a mile from the Troutdale airport. There was a shuttered metal fabrication facility sitting in the middle of a boggy field, within sight of the runway. The place was huge and surrounded by a six-foot chain link fence. We paused to get buzzed through the gate, and I could see cameras everywhere.

The parking lot was mostly deserted. There were maybe half a dozen cars. I was glad to see they looked like real cars, not bland, obviously government issue sedans, or the behemoth of a Suburban we were riding in. We drove around the back to a big roll-up garage door and paused while it rattled upward. The inside was a cavernous space, easily the size of a football field. Huge pieces of machinery were pushed up against one wall, leaving plenty of room for the half dozen or so painfully obvious unmarked cars.

We stepped out of the Suburban. Inside the factory smelled like machine oil and welding slag. Our footsteps echoed as Bolle led us to a door on the far side. The empty space on the production floor was full of nearly a dozen or so travel trailers, the kind people towed behind their trucks on vacations. Electrical lines and plumbing hoses were attached. Bolle had created his own little RV village in here.

On the other side of the door were administrative offices. We wound our way past office doors and cubicles to a large meeting room. Large flat screens had been mounted on the walls, and cables had been duct taped to the floor. A coffee maker was burbling over in a corner and the smell reminded me of how tired I was.

There were three people in the room, all staring intently at computer screens. Two of them, a man and a woman, I didn't recognize. The third was Henry, Bolle's chief computer hacker and all around geek. He stood up and smiled at us, or more properly, he smiled at Casey, then the rest of us. He'd always been a little sweet on Casey.

Bolle motioned everyone to have a seat around the table. Everybody else but Henry left. Bolle took a second to fetch a cup of coffee. He took a small sip and gave a slight wince.

I'd been studying Bolle out of the corner of my eye. Last year, I'd aligned myself with Bolle out of desperation. He'd had an arrogant, cocksure attitude I'd found grating, and there was always something he was holding back. I never felt like I'd gotten the whole story. Everything had literally blown up in our faces that night on the tarmac, and I'd lain awake at night, wondering how much I blamed Bolle, and how much I blamed myself for following him.

Something seemed different about Bolle, something I couldn't quite put my finger on. I felt like I was seeing a man that had been humbled by experience. I wondered if that was a good thing or a bad thing.

"I'm going to be upfront with all of you," he said. "Henderson Marshall is going to try to become a US Senator, and I'm going to stop him. I'm not doing it because I disagree with his politics, I'm doing it because he's a criminal. All of us, including me, represent loose ends to Marshall, and he's perfectly willing to kill us to make us go away."

He took another sip from his coffee.

"I'm still a Federal agent, and while the defeat we suffered last year caused me to lose some support, I still have a tremendous number of resources at my disposal, in the form of money, equipment, the force of law. What I need is people I can trust. People who won't be corrupted by Marshall's wealth. If you are willing to help, I could use all of you in one fashion or another."

Casey, Alex and I all looked at each other. Part of me was tempted to stand up, ask them both to come with me, and get the hell out of here. We were smart and resourceful, we could stay ahead of Marshall long enough to find a hole to hide in, particularly if Bolle was keeping him busy.

But I wondered how long that could last. I'd spent the last six months constantly waiting for Marshall's people to make a play for me, and I wasn't keen to spend the rest of my life that way.

I wanted to fight. The tattoo on my chest "Front Towards Enemy" wasn't just a drunken whim, it pretty much summed up my approach to life. I wanted Marshall to no longer be a threat, one way or another.

The question was whether I wanted to do it with Bolle. He was right about one thing, he had resources I didn't. I was nearly broke. My security and investigations company had made about enough money to buy me a pizza and a six-pack every month. I'd been hemorrhaging cash on living expenses and security precautions.

Bolle also was acting under the color of law. More than once, I'd considered finding a place to hide with a good rifle, so I could put a bullet through Marshall's eye, but I didn't relish the idea of spending the rest of my life in prison. Bolle could put a badge back on my chest, and if some blood got spilled, maybe I would still be the good guy.

Casey and Alex were silent, but watching me out of the corners of their eyes. I knew they would both make up their own minds, but they'd also want to know which way I was leaning. Last fall I'd been in that same boat, trying to decide whether to join forces with Bolle or not. In the end, I'd trusted the judgment of Al Pace, Alex's father. It had ended with a burning airplane, a stab wound in my arm, and Al dead. Hopefully, history wasn't about to repeat itself.

"I want to know all of it, from the beginning," I said.

He stared off into space for a minute. I thought I was going to get the usual, evasive Bolle brand of bullshit, but to my surprise, he started to talk slowly.

"I was a young Special Forces Lieutenant, during the initial invasion of Iraq during 2003. I had tried everything I could to get sent to Afghanistan, but the war was still small then, and I couldn't get in. So I was desperate to prove myself in Iraq. I wanted a combat record, and a chance to get into Delta."

The Army Special Forces were one of the two primary pipelines to get into the secretive Delta Force. The other was the Rangers, which I'd been a part of during my stint. We'd provided cover for Delta in places like Central America, and most famously, during an ill-fated mission in Mogadishu, Somalia.

"So I hit the ground in Baghdad in March of 2003, ready to find Saddam's weapons of mass destruction. Instead, I found myself assigned as a liaison officer to Cascade Aviation. You see, Marshall was a business associate of my father's, and he pulled some strings to get me that assignment."

Bolle stood, started pacing around the room.

"The corruption was unbelievable. The Iraq war was our first privatized war. Cascade Aviation had dozens of contracts, not just for aviation support. They had contracts to provide supplies to US troops, to provide aid and reconstruction to the Iraqi people. By the time Cascade Aviation delivered a case of bottled water to troops in the field, they'd charged the US Government a thousand dollars. I saw shrink-wrapped pallets of hundred dollar bills just disappear. Iraqi gold, artwork, cultural relics, all of it was looted and shipped out of the county in the bellies of Cascade Aviation planes."

He fiddled with his coffee cup and apparently thought better of trying another sip.

"So I contacted the investigators at the Pentagon responsible for waste, fraud, and abuse. They treated me like I was crazy. Two weeks later a bomb blew up in my quarters in the Green Zone. It detonated early so I was injured, but not killed. Nobody was ever able to explain how the insurgents were able to sneak past multiple layers of security, or why they chose to plant it under my bunk instead of picking more lucrative targets like the ammo dump or motor pool."

He sat back down. He looked pale. I knew what it was like to relive a particularly bad memory. I especially hated doing it in front of people.

"After I recovered, I was transferred out of Special Forces to a job overseeing facilities maintenance at Fort Leonard Wood Missouri. One night as I was driving home from the base, I noticed an envelope stuck between the seats of my car that I knew I hadn't put there. Inside were baggies of white powder. I threw it out the window. Two minutes later I was pulled over by the local police, supposedly for running a stop sign. They searched my car three times and seemed very frustrated when they didn't find anything."

This time last year, I would have thought this whole story was bullshit, cooked up by some crazy conspiracy theorist. Now I found myself nodding my head.

"I took that as a sign to keep my mouth shut and left the Army quietly. I figured my attempt to join the FBI would be sabotaged, but surprisingly, I found myself as a trainee at Quantico, then the New York Field Office. Along the way, I managed to gain the support of other like-minded people, some of them in the FBI, some in other agencies, even some elected officials."

He got back up, paced some more.

"People like Marshall have always existed. Beneath their veneer of civility and accomplishment, they're savages. But in the first part of this century, they've become emboldened. No longer satisfied with millions, they want billions. They no longer are content to subtly influence from the shadows, they want to own the world. And I intend to stop them, starting with Marshall."

In my gut, I knew what he told us was true. I also expected there was more, things he hadn't told us. My guess was they involved his father, who was an "associate" of Marshall's.

Casey and I had investigated Bolle, as much as we were able, and his story matched what little we'd been able to dig up. Came from an affluent family. Went to the right schools, but sought a commission in the Army anyway after 9/11. A brief time in Special Forces, then a sudden, undistinguished posting, followed by time at the FBI.

I took a deep breath.

"I'm in," I said.

Casey and Alex were both nodding their heads.

I hoped I was making the right call.

CHAPTER NINE

This was the second time I'd been sworn in as a cop. Both were a little anti-climatic. After my stint in the Army, I'd gone to college and started at the Portland Police Bureau a week after graduation. At my swearing in ceremony, I'd been alone, surrounded by new officers that were being congratulated by wives, husbands, parents, kids, and friends. I'd stood over in the corner, watching all the hugs and pictures for a few minutes, then I left. I went to Ringside Steakhouse in Portland, and for the first time in my life, dropped a hundred bucks on a dinner for myself. Eating it alone was a depressing, lackluster experience.

This time I found myself raising my right hand in a dilapidated conference room with fiber optic cables duct taped to the walls and a big coffee stain on the worn carpet. Bolle seemed to sense the situation was lacking in decorum and tried to make up for it by standing there ramrod straight and reading the oath to me as if his life depended on it.

After a few minutes, it was done. Big Eddie handed me a set of credentials fresh out of the laminating machine. Like most federal law enforcement credentials, they looked almost amateurish. He also had a set for Casey, and for Alex. They were receiving special commissions that the Justice Department had developed for technical experts. It was mostly so they could possess and examine evidence. They didn't quite have full law enforcement powers, but they could carry a gun.

Bolle made introductions all around. I already knew Eddie and Henry of course. I'd met Dalton in the car, but now I shook his hand. I wondered what his story was.

The other three, Drogan, Struecker and Byrd were typical feds. Stuecker and Byrd were virtual twins, both guys in their early thirties with short haircuts, nice clothes, and an erect bearing. You could put them in clown suits and they'd still look like federal agents. Drogan was a woman, not quite forty, who had hard gray eyes and short-cropped dark hair. I guessed she'd seen some shit. I wondered how they had hooked up with Bolle.

After the introductions, Bolle turned us over to Eddie to get us settled.

"I assume you guys are heeled?" Eddie asked.

I nodded. Casey lifted the hem of her baggy hoodie, showing the handle of her H&K nestled next to her belly button piercing. Alex shook her head.

"I just got off a plane," she said.

"Well, right this way to the gun locker," he said, gesturing expansively.

Just then, from the room next door, Henry yelled, "Hey! I think I've got something."

We all walked across the hallway. I'd given him the cell phone I took off the dead skinhead. It was plugged into a laptop and Henry was typing away at a screen.

"What is it?" Bolle asked.

"I cracked this guy's phone. It's a pre-paid throw away, but I've been tracking all the numbers in the call history and trying to get into those phones too. I managed to crack the phone he called most frequently."

Cell phones were scary. Henry had gained access to the phone I'd given him, checked out the call history, and had managed to gain remote access to at least one of those phones. This was one of the many reasons I hated cell phones.

He clicked on a file and a picture of a woman bound to a chair appeared on the big screen. She looked scared. It was grainy and poorly lit, but I still recognized her.

Gina.

"Shit," I said.

"When was that sent?" Alex asked.

"About two hours ago, with this text message," Henry said. He clicked on another file and a text message came up on the screen.

We still got the bitch. She is pain in ass. How long we have 2 keep her?

"Then a reply came from another phone," Henry said as he clicked again.

Sit tight. She may still know something.

"And then this," Henry said.

If u wnat to Torcher her, we have 2 move. Shes noisy.

"Last message," Henry said.

I'll tell you when. Busy. Sit tight.

"Torcher?" I said. "They're going to set her on fire?"

"I think they mean torture," Casey said. "That guy doesn't strike me as real literate."

"Shit," I said again. "Can you tell where they are?"

After more typing, Henry brought up a map. Three lines intersected on a red dot.

"They're across the river in Vancouver, Washington. Looks like an apartment complex off 164th Avenue."

"We need to get over there," I said.

Henry shook his head and pointed at one of the big monitors bolted to the wall. It showed live traffic feeds from the two major bridges crossing the river between Portland and Vancouver.

"It's rush hour," he said. "The bridges are gridlocked."

"Call Jack," Bolle said. "I want him and the Little Bird in the parking lot."

He turned to Dalton.

"I'd like for you to take Dent and Henry and try to get eyes on that apartment. Figure out what we are dealing with."

Dalton nodded. "I'll need a vehicle on the other side."

"It'll be waiting for you. I'm going to get a team together and start moving across the river. The helo is too small to ferry everybody and their equipment. If this goes to shit, we may need to use the locals. Their SWAT team is pretty good."

Dalton nodded again, then turned to Henry. "You've got kits for video and phones pre-loaded?"

"I do," Henry said. "But it's going to be hard for me to do video and phones all at once. Can we bring Casey too?"

Dalton gave Casey a look. I could tell he was uncomfortable bringing along people he didn't know, but I could also tell he trusted Henry.

"Ok," he said. "You take Casey and get your gear. Dent, come with me."

With that, he turned and started leading me through a warren of corridors.

"We're going to have to do this quick," he said without turning around. "Tell me about your background."

I would have bet a paycheck he already knew my background. A good way to learn about somebody was to get them to talk about themselves.

"I did four years in the Regiment. I managed not to get killed in the Bakara Market."

The Regiment was army speak for the 75th Ranger Regiment. The Bakara Market was where the infamous Mogadishu shootout had happened in 1993. They made a movie about it. I always fancied that one particular extra who showed up on screen for a few seconds was me.

"Yeah," he said.

"Cop ever since. Well, at least until November. I was a detective the last few years. Never on SWAT."

He nodded, satisfied. I hadn't exaggerated but hadn't downplayed my experience either.

"I spent 15 years in the Army. Last eight were in the Fort Bragg Stockade Rifle and Pistol Club."

That was his way of letting me know he'd been a member of Delta Force, the Army's most elite band of special operations soldiers. Their original headquarters had been at the Fort Bragg Stockade. It was interesting he hadn't done a full twenty, the number of years you needed to retire. I wondered if he'd gotten hurt, or if he'd run afoul of the same people as me and Bolle.

We stopped at a heavy metal door. He typed in a combination and grunted as he pulled it open. The room inside smelled like gun oil. There were long guns in racks. Pistols hung on the walls, and there were lots of black nylon cases and backpacks with labels on them.

He grabbed two backpacks.

"Look, my primary objective is to just get eyes on the target and start passing intel. But I think we need to be ready with a hasty assault plan in case they act like they're going to kill the hostage or move her somewhere before we get resources there."

I nodded. That was standard doctrine. If we had to rescue Gina, we would want to do it at a time of our choosing, with plenty of resources, and a very carefully thought out plan. But if it looked like the bad guys were going to kill Gina, or move her, we'd have to make things happen on her own.

He unzipped one compartment of the backpack, pulled out an AR-15 that had been chopped down to the size of an overgrown pistol.

".300 Blackout. Aimpoint red dot sight. 10" barrel with a brace instead of a full stock. I'm not thrilled with them, but they are easy to hide."

I nodded.

He put the gun back, showed me the other compartments. "Some extra mags, flashbangs, and a rudimentary chest rack. There's only a plate in the front, so don't get shot in the back."

"Front towards enemy," I said and reached for the bag. It was surprisingly heavy.

He swung his own bag on his shoulders. Then picked up a small satchel.

"Demo kit," he said.

I followed him back through the corridors. I was going to have to take some time getting to know this place so I wouldn't get lost trying to find the bathroom. Outside I could hear the clatter of rotor blades. We walked by the conference room and Alex grabbed my arm.

"I feel really useless here," she said.

"Hang tight," I said. "We'll find something for you to do."

"Well, hopefully, it isn't stitching you up. I never liked Gina, but..."

"But she was your dad's wife," I finished for her. "We'll get her."

"Ok," she said. "Be careful."

She kissed me. Then drew away.

I made myself walk away, out to the parking lot, where Dalton, Casey and Henry were loading backpacks and bags. Even though the Little Bird was modified with a long narrow storage compartment under the fuselage, it was going to be a tight fit.

Dalton motioned me into the front right seat and I climbed in. Dalton, Casey, and Henry crammed into the back seat like peas in a pod. There was no way I would have fit back there with a person on each side. There was a set of headphones dangling from a hook beside me. I put them on, grateful for a break from the noise.

Jack's voice crackled over the intercom.

"We set back there?"

Dalton made sure both doors were secured and gave a thumbs up. The Little Bird labored to get off the ground. Instead of springing straight up in the air, we took a sort of running start, with the skids just a few inches over the pavement as we flew forward for fifty yards or so before we gained altitude.

"We're heavy," Jack said.

Great, I thought. I hated helicopters.

He put us in a gentle, right-hand turn to get the nose of helo pointed north. Down below, I could see Alex standing in the parking lot, looking up at us.

CHAPTER TEN

Jack climbed to a thousand feet. I was sitting in what was technically the co-pilot's seat and could see all the instruments. I sat with my arms folded across my chest, hands well away from the stick and collective, and my feet pressed against the base of my seat, away from the foot pedals. The only thing that scared me more than being a passenger in a helicopter was the idea of accidentally bumping the controls.

"You want an overflight of your target area before I set you down?" Jack asked over the intercom. It was clear he was talking to Dalton. I was fine with playing second fiddle on this operation. Hostage rescue was a Delta specialty. In the Ranger Regiment, I'd had plenty of training in urban warfare, close quarters battle and shooting, but that was twenty-five years ago now. Also for every hour of training I'd received, a Delta guy would get ten. For every round of ammo I'd fired, a Delta guy would probably fire a hundred. Hopefully, if something needed to be investigated Dalton would have the good sense to let me take the lead.

"Let's do a single overflight, in a straight line," Dalton said. "Don't circle. We need to look like we're going from point A to point B."

We flew over the river, into Washington state, and Jack banked to take us west. We flew for a minute or two and I tried to orient myself. Even though it was right across the river, I hadn't spent much time in Vancouver. I'd crossed the river a handful of times to pick up a suspect and that was about it.

"That place is huge," Casey said over the intercom. She was on the left side of the aircraft and had a good view of the apartment complex as we buzzed by. I leaned forward in my seat to see around Jack. She was right. The complex was probably a square mile or so, with dozens of buildings, and a half dozen streets that snaked around the complex.

"A couple of hundred units," Henry said. He was alternating between looking out the window and looking at the tablet in his lap. "The cell signals triangulate right about the center of the property. I can narrow it down to a couple of hundred feet, but that's it."

"Ok. We'll figure it out when we get there," Dalton said. "Let's go pick up our vehicle."

We flew a couple of miles further east, then landed in a field just south of a fire station. Two guys were standing in the fire station parking lot next to a minivan and a little subcompact car. I hoped the minivan was for us. Dalton motioned me towards the vehicles as he helped unload the Little Bird's cargo compartment.

After shouldering my backpack, I ran forward. Both guys looked like they were in their late teens or early twenties and were bug-eyed at the sight of the helicopter. I walked up to the one holding a set of keys in one hand, and a clipboard in the other.

"Uhhh... Are you here to pick up a van?" he asked.

"Yep," I said. I took the clipboard from him, scrawled something illegible in what looked like the right places, then held out my hand for the key. He put it in my hand slowly, never taking his eyes off the helo as he did it.

"What are you guys doing?" his slack-jawed buddy asked.

"We're with Fish and Wildlife," I said. "Goose survey."

"Oh," he said, then did a quick scan of the cloudless blue sky. There wasn't a goose to be seen.

"We can't find any in the sky, so we're going to look on the ground."

He blinked owlishly, then the two looked at each other and headed for the subcompact. I got in the van, fired up the engine, and adjusted the mirrors to my liking. Everybody else piled in and we were off.

"So, I was thinking," Casey said. "Dent, you and Dalton look like cops. Why don't you drop me and Henry off? We can act like we're checking out apartments and text you if we find anything interesting."

My first impulse was to tell Casey to keep her ass in the car, and not get within range of target house, but I just as quickly dismissed it. Her plan was sound. Casey and Henry both could easily pass for a young couple looking for an apartment.

Beside me in the passenger seat, Dalton was nodding.

"Sounds good. We'll be close."

We dropped them off on the north side of the complex. They strolled down the street, and Casey linked her arm in Henry's, which he seemed to enjoy tremendously. Hopefully, there would be enough blood still flowing to his brain that he could keep working his gadget and home in on the cell phones.

"Let's find someplace close, but inconspicuous," Dalton said.

"I need food, and coffee," I said.

Dalton checked his phone. "Go north. There's a burger place."

I nodded, pulled out into traffic.

"When did you last sleep?" Dalton asked.

"I napped on the helo. Other than that, going on two days."

He nodded. There was no judgment. It was just a piece of information. Just like you needed to know if the engine of your truck had enough oil, you needed to know the sleep state of your men.

I parked at the Burgerville a couple of blocks north and ran inside rather than using the drive-through. I didn't want to get stuck behind a soccer mom ordering a meal for her family of five if things went to shit with Casey and Henry. I was back in the van in a matter of minutes. I parked us in a far corner of a shopping center parking lot and tore into the food like a ravenous wolf.

My phone sat on the dash between us. When it buzzed I wiped my fingers on a napkin and reached for it.

Found the place. Did a circle and Henry's detector tracked the cell. Also car with "White Pride" stickers out front. Blasting music from inside. Pretty sure it is Skrewdriver.

I looked at Dalton. He shrugged. The phone buzzed again.

Skrewdriver = White Power band.

We both nodded.

"Tell them…" Dalton started, but the phone buzzed again.

Apartment next to them is empty! We are inside. I bumped the lock.

Dalton's eyebrows went up. The phone buzzed again.

Hope that's ok???

"Ask them the apartment number," Dalton said.

I started typing out the message, messed up, corrected it, then messed up again. Beside me, Dalton sighed.

"Here," I said, handing him the phone.

His fingers flew across the keypad.

You can park here, Casey sent, accompanied by a picture taken from inside the apartment of an empty visitor parking spot. When I see you pull up, I'll go knock on their front door, tell them I just moved in, ask for a roll of toilet paper. You come in the back while they are distracted.

"Maybe we should just let them handle this," Dalton said. "We could go catch a movie or something."

"I don't think Henry can shoot very well," I said as I put the van in drive.

It worked out just like we planned it. We pulled into the empty spot and Henry motioned us in. Dalton and I each wore a backpack and carried another duffel bag full of surveillance equipment. It would have looked suspicious as hell, except nobody was out and about to see us. It was still the peak of rush hour, so folks commuting from Oregon wouldn't be there yet. Most folks here probably went inside and stared at one screen or another when they came home anyway.

The inside of the apartment was dark and smelled like carpet cleaner. It was small and narrow, with a living room and kitchen downstairs, and a staircase leading up to what I assumed would be the bedrooms. We were at the end of the building, the target apartment was next to us, and there were two more apartments on the other side.

Through the wall I could hear pounding bass and what sounded like screaming vocals. I instantly started developing a headache.

Casey came back in the door, carrying a roll of toilet paper.

"One guy opened the door just enough to talk to me, so I couldn't see in the house. Early twenties, shaved head, bad teeth, lots of crummy tats. He talked to my boobs the whole time." She kept her voice low, although odds of somebody hearing over the music were pretty low.

Dalton pointed up and started towards the stairs. We all followed him and congregated in the hallway in the center of the apartment, the farthest point from the front and back windows.

"Ok," he whispered as he reached in his backpack. "Henry, you and Casey get started on phones and cameras. Dent, we're going to cut some big strips of carpet off the floor and duct tape them over the windows."

He handed me a roll of duct tape from his bag and headed for the back bedroom. I went to the front bedroom, flipped open my Benchmade folding knife, and with a few minutes' work had a strip of carpet cut loose. I affixed it with plenty of tape and put my knife away. To anybody standing in the street, it would just look like a curtain, if they even noticed it at all.

I went into the back bedroom. Casey was setting up the cell phone monitoring equipment. She had two devices called Stingrays hooked up to a laptop. The Stingrays were clunky-looking gray boxes that looked like something a high school kid would build from a kit for a science fair, but they let Casey basically own any cell phone within half a mile.

"I've got two associated phones extremely close. Probably next door."

By "associated phones" Casey meant she'd managed to delve into the call histories of the two phones and determine that they'd called each other. She would download the histories of each phone which would give us more numbers, then set the Stingray to search for all the phones in those histories. When one of those phones came in range, it would attempt to download the history from those phones. The amount of information could grow exponentially with each new phone. The laptop would sift the data and build what was called an association matrix. We could analyze it in dozens of ways, to determine who called whom when, and how frequently.

Given enough time, we could also retrieve text messages, pictures, and anything else stored on the phone. We were engaging all sorts of warrantless electronic searches. If this ever went to court, we would have some big problems.

"You want me to turn on their audio?" Casey asked.

Dalton nodded as he walked over to the common wall shared between this apartment and the one next door. He held what looked like an over-sized electronic stud finder. I recognized the device as Range-R, a cutesy name for a handheld doppler radar unit that could see through walls and tell us if a human-sized object was moving around on the other side. I did some quick math in my head as I watched Henry unpack several pin-hole fiber optic cameras. We probably were toting close to a quarter of a million dollars worth of electronic surveillance gear with us. Whatever Bolle's other faults, the man knew how to secure a budget.

As Dalton pressed the device up against the wall, Casey patched an audio feed into the earpiece in my ear. She'd remotely commanded one of the cell phones next door to turn on its microphone and we were using it to eavesdrop on the room.

This was one of the many reasons I didn't like cell phones.

At first, I got a double dose of the pounding music, then I heard what I thought was gunfire. I must have jumped because Casey waved at me.

"Video game," she said.

I nodded.

She worked at the controls of the laptop for a second and the music level dropped in volume. I could hear male voices utter the occasional expletive, and hear the clicking of controls.

"I got you fucker!" one of them said, his voice rendered tinny and metallic by all the audio processing and filtering Casey was using.

Dalton checked the display of the Range-R. Nothing moving. He pointed at the wall to Henry, who stood on tiptoe and used a silent drill with a slender bit to drill through the wall near where it joined the ceiling. The drill had a depth gauge that stopped just before the bit poked through the drywall on the other side. He pulled out the flexible bit, leaving a long plastic tube behind. He fed one of the fiber optic cameras through the tube, and by feel pushed it through the last few millimeters of the drywall on the other side. The camera went live.

The two apartments were mirror images of each other. We were looking through the common wall at an empty bedroom. The fisheye lens of the camera showed up some sleeping bags, some crumpled up clothes and nothing else. We repeated the process with the front bedroom. It too was empty.

Dalton gathered us together.

"Ok, we need to get cameras downstairs, but we need a quick plan in case this goes to shit. All of our options suck right now, but if we think they are going to harm the hostage, we need to act. Bolle is on his way, but he's at least half an hour out."

There were nods all around.

"We've got two ways in the front door and the back door. Both are absolutely terrible approaches. They'll see us coming. I want to work on a better plan, but if we go right now we'll take the back door."

I nodded. The back door had big windows on either side, but then again, so did the front. Hopefully, they wouldn't be expecting anybody at the back door.

Dalton pulled a flashbang grenade off the front of his vest. Unlike a military fragmentation grenade, which sent out a cloud of lethal fragments, the flash bang relied on concussion and a blinding flash of light to disorient and stun opponents.

"Casey, do you think you can throw one of these?" he asked.

She nodded.

"The command to go will be the word 'execute' three times. Got it? Execute. Execute. Execute."

She nodded again.

"Pull the pin, release the lever, throw it right by the front door."

"Ok," Casey said and took the grenade from him.

"Dent and I are going to stand by the back door, while Henry places the cameras," he said.

Through-wall cameras were great. The intelligence they could provide was invaluable. But there was a small chance that somebody would see the tiny little hole appear in the wall. Placing them took a deft touch to avoid sticking them out too far, and there was always a chance a paint chip would drop off the wall when the camera penetrated.

Henry looked cool as a cucumber as he went to work with his tools on the walls of the kitchen. Casey stood by the front door with her grenade, and Dalton and I stood by the back door. I stood there for long minutes with nothing to do but listen to the sounds from next door. The music cut off, leaving only the sound of computer-generated gunshots and screams from whatever video game they were playing. The absence of the pounding music was like a weight being lifted off my shoulders.

I heard what I thought was a woman crying and strained my ears.

"Shut up!" a man screamed from next door. He was loud enough that the sound in my earpieces was distorted, but I could hear him through the wall too.

"Settle down, man." Another voice. Also male, but younger.

Henry walked in the living room, gave us a thumbs up. He held up the tablet and showed us the view from the camera he'd just placed. It was working great. There was nobody in the kitchen.

This was the tricky one. There were at least three sets of eyes in the tiny living room of the apartment next door. Presumably, Gina wouldn't say anything, but we had a real problem on our hands. Casey walked up, leaned in close to me and Dalton.

"Once Henry finds his spot, I could go over and ask to borrow something else, a corkscrew maybe."

Dalton nodded. Henry pulled a thermal scanner out of his bag. Unlike in the movies, it wouldn't let him see through the walls. He held it a few inches from the wall separating the two apartments and started moving it around. The ghostly images of the studs and the electrical wiring showed up on the screen, then he moved it up and back and forth in a zig-zag pattern. I realized there was a faint rectangle on the wall that was slightly warmer, several feet wide by a couple of feet high.

"TV," he said. "A big one."

It would do little good to place the camera behind a TV. It was also the focal point of the room, where the two men would be watching.

Instead, Henry picked a spot near the back door and started drilling at an angle so the camera would aim toward the front of the apartment. I heard Gina mutter something, then sob.

"I said shut up! I'm tired of you."

The guy sounded a little unhinged. Not good.

"Hey man, be cool. Curtis told us it wouldn't be much longer."

"Fuck Curtis! Fuck you! And fuck this bitch! Where's my pipe? I'm tired of this shit."

"Curtis told us he wanted us to stay clean while we had the woman."

"Fuck Curtis! Where's my pipe."

Henry nodded and gave Casey a thumbs up. He was almost through. Balanced on tip-toe, he pulled the drill out, and fed the fiber optic camera into the plastic tube in the wall. The only thing between us and a view of the room was about a millimeter of drywall and some paint.

Casey carefully laid her grenade on the floor, took a deep breath, and walked out of the apartment. A few seconds later we heard her knock and a man appeared on the camera aimed at the foyer and kitchen. He was short, kind of chubby with a hoodie and a smear of acne across his face.

"Hey," he said as he opened the door.

"I'm really sorry to bother you again," Casey said, putting on her best airhead impersonation. "But I like totally forgot a can opener. Do you have one?"

"Uhhh... Let me see."

With the slightest push, Henry put the camera in place. He'd set the tablet on a split screen view, half of the kitchen and foyer, the other half the living room. As the camera broke through the wall on the other side, the screen lit up with a picture.

We were looking at the back of a shirtless man. A giant Nazi eagle was tattooed across his back. He was big and had the kind of muscles I'd come to associate with prison inmates who had way too much time to pump iron.

Gina was bound in a chair, just like we'd seen her in the cell phone picture. The guy with the tattoo was pointing a gun at her face. The muzzle was inches from her nose. Tattoo Guy had his back to the camera and was looking towards the front door, but Gina's eyes were looking directly into the camera.

"She saw it come through the wall," Henry whispered.

"Yeah. Hopefully, she won't blow it," I said.

"If she does, we go," Dalton said.

"Ok." I busied myself making sure my gear was arranged correctly and breathed deeply.

On the kitchen side of the screen, Pimple Face went back to the front door.

"Sorry, can't find it," he mumbled. He seemed like he was in a hurry to get Casey out of there.

"No worries. Thanks, dude!" Casey chirped.

She hurried back through the front door of our place and picked up her grenade again. On the screen, I watched as tattoo guy stuck his pistol in the waistband of his jeans. He started rooting around in a duffel bag on the floor. I realized I recognized him. The night I'd been ambushed by the skinheads in Portland, he had been the younger man who had muscled Gina into the SUV.

Gina was no longer looking at the camera, she had her eyes closed and her lips were moving silently. I wondered if she was praying.

"Nice work," Dalton said to Casey. He motioned us to follow, and we all went upstairs to the back bedroom. Henry slaved all the cameras to a single laptop and we now had a view of the whole apartment. Tattoo Guy was puffing on a pipe. Meth. The windows in both apartments were open, and the sweet, chemical odor of burning methamphetamine wafted through.

Tattoo Guy took a big drag, then handed the pipe to his partner, who took a puff reluctantly. This wasn't good. If they'd been passing a marijuana pipe around I would have welcomed it. Tattoo Guy's raging meth withdrawal symptoms were now going to be replaced by an actual manic high. He started pacing around the living room. He pulled the pistol out of his jeans and started playing with it.

"I think we should just have some fun with her and then do her, and then get out of here," he said, sighting down the barrel of the pistol at Gina's head.

"Curtis said..." Pimple Face started.

Tattoo Guy wheeled and pointed the gun at Pimple Face.

"I don't give a FUCK what Curtis said. I'm in charge here."

Dalton keyed his mic.

"Bolle, this is Dalton, how far out are you?"

Bolle answered right up. "We are just now crossing the river. There was a four-car pile-up on the Glen Jackson Bridge. We're monitoring your feeds. I'm guessing twenty minutes minimum, maybe as much as thirty."

"Copy. We may go early."

Bolle didn't answer for a few seconds. "It's your call," he said.

"New plan," Dalton said. He grabbed a satchel off the floor. "Bring the laptop in here."

We all followed him into the front bedroom. He used the thermal imager to find the studs in the walls, then opened his demo kit. He pulled out a reel of cord that looked like clothesline, but I recognized it as explosive detonating cord, or "det-cord." Dalton handed me his roll of duct tape.

"I need pieces three inches long," he said.

Dalton started making a rectangle on the wall, wide enough to bridge across two wall studs and tall enough for us to walk through. As I handed him strips of tape I kept one eye on the monitors. Tattoo Guy was pacing around the apartment mumbling to himself and playing with his gun. Pimple Face guy was back to playing video games. Gina looked like she was shivering. It was warm, so it had to be from fear and not cold.

Dalton finished his rectangle, and with a speed clearly born of long practice, hooked up a pair of blasting caps and connected the whole thing to a firing device. He motioned us out of the room and followed behind, trailing electrical wire behind him.

I looked over Henry's shoulder at the screen. Tattoo guy was still pacing around. Pimple Face had apparently resigned himself and was sitting on the floor puffing on the meth pipe. Gina sobbed and Tattoo Guy whirled.

He put the gun against her head.

"I can't take it anymore. BE QUIET!"

"Shit," Dalton said.

Gina had reached her breaking point. She gave a scream.

"We're going," Dalton said. He looked at Casey. She was still carrying her grenade.

"You bang the front door," he said. Casey nodded.

He pulled a flashbang off the front of my vest and handed it to Henry.

"You bang the back."

Henry took the bang without hesitation and he and Casey headed downstairs.

"I'm ready," Henry said.

"Me too," Casey said a few seconds later.

The laptop was on the floor where we both could see it. Tattoo Guy still had his gun pointed at Gina's head. His finger was on the trigger. We now had to choose between watching him shoot Gina, or detonating the explosions, which might startle him into pulling the trigger anyway.

Pimple Face put the meth pipe down. "What will we do after we shoot her?"

Tattoo Guy turned to face him. The muzzle was no longer pointed at Gina's head.

"Execute. Execute. Execute," Dalton said.

CHAPTER ELEVEN

We didn't have enough people to do this correctly, so we were making up for it with explosives. The two flashbang grenades detonated within half a second of each other. Score one for the nerds. Then Dalton pushed on the detonator for the wall charge.

The flashbangs had been loud enough to rattle the windows. I remembered to open my mouth right before Dalton blew the wall, but it still felt like an icepick shoved in my ears. Instantly everything sounded like it was underwater, except for a high keening whine in my ears. The lights went out and the room in front of us filled with drywall dust and smoke.

Dalton charged forward. I was right behind. I flinched when a bunch of water hit the top of my head and ran down my back. I'd noticed that this apartment complex had a sprinkler system in the ceiling. Apparently, the explosion had ruptured one of the pipes.

The hole in the wall was big enough that I didn't even have to duck. We entered the other apartment at the top of the stairs. We turned left and started down. Dalton paused two-thirds of the way down, plucked a flashbang off his vest and held it up where I could see it. I slapped him on the shoulder with my left hand to let him know I was ready. He pulled the pin on the grenade and tossed it. He banked it perfectly off the kitchen counter so it dropped into the living room.

The blast felt like a punch in the chest. My ears shut down completely. I couldn't hear anything but a sound like waves at the ocean. We charged down the stairs. I looked through the red dot scope mounted on the little rifle in my hands, careful not to point it at Dalton's back as we charged into the living room. Dalton broke left, hugging the wall, so I followed the wall on the right.

Pimple Face was lying on the floor with his hands over his eyes, screaming. Dalton soccer kicked him in the abdomen and he went still. Gina's chair had tipped over and she lay on the floor screaming. Tattoo Guy was behind her on the floor, sitting on his ass with a dazed expression on his face. Somehow he'd managed to hold onto his pistol the whole time.

I screamed, "Police! Drop the weapon!" as loud as I could. It sounded like my voice was coming from miles away. Gina was on the ground squirming, still bound to the chair. I hoped she didn't figure out a way to stand up, because she'd be right in my line of fire.

The skinhead had a blank, thousand-mile stare like he was somewhere else. No doubt he was concussed, and maybe even blinded by the grenade. His head swiveled from side to side. The pistol was aimed at the ground, but his finger was on the trigger.

"Drop the gun!" I screamed again. I put the red dot of the sight on his face. I kept both eyes open, so I could see his hands.

He started to raise the gun, so I shot him, taking the quarter of a second to settle the red dot of the scope on the bridge of his nose. I was shooting over Gina, so it had to be precise. The little carbine barely recoiled, giving me the slightest tap on the shoulder. The sound of the shot didn't even register to my abused ears.

A fan of red hit the wall behind him and he hit the ground in a boneless slump. The pistol fell from his hand and didn't fire. It was over.

Gina's mouth was open, and she was screaming, but I could barely hear her.

Dalton was getting Pimple Face into flex-cuffs, so I walked over to Gina and started cutting her loose from the wraps of duct tape that held her to the chair. I helped her up, and she leaned against me.

"Dent? Dent?" I could barely make out Casey's voice in my earpiece over the whooshing noise.

"Standby," I croaked into my microphone. My throat felt like it was full of dust.

Dalton had Pimple Face well under control. He had a knee in the guys back and was turning out his pockets. Tattoo Guy was lying in a puddle of his own brain matter, so we didn't have anything to worry about there.

"I'm walking one out," I said. Dalton gave me a thumbs up.

I steered Gina around some skull fragments on the carpet and out the back door. A couple of people were standing in the green space between the apartment buildings, at least one woman was holding her cell phone up, taking pictures or video. Another reason to hate cell phones.

We went inside. Henry was talking on the radio with Bolle. I could hear bits and pieces of their conversation if I concentrated hard enough. It sounded like Bolle was succeeding in letting the local cops know they shouldn't come and shoot us. That was a bonus.

"Stop," Gina said and bent over. I managed to get my shoes out of the way just in time to avoid the vomit. She collapsed to the floor, crying.

I sat down next to her. As the adrenaline burned out of my system I felt a wave of fatigue wash over me that felt like I was being crushed to the floor by a massive hand. I wanted to just curl up there on the carpet and go to sleep. My hearing was slowly starting to come back. I could hear Casey trying to comfort Gina.

Dalton's voice came over my earpiece.

"We're drawing quite the crowd outside, and it sounds like the cops are on their way."

Come to think of it, I could hear sirens off in the distance.

"Jack is in the air over you," Bolle said. "I'd like to get the hostage out of there before the locals show up and we have a jurisdictional dispute."

"Dent, get the hostage into our vehicle," Dalton said. "Casey can drive you back over to the fire station. Send Henry over here to help me with the other guy."

I made myself get up. Casey coaxed Gina to her feet.

"Come on. We're going somewhere safe," she said.

We walked out the back door, with Gina supported between us. The crowd had grown and there were more cell phones out, but nobody approached us. The word "police" stenciled on the front of my vest, coupled with the wicked looking gun hanging around my neck probably helped.

"Need you to drive," I told Casey as I dug in my pocket for the keys. I felt like I was moving in slow motion. My hearing was better, but I still felt like I was underwater. I was probably mildly concussed from the blasts.

We saw red and blue flashing lights heading towards the apartment complex as we pulled out, but nobody tried to stop us. Jack was circling the fire station in the Little Bird and landed as we pulled in. I helped Gina out of the minivan and started walking her towards the helicopter with my arm under her shoulders. I was afraid she would collapse if I didn't hold her up.

Eddie and Alex got out of the helo. Eddie clapped me on the shoulder as he ran by to join Casey in the van. Alex's face was blank as she helped me load Gina into the helicopter. I climbed in beside Jack and we were off.

Jack circled the apartment complex once. There was a sea of red and blue lights in and around the complex, with more coming from all directions. Bolle had been smart to get us out of here when he did.

I looked over my shoulder. Alex took Gina's blood pressure and other vitals then pulled a syringe out of her bag and injected it in Gina's arm. Whatever was in the syringe, it worked quick. Gina became glassy-eyed and still.

"How is she?" I asked over the intercom.

"Bumps and bruises," Alex answered. "And really freaked out. I gave her enough Ativan to chill her out for a while."

"So we don't need to go to the hospital?" Jack asked.

"Nope," Alex said. She didn't sound particularly sympathetic towards Gina. I didn't blame her.

"Ok. I'd like to land at the airport and transfer you guys by vehicle. Landing at the factory is liable to attract a bunch of attention."

Alex looked at Gina, who was staring out the window. Her mouth hung open and she was blinking.

"She'll be fine."

Speaking of attracting attention, I was still wearing an assault vest and a gun slung around my neck. I started pulling them off.

"There's an empty duffel bag under the rear seat," Jack said.

It was hard in the cramped confines of the Little Bird, but I managed to pass the stuff back to Alex so she could stow it in the bag. She didn't make much eye contact with me, but once when our hands touched, she gave it a little squeeze.

Jack slowed the Little Bird down and flared for a landing in a far corner of the Troutdale Airport, where one of Bolle's ubiquitous black Suburbans was waiting for us. I'd seen the gridlocked traffic and had to admit the Little Bird was an excellent idea, even if it did attract attention.

Jack handed me the keys to the Suburban and we transferred Gina to the back seat. She was glassy-eyed and stoned, but much easier to manage. I felt like I could drive but I still took it slow. As I approached the back door to the factory it rolled up, courtesy of whoever was watching the cameras. I helped Alex settle Gina in the makeshift infirmary, which had once been the plant safety supervisor's office, and went in the watch room.

Drogan was manning the phones, radios, and cameras. She seemed non-plussed to be left out of the action. I monitored what was going on for a while. Bolle was working with the local cops to secure the apartment building until he could get a warrant to search it. Reading between the lines, there was more than a little friction.

"I don't think there's much I can do here," I said. "I'm going to get some food and some rest."

"There's food in the break room, and nobody's using that trailer over in the corner," Drogan said as she pointed at the camera feed that covered the factory floor.

"Thanks," I said, and she replied with a grunt. I wasn't much in the mood for conversation anyway.

Still carrying my bag of gear, I went in the break room and made myself a giant sandwich. After eating it, I made another one and ate it too. I was too mentally fuzzy to do the math and figure out how long it had been since breakfast at the Williams' house, but I knew it was a few helicopter rides and one shootout ago.

The inside of the trailer was small but clean. This was another good idea. Instead of trying to turn the old factory into living quarters, they'd just hauled a bunch of trailers inside and hooked them up.

I set the bag of gear down on the inviting-looking bed. As I showered, the rescue played back over in my mind. I didn't feel any particular remorse over the man I'd shot. He'd kidnapped Gina and was going to kill her. It bothered me sometimes how cold I could be about something like this, but the bottom line was he was dead, and I wasn't. That was what really mattered.

I was toweling off when there was a knock at the door.

"Dent?" It was Alex.

"I'm in here." I wrapped the towel around my waist.

She walked in, saw me standing there dripping, then looked around the trailer.

"I've never been inside one of these before," she said.

"I grew up in one not much bigger than this. How's Gina?"

"Asleep. She's stoned out of her mind on Ativan." She took a step towards me. "Thank you for saving her. Are you ok?"

"Yeah," I said. "Didn't do my hearing any good, but I'm fine."

Things still sounded a little muffled, and I hoped the tinnitus would go away soon so I could sleep. I stood there with the towel around me, dripping on the carpet and trying to figure out what was going on. I didn't know where I stood with her. I wanted to get dressed but wasn't sure if it was ok to be naked in front of her. We'd spent two long, intimate days together last year, then she'd dropped out of my life for six months. I felt two equally powerful emotions at the same time. On one hand, I was pissed at her, wanted to yell at her for ditching me and being mostly silent for months.

On the other hand, I wanted her. I'd always been attracted to Alex. For years it had made me uncomfortable, because she was so much younger, and was Al's daughter to boot, but it was there, a primal attraction that I couldn't deny. I wanted to hold her, and smell her skin so bad just then. I was glad I was holding the towel, but soon it wouldn't be hiding much if this kept up.

She took another step towards me.

"I'm sorry," she said.

"For what?" I asked, taken aback by the change in direction.

"For leaving you. For not talking to you."

"Why did you?" It came out almost like a cry. I'd been asking myself that for months, had stared at the ceiling at night wondering it. It was like I'd lost her and Al both at the same moment.

"I..." She looked away, ran her hand through her hair. "I can't explain it all right now. But it wasn't you. You didn't do anything wrong."

"What are we doing right now?" I asked. She'd spent the last six months in de-facto control of our relationship, and part of me was still pissed about it. I was going to be damned if I was going to stand there in a towel for much longer.

She took another step towards me.

"Is that shower big enough for both of us?"

"Uh. No."

She peeled off her shirt.

"I guess you'll just have to stand outside and watch then."

CHAPTER TWELVE

Later, we lay there in a tangle of arms and legs on the bed, not talking. I was enjoying running my hands over her and feeling her pressed up against me. I didn't want this to end. This moment was simple and free of all the complications that were between us. Before, when I'd been with somebody, I'd accepted the fact that someday the relationship might end, and to be honest, given my track record, probably would. But with Alex, I was terrified that now that she was back, something would happen to drive her away again.

We'd been quiet for a long time, and when she spoke, it startled me.

"At first, I drank, and I didn't want you to see that," she said. "I went on a hell of a bender in the week after my dad died."

I didn't know what to say about that, so I kept my mouth shut. Alex's mom had been an alcoholic. Her dad had never quite been a full-blown alky, but after Alex's mom committed suicide he'd hit the bottle pretty hard. Alex had her own issues, from time to time. She'd gotten a DUI a couple of years ago, and that had been a wake-up call for her.

"I woke up one morning embarrassed. If my dad had seen me, he'd have been ashamed. I didn't want you to see me that way either. I'd had you on my mind for a long time, and now I was screwing up. I wanted to be around you, but I just didn't know how to go forward after what happened. So I left. I sold everything. The house. The Mustang. Cashed out my retirement. Then I got on a plane"

"To Hawaii," I said. I knew that much at least.

"At first," she said. "I surfed. I hiked. Every time I wanted to drink I went for a run, or a hike. I found a Kajukenbo school and started training."

I was vaguely familiar with Kajukenbo. It was a martial art that blended techniques from all over Asia, with some western boxing thrown in for good measure.

"I was the only woman there. It was a nasty little place. It smelled like balls and ass and there was a hole in the wall where somebody's head went through one day, but they trained hard. Every day. After a while most of them accepted me. It helped that I could do stitches and stuff on the side. One guy though, just couldn't handle it, just couldn't take no for an answer."

She smiled a little. It was a smile I'd seen on her dad's face, more than once.

"I left him needing some dental work, and probably unable to have children. I decided to leave Hawaii for a while. I went to Japan and trained at the Kodokan."

The Kodokan was the home of Judo, the Japanese grappling art. The people there were hardcore. I'd always meant to try Judo one day. Alex had been doing it since college, which strangely had made me avoid it. Before, I'd always been a little uncomfortable when our paths crossed.

"I lived there. I trained hours every day. I kinda had a big head on my shoulders walking in. I won some tournaments and stuff in college. These people made me look like an amateur. I loved it. All I had to do was move my body. While I was practicing I didn't have time to think. I didn't have to remember my dad's head exploding. After I practiced, I was too tired to do anything but sleep."

She rolled onto her side, propped her head up on one hand, and ran the other hand over my chest.

"I missed you though. I thought about you every day. I just couldn't talk to you because there just wasn't space in my head. I just needed to do what I was doing. Then one day, I managed to throw five opponents in a row, people that could toss me around like a rag doll when I first walked in the door. Then it clicked. I was done. I'd done what I needed to do. It was time to come back here, and see what was left. I wanted to see you."

I was quiet for a while. I liked the way she felt next to me, liked the way she touched me, liked the way she smelled. There was a rough callous on the bottom of her hand, from gripping those heavy canvas Judo uniforms, but it didn't bother me. I wasn't really into women that were China dolls. I was tempted to ask her to get dressed and go get in one of the cars outside. We could just point it in a direction and go, away from all this madness and violence.

"What is it about me? What makes you want me?"

I was used to being attracted to women. There had been more than a few over the years, ranging from mild interest to outright infatuation. But I was used to them not being attracted back. When a woman did seem interested in me, it usually took me by surprise. I wasn't any good at this.

"I think part of it is pheromones," she said. "I think there's something about you that my body is drawn to, probably because your genetics are a good match for mine."

"Oh," I said. I wasn't sure how I felt about that.

She laughed. "That's not the only thing silly. People like that come along from time to time. There was a guy in college. Good grief. From the neck up I knew he was an asshole, but from the waist down I totally wanted to have his babies."

Part of me wanted to know how that ended, but I decided it was best I didn't ask.

"The other part is you're a good man. Like my dad. I don't mean that in a creepy way. It's just that I grew up thinking all men were like my dad. It really wasn't until high school I started to realize most of them weren't. You were a good guy though. My dad thought the world of you, which made me even more interested in you. I could tell you were attracted to me, but you'd never do anything about it, at first because you were so much older than me, then later, I think because you'd gotten it into your head that it just couldn't happen."

"I'm still older than you," I said before I had a chance to think. I thought about that frequently.

She shrugged. "When I was sixteen, and you were twenty-six, it would have been creepy. Now though? Every guy I know that's my age is like a giant overgrown man-boy. I need to be with an adult."

I realized I was fighting sleep. I felt like I was having one of the most important conversations of my life, and I was fighting to stay awake. Maybe I was too old.

"Your dad would have killed me."

"Yeah, he would have, then. Now he would be happy for us." With that, she sobbed a little and buried her face in my shoulder. I held her and stroked her hair. Then I cried too.

Finally, exhausted, we both fell asleep.

CHAPTER THIRTEEN

If Bolle had a problem with two of his people sleeping together, he didn't say anything. Alex and I had felt a little conspicuous walking out of the trailer together the next morning, but there was nobody on the factory floor to see us. Bolle was in the kitchen, pouring himself a cup of coffee when we walked in.

"Good work yesterday, both of you," he said. "I'm glad you're rested. Things were a little rough."

Considering I'd shot a guy in the face, after running through a hole blown in a wall, I thought rough was a little bit of an understatement.

"Gina is doing better, and I think it's time we try to find out what she knows. How would you feel about doing a soft interview?"

I was a little taken aback. I was technically a Federal law enforcement officer. During my years in the Portland Police Bureau, I'd killed two men, and both times I'd been on paid leave, subjected to endless rounds of interviews, after action reviews, tactical debriefings, and a psych eval. On Bolle's squad, I could apparently smoke a guy one day, and go right back to work the next day.

"I'll give it a shot," I said.

Bolle had done a decent job of turning one of the old offices into an interview room. The pastel walls still smelled faintly of fresh paint. I was already seated in the interviewer's chair when Drogan led Gina in.

Somebody had found her a pair of sweatpants and a sweater, definitely not her usual standards of couture. She looked tired and haggard, but not stoned out of her gourd like she'd been last night.

"How are you, Gina?" I asked.

She was nervous. Her eyes darted around the room and she kept picking at the hem of her pants.

"Better than I was last night, Dent," she said. "When can I leave? No one will tell me. I just want to go home."

"Well, Gina, we want to make sure you're safe. The people that took you were some pretty bad dudes. We're not clear about some of the details, so we want to work with you to understand exactly what happened."

I was trying to create a sense of rapport with her, make her feel like we were both on the same team and my biggest interest was in making sure she was safe. To a certain extent, that was true, but I also smelled a rat. I strongly suspected there were some things Gina wasn't telling me.

"They... Took me," she said, not meeting my eyes.

"The men at the house? Where they tried to kill me?" I asked.

"Yes," she said. "The ones you shot."

"Had you ever seen them before?" I asked.

"I'd never seen those men before. They took me to that house, told me I had to call you and to try to get you inside. They made me."

"You said 'those men,' but there was somebody else, somebody you had seen before, and he was behind all this, wasn't he?"

"I don't know what you're talking about," she said quietly. She didn't meet my eyes.

I scooted my chair closer, moved in towards her.

"Gina, I think you need to understand a few things. This is a big deal. That man out there is a Federal investigator from the Justice Department. We think the men you were involved with were terrorists. The normal rules don't apply when it comes to terrorism cases. One of the decisions we need to make real soon is whether we're going to treat you like suspect or like a victim. The guy in charge of this doesn't buy your story. He thinks you're a suspect. Right now I'm the only friend you've got in this building, and I don't think you're being honest with me."

I didn't believe her either, but by making Bolle out to be the bad guy, I was hoping she'd see me as her only salvation. She kept her eyes down. She was picking at one of her nails now. She probably didn't realize she was doing it, but if she kept at it she was going to draw blood.

"Why don't you start by telling me his name?" I asked. I tried to keep the tone of my voice level and low like I was soothing a child.

"Bill," she said, keeping her eyes down. "He told me his name was Bill. I don't think it was his real name though."

"What did he look like?" I asked, already knowing what the answer would be.

"He was big. As big as you. Maybe taller. A few years older than you. Maybe as much as ten. He was super fit, and athletic. His head was always shaved. He had blue eyes, pale blue eyes."

Todd. That description fit him down to the last detail.

"But you knew him before the night they took you, didn't you. Gina?"

"Yes," she whispered, staring over into a corner of the room.

"You knew him while you and Al were married, didn't you, Gina? While Al was still alive?"

"Yes." This time she was barely audible. I wasn't sure the microphone in the room would pick it, but she was looking right at one of the hidden cameras.

"When, Gina? When did he approach you?"

"About a year before Al died. When he took the new job, working for the Feds."

That was louder. The microphones would have no trouble with that.

"What did you tell him?"

"Whatever I knew. When Al was traveling. What city. Whatever I could overhear on the phone."

I could feel a rage building that I knew I had to control.

"What did he give you, Gina?"

"Money. Jewelry." Her voice broke. "But that wasn't it. I was alone so much. When Al got his new job, he was gone. Even when he was there, he wasn't really there. Bill was... Nice to me. At first."

"At first?"

"At first. Then after he had me hooked, he started threatening me. Told me he'd make sure Al found out about us if I didn't do what he wanted. That's when he wanted me to start seeing the other guy."

"The other guy?" I asked. I hadn't seen that one coming.

"He was a cop too. You knew him. Steve. Steve Lubbock."

Lubbock. That explained all the missing things his wife had taken from the house. Apparently, it hadn't just been about Lubbock losing his job.

"Then, after Al... died, Bill just disappeared. I didn't hear from him for months until he showed up at my house with those awful men. He told me I needed to do what they said, or..."

This time she did break down, she sobbed for a few seconds, then collected herself.

"They told me I needed to do what he said, or he'd fly me over the

Pacific Ocean and drop me out of a plane, somewhere between Oregon and Japan."

There was no doubt in my mind that was true. That was Rickson Todd's preferred way of tying up loose ends. Casey had been on her way to being tossed out of a plane when I'd rescued her. No doubt Todd would have been happy to do it to me if he could have grabbed me.

"You must have been really scared," I said. I fought to keep my tone level, sympathetic. I wanted to build the level of rapport back up.

"I was. It was horrible," she said.

"One last question, Gina," I said. "It's important that you're honest with me. There's no holding back now."

She nodded her head.

"The day Al was killed, did you tell him where Al was going to be?"

"Yes," she whispered. "But he mostly wanted to know if you would be there."

I replayed it all in my mind again. I had relieved the moment Al had been killed over a thousand times. I'd stumbled right before the shot came. The bullet had whizzed past my ear and hit Al in the face.

I'd suspected I'd been the true target. Now I was sure I was right.

Gina looked at me hopefully as I stood. I'd never hit a woman before, but right now I wanted nothing more than to smash her head in the wall. Al had been more than a friend to me, more than a mentor. He'd been my father, much more than my real father ever had been. Gina had betrayed him and helped get him killed.

I needed to get out of this room.

"What now, Dent? Can I go now? Can I go home?"

I looked at her, my anger had turned cold. She was pathetic.

"That's not up to me," I said. "But honestly, I hope we figure out a way to put you in prison for a long time."

With that, I turned, walked out and gently shut the door behind me. From the other side came a wail like a wounded animal.

I stood in the hall, breathing long and slow. The next door down the hall opened and Alex stepped out. She was deathly pale.

"She spied on him. Set him up," she said.

I put my hand on the doorknob to the room Gina was in.

"You can't kill her," I said.

Alex's eyes were big and round. Her fists were clenched.

"I want to, so bad."

"I know, but you can't."

Her nostrils flared, and for a second I thought she might try to push past me. Thanks to her months in Japan, she probably knew some ways to break Gina's neck.

"I think they were aiming for me," I said.

Alex nodded. "I wondered."

Bolle stepped out then. Looked at each of us.

"I'm going to transfer her to another facility," he said, deadpan.

"That might be best," Alex said. "I don't think I can provide her with any more medical care. There's a conflict of interest when you want to kill your patient."

With that, she turned and walked down the hall.

CHAPTER FOURTEEN

Bolle called a meeting and we all gathered in the command center. At first, I didn't think Alex was going to come, but she finally showed. She took the last available seat, across the table from me. Her mouth was set in a hard line, but she seemed calmer, more focused. I think she'd just walked through the same process I had: starting out wanting to kill Gina, then realizing that the real offenders were Marshall and Todd.

Dalton was there, nursing an oversized mug of coffee. Also around the table were Eddie, Casey, Henry, Drogan, Byrd, Struecker, and Jack. The gang was all here.

Bolle cleared his throat.

"We attracted some attention yesterday. That's not a criticism of those of you that rescued Mrs. Pace, just a statement of fact. We can't throw flashbangs and fly helicopters around without people noticing."

I saw Alex wince at "Mrs. Pace." Maybe I could ask Bolle not to call Gina that anymore.

"We did well to get our hostage out of there when we did. We weren't so lucky with the surviving suspect. In order to make peace with the locals, we housed him in the Clark County Jail."

Bolle's little facility was totally off the radar. If we started housing prisoners here, we probably could be fairly accused of running a "black site," an off the books detainee camp. What we were doing with Gina was pretty sketchy, but at least we could argue she was a witness that needed protection.

Bolle hit his remote, and Pimple Face from yesterday stared back at us from one of the flat screens mounted on the wall. It was a booking photo, taken yesterday.

"His name is Alvin Tolly. Juvenile record. Mostly minor stuff like dealing weed and vandalism. He recently became a probationary member of the West County Hammerheads, a white supremest group."

I'd heard of the Hammerheads before. They were a bunch of vicious losers. They were mostly a problem in the counties to the west and east of Portland, but we'd had the occasional run-in with them when I worked for the city.

Bolle hit the remote again. Now we were looking at an old booking photo of Tattoo Guy. He looked a little younger and skinnier than when I'd last seen him, but I'd recognize him anywhere.

"This man is Clarence Coban, but as an adult, he changed his name to Thor Wulfguard. He was, until yesterday, a fully patched member of the West County Hammerheads."

Eddie gave me a wink and a thumbs up. I felt like I shouldn't take pride in killing somebody, but truth be told, I felt like the world would spin a little more freely on its axis. If the West County Hammerheads let Clarence, or Thor, or whatever the hell his name was, wear their patch on his jacket, it meant he'd done some bad things. The usual price of admission was something like beating a person of color until they were either dead or had some broken bones or raping a woman or something similarly heinous.

"The local police did let me spend some quality time with young Mr. Tolly. After some initial resistance, he became enthusiastic about talking to me."

Bolle clicked his remote again. A video of Tolly started playing. He had on a prison orange jumpsuit and had a slack-jawed expression on his face.

"So it was all Thor's idea?" Bolle's voice said from the speakers.

"It totally was, man. I had to go along with it or Thor was going to kill me. I was looking for a chance to escape. I was going to run away and call the cops when those guys charged in and shot Thor. I thought we were being bombed man, it was crazy."

"So I'm sure Thor didn't think of this by himself," Bolle said. "Who put him up to it?"

"It was all Curtis, man. Him and that big bald dude."

"Tell me about the bald man."

"He's big, like really big. He's old too but still fit. He's scary. Even scarier than Curtis."

"When did the bald guy show up?"

"A couple months ago, far as I know. I used to be Curtis's driver. I kept his ride clean, fetched him shit, picked up his women, stuff like that. I would take Curtis somewhere and he'd meet with this dude, but they'd always leave me in the car while they talked."

"Where did they meet?"

"Restaurants mostly. But one time I drove Curtis out to that big nature park in Portland. He met the dude out there and they just walked around for a couple of hours while I sat in the car. It was like they were on a nature hike or something. Weird."

"Powell Butte?" Bolle asked. "Is that the place you're talking about?"

"Yeah, that's it. Powell Butte. Look, can I get a sandwich or something? And when can I get out of here?"

The video cut off.

"Needless to say, Alvin isn't getting out of there any time soon. I did get him a sandwich though."

Bolle clicked again. Now we were looking at an aerial photo of a big green space.

"For those of you who didn't recognize the significance of that, Powell Butte reservoir is where the majority of the drinking water for the city of Portland is stored. The city built a giant underground water storage facility there a few years ago, to replace the open reservoirs that were over a hundred years old."

Bolle let that sink in for a second.

Dalton leaned back in his chair.

"Yeah, on the surface, that sounds troubling," he said. "But that's a hard target. You can't poison that much water without attracting attention. Even with something really lethal, we'd be talking tractor-trailer loads of contaminants."

Bolle shook his head. "But what if you just want a display? What if your goal isn't to kill people necessarily, but just scare people?"

The room was silent for a minute while everybody chewed on that.

"The drinking water for a million people passes through this system. All it will take is a hint that something is wrong with it and it will cause a mass panic that will cost millions of dollars. Marshall has been screaming for years that we aren't doing enough to protect ourselves against terrorists, that our borders are too weak. A terrorist attack in Portland would play right to his strategy."

Casey spoke up. "But why these white power assholes? Isn't Marshall's whole shtick about how vulnerable we are to foreigners?"

Bolle shrugged. "I think he would prefer to use somebody from overseas. In fact, we strongly suspect that's what he was doing last fall.

We think those men on the plane were destined to be used as patsies for some kind of attack. But time is running short. His election is coming up. I think what we're seeing is their plan B."

That made sense, in a warped way. I'd long ago given up being shocked at the things other people would do to advance their own agenda. I'd met sociopaths who lived in boxes down by the railroad tracks, but the ones that really scared me were the ones that lived in mansions.

"Who is Curtis?" I asked.

"Good question," Bolle said and clicked again. Another mug shot appeared on the screen. This one was of an older man. He was still a skinhead though. You could tell not only by the shaved head but by the tattoos. He didn't have any on his face, but the Nazi eagle on his chest came up all the way to his neck. I recognized him. He'd been at the house when the skinheads had tried to kill me. He was the older guy who had pulled up in the black Suburban and shot at me with the rifle.

"He was out the house," I said. "Where they tried to hit me."

Bolle nodded.

"I'm not surprised. His name is Ragnar Curtis. He's another name changer. He was originally named Marion Curtis, but changed it after his first stint in prison."

"Can't say I blame him there," Eddie said.

"Hey, John Wayne's real name was Marion," Dalton said.

Bolle looked annoyed at the interruption. "Curtis has worked his way up to leadership of the West County Hammerheads by virtue of brutality and animal cunning. The locals have gotten close to getting him on methamphetamine distribution charges on a couple of occasions, but they've never managed to get a good case on him."

The cops in Washington County had their hands full. In addition to the usual criminal street gangs, they had white supremacist gangs, some Asian organized crime, and a growing influx of Eastern European gangsters to boot. It was like playing whack a mole over there. While they were busy taking down one group, another one would metastasize.

"I'm confused," I said. "Marshall and Todd have a tremendous number of resources. They've got former Special Forces guys, SEALs, people like that on their side. If he had sent four of those guys to kill me in that house, I'd be in a bag right now. Why is he screwing around with these peckerwoods?"

Bolle sat down. "Getting into Marshall's organization is like peeling an onion. On the outside, you've got a legitimate government contractor. Maybe legitimate isn't the right word for a company that rips off the taxpayers to that degree, but the men who are involved think they are carrying out a worthy mission, just like when they were on active duty, only making more money."

I saw Dalton nodding his head. It made sense to me too.

"The next layer is the drug smuggling and human trafficking. We suspect quite a bit of heroin made it into the country via Cascade Aviation planes. Most of those former military men didn't know about that, but enough of them did to make it happen. Those men made hundreds of thousands of dollars."

Dalton was nodding his head at that too. Interesting. Not for the first time, I wondered what his story was.

"We think fewer than half a dozen people at Cascade Aviation and Transnational Solutions knew about the human trafficking. Even men that could countenance heroin being brought to American shores would put a bullet in Todd's head if they found out he was shipping American women overseas."

Dalton nodded at that too.

"How many of those former military men are going to support a terrorist attack on American soil? Even one that is only designed to make a statement?"

At one point in my life, I would have thought that number would be zero, but Todd himself was proof that wasn't true.

"So Todd and Marshall need cannon fodder," Bolle said. "They've found that in the Hammerheads. They may honestly have some sympathies towards their beliefs too."

Bolle stood. "Today, I want us to take a two-pronged approach. Dent, Dalton, Eddie, and I are going to pay a visit to Powell Butte Reservoir. Everyone else is going to work on finding Ragnar Curtis. We're going to run a combination of physical and electronic surveillance until we find him."

He looked at his watch. "We leave for the reservoir in an hour."

Everybody stood up and Alex headed for the coffee pot, which seemed like a good idea to me. I walked over to her. I wanted to ask her how she was but didn't want to do it in front of everyone. She reached over, gave my hand a quick squeeze and gave me a half-smile. I guess in the back of my mind, I'd been worried she'd blame me for her dad getting killed by a bullet meant for me.

"Guess while you're out investigating, I'll be standing by here in case somebody gets shot," she said. "Try not to drum up any work for me, ok?"

Bolle stepped forward. "Actually, I was hoping you could help us out with some other things. We're short of people, and I was hoping to work you into the watch officer rotation."

Alex seemed grateful for something to do. As Bolle and Henry led her off to show her how all the radios and other equipment worked, she gave me a little wave. Before I left the room, I made sure Casey was the one sitting by the cell phone monitoring equipment. She gave me a little wave.

I fueled up on coffee and headed back to our little trailer for a few minutes. I dug a burner phone out of my satchel and checked a Facebook group for buying and selling guitars in the Portland Metro area. There was an ad for a 1978 Shell Pink Fender Stratocaster, modified with Dimarzio pickups and a Floyd Rose tremolo.

I dialed the number in the ad. Dale Williams answered.

"Hello."

"It's me," I said. "How's it hanging?"

"Low and slow."

That was our all clear code. Anything else and we'd know the other man was in duress.

"I think we underestimated the amount of attention that ad would generate," Dale said. "I've gotten twelve phone calls since I posted it. I don't even know what a Floyd Rose tremolo is."

"Huh," I said. "I would have guessed the color would turn people off."

I briefed him about what was going on.

"I wondered if that was you I saw on the news. I'm just sitting here in my hotel, avoiding the mini-bar, and watching too much cable TV. Portland really isn't my kind of town. My boys are chomping at the bit to come out here and join in the fun, but so far they're listening to their old man and running the ranch. I'll check out this Powell Butte place. I'm in the mood for a little nature hike."

"Sounds good, Dale. I'll keep you posted. You keep that guitar case handy."

"Will do, son. If I have to open it, I'll sure as hell be playing somebody the blues."

I shut the phone. The conversation had been short, and since Casey was running the monitoring equipment, there wouldn't be any record of the call in Bolle's records.

It wasn't that I didn't trust Bolle, exactly. It was that I trusted Dale Williams more.

Dale was my ace in the hole. If this thing went totally to shit, having a cranky old man on my side who could put .308 caliber holes in someone's head from half a mile away seemed like a good idea.

Part of me wanted to protect Dale. He had much more to lose than me.

I wondered if, by the time this was over, he would wind up protecting me.

CHAPTER FIFTEEN

Dalton and I drove in one car. Bolle and Eddie went in another. Bolle apparently had another meeting later, and he wanted me and Dalton to be ready to roll in case something happened. We were driving around in a black BMW with a trunk full of guns. It was nice to work for an employer that understood the importance of quality vehicles that didn't look like cop cars.

It had been a long time since I'd been to Powell Butte park. I'd worked a case where a homeless man had been beaten nearly to death on one of the trails and never found a reason to go back. On the rare days that I did something to relax, I usually left Portland. I knew bad things happened everywhere, but when I visited other cities, I didn't know exactly what those bad things were.

There were a few more roads through the park than I remembered. They were all blocked off by two simple posts with a padlocked chain strung across them. It wasn't exactly high security. The new parking lot and bathrooms were nice though. The parking lot was empty except for us.

I got out and stretched. Two vehicles were approaching. First was a pickup truck with a police-style light bar with "Water Bureau Security" stickers on the hood and sides. Then came a compact car I recognized because it had been parked in front of Lubbock's house.

Eddie and Bolle walked over to join us.

"Looks like we're about to meet my old boss," I said.

"This should be interesting," Bolle said.

The uniformed security guy got out first. He was a burly dude in his 50's. At a few paces, you could confuse him for a cop. The uniform was a gray shirt over black pants, instead of the blue over blue the Portland cops wore, but he was wearing a badge and a duty belt. When you looked close though, you could see there was no gun hanging from the belt, and the badge said "security" instead of police. It looked like to me he had all the right stuff on to make somebody want to shoot at him, but nothing to shoot back with.

He looked at each of us, probably trying to figure out which one of us was in charge. Bolle stepped forward and stuck out his hand.

"Special Agent Sebastian Bolle."

"Zach Wilson." He shook hands all around. The guy looked like a professional. His uniform was pressed and neat, boots were polished and his gear looked squared away.

Bolle actually treated the security guard with some respect, I'll give him that. Bolle not only came from the FBI, but he came from a rich east coast family to boot, but he greeted the security guy like a colleague and not an inferior. Bolle's stock rose a little with me because of that. I'd been raised around blue-collar, working people who were doing whatever they needed to do to put food on the table.

I couldn't say the same for Lubbock. He walked up and didn't even acknowledge his own guy with so much as a nod.

"Special Agent Bolle," Lubbock said, extending a hand.

"Lovely to finally meet you, Lieutenant Lubbock," Bolle said with a shark's grin.

Lubbock wasn't technically a Lieutenant anymore. He'd taken early retirement from the police bureau, and the new gig at the Water Bureau was a civilian position.

"I believe we have a mutual friend," Bolle continued. "Gina Pace sends her regards."

Lubbock looked like he had been punched in the stomach. Bolle turned to Zach, the guard.

"So, what can you tell me about this place?" he asked.

Zach knew his stuff. I had to give him that. He pulled out a map, gave us a high-level overview of how the system worked. He did an excellent job of explaining where the water came in from giant conduits up in the mountains, how it was stored in a pair of giant underground tanks, and then distributed all over the system. He kept giving sidelong glances at Lubbock as he talked as if expecting his boss to weigh in on something, but Lubbock stayed silent. Lubbock probably only had a vague understanding of how all this worked.

"We do a combination of random vehicle and foot patrols through the area," Zach said. "We can cover more ground in the vehicles, of course, but we need to get out periodically on foot to really see stuff. I was just about to make a round on foot."

He looked around, obviously nonplussed at the idea of leading a gaggle around, but willing to do it anyway.

"I appreciate the briefing, Officer Wilson," Bolle said. "I have a commitment downtown. I was hoping Special Agent Miller and Special Agent Dalton could accompany you."

He looked at us, then unconsciously looked at our shoes. I was wearing a pair of Danner boots and Dalton was wearing a pair of those Scarpa mountaineering boots the Delta Force guys had always loved so much. I saw him relax a little. The guy probably put on some serious miles in this job and didn't relish slowing down for some office weenies.

Lubbock begged off too. He seemed hell-bent on getting out of here as quickly as possible. Wilson grabbed a waist pack from his vehicle, checked out on his radio and we were off.

At first glance, you'd never guess that a substantial chunk of the city's drinking water passed through this area. The park looked like a series of big, open grassy fields surrounded by patches of woods, but if you looked closely you started to see utility vaults, little concrete bunkers, and the occasional pipe here and there. Wilson went about his job as we shadowed. It was clear the guy knew the place well. He checked lots of nooks and crannies that no one would notice at first glance. In a particularly dense stand of trees, he found the remains of a homeless encampment. There was a small fire ring, some trash, some unburied human waste. He took some pictures and jotted down a few notes.

"So what's the biggest problem you guys have out here?" Dalton asked.

"Graffiti. Vandalism. Issues with homeless people like this. Kids come up here and screw around and smoke dope. We get the occasional lost or injured hiker."

"But no real attempts to tamper with the water system?" I asked.

He almost laughed. "No. This isn't the place for that. I'm not sure what type of tip you guys got, but there are much more vulnerable places than this."

Dalton nodded. "I've read the vulnerability assessment."

Wilson seemed impressed by that. He and Dalton launched into a discussion about the water system that quickly left me in the dust. They talked about buried and unburied conduits, seismic vulnerability, backflow prevention and a bunch of other stuff that only vaguely made sense to me. It was clear Dalton had studied up.

The whole trip around the complex took a couple of hours. I wasn't the expert that Dalton was, but I could tell that breaching the actual reservoir would take massive amounts of explosives, and plenty of time to prepare them. It wasn't like a guy could drive up with a bomb in a backpack and do significant damage. Wilson showed us some valves and distribution equipment. It would be problematic if they were damaged, but the system could be back up and running in a matter of days.

None of this made any sense. The only real value of an attack here would be the symbolism. Todd and Marshall were evil. That was an old-fashioned word that people were uncomfortable with these days, but I thought it fit. Maybe there were limits, though. Maybe they balked at the idea of wholesale slaughter and would launch an attack here that would get attention, and cost millions of dollars, but not take many lives.

Wilson seemed like a steady dude. He obviously took his job seriously but didn't come up as a hyperactive cop wannabe the way so many security people did.

"So what did you do before this?" I asked, genuinely curious.

He gave me a sidelong glance. "I was a licensed clinical social worker for fifteen years. I got burned out and one morning I walked in to work, meaning to ask my boss for a vacation. What came out instead was 'I quit.' I've got a kid I'm raising, so I took the first gig that came along, which happened to be this."

He walked over to a utility vault set in the ground and gave the lid a little tug to make sure it was locked.

"It's not the most glamorous thing in the world, but it pays the bills. I get paid to walk around and I don't have to try to solve anyone else's problems."

That made sense to me. I'd known some social workers during my time as a cop. The young ones always seemed like they were ready to save the world. The older ones all seemed like they would rather have their teeth drilled than go to work.

After our circuit of the complex, we wound up back in the parking lot by the vehicles.

"Look," I said, pulling out my phone. "I'm not sure what's going on here, but I need you to look out for two guys for me."

I showed him pictures of Curtis and Todd, then forwarded them to his phone.

"If you see these guys, call us. Don't approach them. Just give us a call at this number. Somebody will answer 24 hours a day."

He nodded and I put the phone away. Zach got in his vehicle and we got in ours.

I could tell Dalton was a little surprised I was sharing intel with the security guy. In my time as a cop, I often trusted the ordinary people I met on the street with a little information and asked them to help. It had paid off more times than I could count. I had received tips from store clerks, utility workers, mail carriers and nosy little old ladies that helped me put murderers in prison.

"What do you think?" I asked him as we drove through Portland.

Dalton shook his head. "It's not a hard target. Getting in isn't the problem. It's doing any damage. I could blow that reservoir. You give me enough explosives and enough time to prep it, I can blow up anything. But the only way to blow that reservoir is to dig some giant holes, lower in hundreds of pounds of explosives, then tamp it all down with earth. I'd need, half a dozen, maybe a dozen charges. Each one would take hours and a backhoe to prepare."

He signaled a lane change, accelerated to take us onto the freeway.

"The distribution stuff? It's more manageable. I could blow some of those valves and pipes with a cutting charge, take me fifteen minutes to prep it. But there are so many fail-safes, you can't create a flooding event that way. You'd have to blow multiple sites, so then we're back to the problem of being there for hours, undetected."

"All that assumes they have a professional blaster at their disposal," I said.

"Exactly," Dalton said and nodded. "And access to professional grade explosives. If they've got an amateur who is making his own stuff with instructions he downloaded off the Internet, that changes everything."

"How about poison?" I asked.

Dalton shook his head again. "It's a delivery problem. Biologicals like bacteria or viruses, even something like ricin, you'd need massive amounts. We're talking forty-foot tanker truck loads. If you pull an eighteen wheeler in there, somebody is going to notice. Your best bet would be to drop some kind of low yield radiation source in there, like a Cesium-137 capsule from a medical device. It wouldn't kill anybody right away though. It would take years to figure out what was going on, but that doesn't work as a terrorist incident either. They want an immediate bang."

"I think Powell Butte is a diversion," I said.

"Either a diversion or just a symbolic attack," Dalton said. "It just doesn't make sense any other way."

I felt like there was something I was missing. I just couldn't see it. Todd had played us before. Last year he lured us into an ambush down at the Albany Airport. It had been a big gamble on his part. It hadn't really worked out for either side. We'd busted the ambush, well enough to rescue the women before they could be shipped out of the country, but we hadn't obtained the evidence Bolle needed to go public and start seeking indictments. Todd had dealt us a heavy blow, but he'd also lost the group of middle-eastern men he was shipping into the country for whatever he was planning.

I wondered if he was playing us now. I remembered Bolle's onion analogy. I wondered if there was one more layer to the onion we weren't seeing.

My phone rang and I dug it out of a pocket.

"Dent," I said.

"Hey." It was Alex. "Turn your radio onto the Portland Police channel. There's a big disturbance downtown with a bunch of skinheads."

"Wonderful," I said as I started twiddling dials on the police radio installed in the BMW.

"Bolle wants everybody to head to the general vicinity of downtown, in case Curtis and his people are there."

"Ok. We're on our way downtown now." Beside me, Dalton nodded. He couldn't hear her but was apparently picking up on the gist of the conversation.

"Be careful," she said.

"Will do."

There was a long pause. I wasn't sure what to say next. I wanted to say "I love you" but I wasn't sure if it was the right thing to say, and even if it was, I wasn't sure if saying it for the first time as I was barreling down the interstate next to a former Delta guy was the right way.

"Bye Dent." She sounded a little miffed.

This was new. I'd never had a romantic relationship with a co-worker. There had been plenty of female cops at the Police Bureau, and a handful of them had expressed what I thought was some interest, but I'd always kept them at arm's length. Alex and I were going to have a talk soon, and figure some stuff out.

The BMW had red and blue lights mounted behind the grill. Dalton flipped them on and accelerated around a landscaping truck.

Apparently, he was also reading my mind.

"Shouldn't get your honey where you get your money," he said in a sing-song voice.

I just sat there and glowered.

CHAPTER SIXTEEN

The center of the unrest seemed to be the Plaza Blocks, a park directly across the street from the Portland Justice Center, which housed the Portland Police Bureau's Central Precinct. As we drove into the heart of the city, I could hear yelling and drums. There were sirens all over the place as police units converged on the area.

"I saw in the news this morning there was supposed to be some kind of peace rally downtown today," Dalton said as he weaved around a bicycle courier. A woman in a long flowing dress was walking down the street holding a sign in one hand that said: "give peace a chance." She was bleeding from the head and had a dazed expression on her face.

"Let's get some high ground," Dalton said and turned into a parking garage at 1st and Jefferson. My heart did a little double clutch when I realized where we were. The sniper that had killed Al had hidden in this parking garage. I broke out into a cold sweat as we drove up the circular ramp to the top floor. I hadn't been back here since the day Al died. I'd managed to avoid coming downtown until now.

I felt sick to my stomach and it was hard to concentrate on what we were doing. Dalton drove all the way to the top and stopped the car. He popped the trunk release and got out. I followed him on shaky legs. Dalton pulled a tennis racket bag out of the trunk. It held one of the little .300 carbines he was so fond of. He handed a pair of compact binoculars to me, then pulled out a pair for himself.

There were three kinds of people moving around on the streets. First were the folks who I figured had been involved in the original march. They were all carrying signs that said stuff like "love wins" and "be the change you want to see in the world." A good number of them were white and young, with that earnest look I'd come to associate with Reed College and Lewis and Clark College, but there were plenty of black folks, Latinos and a scattering of Asian people as well.

The second group was the assholes. I could see at least half a dozen skinheads in a tight little knot. Dressed in green bomber jackets, jeans and engineer boots, they were screaming obscenities and racial slurs. A couple of them carried honest to goodness wooden shields, like something an ancient Viking warrior would have carried.

The third was a handful of cops. Since this was supposed to be a peace rally, the Bureau probably hadn't pulled in a bunch of staff. They certainly hadn't called out the Rapid Response Team, our politically correct term for "the riot squad," so the cops that were out there were in their regular patrol gear, not full armor and helmets. Before I got out of the car, I'd tuned my portable radio to monitor the Portland Police central frequency, and I heard the order for all the cops to pull back and consolidate.

As I watched, one of the skinheads pulled a string of firecrackers out of a jacket pocket and lit them. The concussions rattled up and down the glass and concrete canyons of downtown, sounding just like gunshots. People screamed and started to run. His buddy flicked open an expanding metal baton and started smashing windows. I heard the sound of glass breaking from other places echoing through the streets.

"This is bullshit," I said. I wanted to go down on the street and start breaking some skinheads. As I watched, two of them charged a pair of women in headscarves, shouting obscenities. The women screamed and ran, and they laughed.

"Yeah, it's bullshit, but it's not our problem. Do you see Curtis?" Dalton asked as he scanned the area with his binos.

Dalton's detachment from what was unfolding in front of us pissed me off. I wasn't a Portland cop anymore, but I'd fought and bled and nearly died for this city, and seeing these assholes busting up the town and frightening people made me angry. I also didn't like bullies. I never had. I'd learned at a young age that the best way to deal with a bully was hit them as hard and as often as you could.

I made myself scan the street methodically. All the skins I saw were young, in their late twenties at most. They were foot soldiers, sent to go out and do stupid stuff and get arrested for the cause. I doubted Curtis would be out there among them. He'd be behind the scenes.

As we watched, more police cars started pulling into downtown. I even saw units from outlying police departments and sheriff's deputies from three counties, along with a couple of State Troopers.

"Looks like they're getting this in hand," I said.

"Yeah, I think it's a dry hole for us. I don't see any sign of Curtis or Todd," Dalton said. He took his eyes away from the binoculars and looked at me.

"We should circulate a little bit," he said. "Let's switch the radios to our frequency and walk around a little. If one of us sees Curtis, we'll sing out."

I nodded. It made sense. Our view here was limited by the surrounding buildings. Most of the action was happening just a couple of blocks northwest of us. Dalton stowed his tennis racket bag and our binoculars back in the car and we trotted down the stairs of the parking garage.

"I'll go north," I said pointing up the street.

Dalton headed off. The streets right here were deserted, but over towards the Plaza Blocks, I could hear yelling and commands being shouted over a bullhorn to disperse.

I don't know why I walked past the spot where Al died, but I did. Thankfully, six months later, there was no stain on the pavement, but I could still see a chip in the concrete where the second bullet had hit. It had narrowly missed my face. I still had tiny little scars around my eye from the flying concrete chips.

I stood there a minute, acutely aware that there were two cops just on the other side of the glass doors inside Central Precinct. I didn't recognize them, and they stared at me intently. No doubt their job was to keep the violence in the streets outside from spilling over into the building. I knew I probably looked pretty weird, just standing there staring at the pavement. I knew I should move along down the street before they came outside and braced me, but I couldn't make my feet move. I thought I was over that day but now that I was back to the spot where Al had died, I felt myself seizing up. For a second I smelled the awful cigars he liked to smoke.

Out of the corner of my eye, I saw the older of the two cops turn to the younger one. He said something and they both took a step forward towards the door. I willed my feet to move.

Ahead of me a woman with long blond hair wearing one of those flowing hippie dresses ran across the street, being chased by two of the Hammerheads. She stumbled on the curb and the two guys each grabbed one of her arms and started dragging her down the street.

That broke the spell. I charged after them. I felt a surge of anger at what I was seeing, but also a surge of gratitude. I desperately wanted to unload on somebody right now, to clear out some of the pent-up frustration and anger I'd been carrying around. Punching the ticket of two skinhead assholes seemed like the perfect opportunity.

I pulled my radio out as I went.

"I'm with two at Second and Main," I said. It was almost like being back on patrol duty again.

"You see Curtis?" Dalton asked over the radio.

"Negative," I said. "Two skins just grabbed a woman."

There was a pregnant pause. Then Dalton said, "Ok, I'm on my way."

I ran across the street. I was making good time and I was proud to not even be out of breath. The workouts were paying off. I closed to within a dozen feet in a matter of seconds.

The two skins didn't see me coming. The woman was kicking and squirming, but not screaming or yelling. I wondered if she was too scared to even say anything.

"Hey! Let her go!" I yelled. They stopped, then turned and looked at each other.

"Ok," one of them said with a smirk, and then both let go of the woman.

Something was wrong. The woman ran towards me and I had just enough time to realize the long blond hair was a wig that was askew on her head. Underneath the dress, she wore jeans and combat boots.

She kicked me in the balls.

We frequently practiced defending against groin shots in Krav. I had just enough time to twist my hips a fraction, so the toe of her combat boot glanced off the inside of my thigh and then traveled into my groin, instead of landing squarely. That made the difference between staying on my feet and hitting the ground. Still, I hunched a little and fought to breathe. It felt like a bomb had gone off in my groin.

She made the mistake of trying to kick me in the same place, the same exact way. She teed off for another ball shot, and this time I was ready. I brought my left leg over and intercepted the kick, disrupting her balance. As soon as my left foot hit the ground again, I threw a lunging left jab at her face. I was off balance from the ball shot, so it lacked power, but it still nailed her square between the eyes. The wig slipped off, revealing a bald head underneath and she staggered backward.

Then the two Hammerheads were on me. One threw a wild haymaker, which I ducked under. I came back with an uppercut to the body, but I was off balance and still rocked by the groin kick, so it didn't land with much force. The other guy slipped in, grabbed me in a bear hug around my arms, and slammed me against a parked car. I tried to stomp on his instep but missed. I head-butted him and was rewarded with a sick crunch as his nose flattened against my forehead, but he hung on, and immediately headbutted me back. I managed to drop my chin, so his forehead slammed into mine.

I fought to get free, but the guy was huge, easily my height, and yoked out with muscles that were the obvious products of free weights and steroids. I felt like my ribs were going to crack under the pressure, and fought to take a breath.

His buddy was trying to maneuver around and throw punches but succeeded only in hitting the guy bear hugging me. The woman ran up and started stomping at my feet and kicking at my shins. I fought to maintain my balance. The last thing I wanted was to get thrown on the ground so they could have a boot party on my head. My arms were pinned to my sides, so I couldn't access my guns, knives, or sap. I tried to turn so the gun on my right hip was pressed against the car, out of fear one of them would see or feel my pistol.

I was screwed. This couldn't last much longer. I kept fighting to get free, but I knew it was futile. My only hope was for one of the cops to see what was going on, or for Dalton to show up. I buried my face against the chest of the man bear hugging me, both to keep him from headbutting me again, and make it harder for his buddy to punch me in the face. I tried to lower my weight and spread my legs to keep him from throwing me. The woman teed off and kicked me in the side of the calf and my leg almost buckled.

There was a screech of brakes, and I felt a moment of hope, thinking it was a cop car.

"Move," I heard somebody say, and the woman and the guy throwing punches stepped back, while the guy clinching with me held on.

I heard a hiss, then I felt two pinches on my right side and leg, and then I felt like my whole body was on fire. I'd been shocked with a Taser before, but that didn't make it any easier. The guy bear-hugging me groaned. Apparently, he got to feel a little of the effects too.

The ground came up and hit me. My muscles jerked I flopped around as the guy kept shocking me. More hands grabbed my arms, and I felt my hands being bound together. Then I was picked up and thrown into a van that was waiting with its door slid open.

There was a big bald man sitting inside. I had just enough time to recognize Rickson Todd before a black hood was drawn over my face.

CHAPTER SEVENTEEN

The van door slid shut and I started kicking, which immediately earned me another ride on the Taser. I felt like my brain was rattling around in my head. I tried to scream, but couldn't make my mouth work right. All that came out was a low "nnnnnnnnnnnnnn" sound. The guy with the Taser let up, and I immediately started to roll. The Taser fired little barbs that were hooked up to the weapon by a thin wire, and I rolled hoping I could pull the barbs out.

He immediately shocked me again, and this time it felt like it lasted forever. My chest seized up and I felt like I was drowning. I tried to struggle to sit up, but couldn't move.

Finally, the electricity stopped and I fell limp and exhausted, like I'd just run a dozen miles. I hurt all over.

"Yeah. He's breathing," I heard a man say.

Barely, I thought. I felt like I was struggling to pull enough air through the thick cloth that was over my face. With each gasping inhalation, the cloth got sucked into my mouth. I felt like I was right on the verge of asphyxiating. I wanted to fight if for no other reason just to make them earn it, but I couldn't make myself move.

"We disabled the timer on the Taser," a man's rough voice said. "I can shock you as long as I want."

The Taser had a built-in safety feature and shut off the juice after a prescribed period of time. I wasn't sure what would happen if it was applied indefinitely but I didn't want to find out. I decided to quit fighting, for the moment.

First, my shoes were pulled off, then I felt my clothes being systematically cut away, probably with EMT shears. In only a couple of minutes, I was naked on the floor of the van. I realized this was probably how the first ambush, back at the house in Hazelwood, was supposed to end. I was lucky that time. Not so much now.

"Here," I heard one of them say. The van's window rolled down, there was the clatter of something hitting the street outside, then the window went back up. I guessed that was my radio and phone.

I made one last effort to sit up and was rewarded with a punch to the kidney for my efforts. I gagged and then threw up in my mouth a little bit. I fought to hold the vomit in my mouth, then swallow it, afraid that I'd suffocate if it got all over the bag over my head. I choked it back down and lay there panting. I wanted to resist, just to be defiant, but I knew there was no sense in getting my ass stomped just for the sake of my ego.

They turned on talk radio, as loud as the cheap speakers in the van would go. They were trying to keep me from hearing anything outside. I had no idea where we were. I tried to estimate how long it had been since they threw me in the van, and realized I didn't really know. It couldn't have been that long. I guessed we were probably still inside the city limits. The van slowed down and sped up, and took the occasional turn. We stopped completely a couple of times, I guessed for stop lights or stop signs. Then we settled into a steady speed. I wondered if we were on an interstate or state highway.

My hands were bound, I thought with flex-cuffs, and so were my feet. I pulled gently and realized both my hands and my feet were attached to something inside the van, probably a seat post or something similar. So even if I were able to get the door open, I couldn't fling myself out.

My efforts were rewarded by a kick to the ribs.

"Hold still."

I lay there and fought a rising panic. I was naked, bound and had a hood over my face that barely allowed me to breathe. Nobody knew where I was. Todd was going to kill me. That was a given. As I lay there, I tried not to imagine all the nasty shit he might want to do to me first.

After that last command, no one spoke. I wasn't even entirely sure how many people were in the van. This was all calculated to keep me as disoriented and as off-balance as possible. It was working. I tried to count my breaths. I figured about fifteen breaths a minute and tried to keep track of how many minutes. I wasn't sure if it actually gained me anything. It just made me feel like I had a little bit of control and helped me keep the feelings of panic and helplessness at bay.

I had one thing going for me. The longer I stayed quiet and

compliant on the floor of the van, the more comfortable my captors would be with me being there, and more they would subconsciously assume that I would continue to not be a threat. Right now, I had no way out, but it wouldn't always be that way. I would need to feign compliance, then if an opportunity presented itself, explode. I'd probably die trying, but in some ways that didn't bother me that much. I just wanted some input on how it happened.

So I tried to get comfortable on the floor of the van, and ignore the voice screaming in the back of my head that I needed to get out now. I tried to rest, and take stock of my body. I hurt all over, but nothing was broken. I tried to shift every now and again ever so slightly, to keep my legs and feet from falling asleep. I realized there was very little chance I was going to get out of this, but if an opportunity presented itself, I didn't want to blow it because my legs buckled under me due to lack of circulation.

Somehow it was easier to be naked with the hood over my head. Stripping me wasn't just a way to see if I had any hidden weapons or escape tools. They also wanted me humiliated and off balance, more concerned about the shame of being naked in front of other men than concerned with trying to escape. It didn't bother me as much as it would some people, but I would have greatly preferred to have some clothes on.

What concerned me more was being barefoot. Like most Americans, the soles of my feet were pretty tender. I wore shoes most of the time, and I didn't much relish the idea of running off barefoot. If I couldn't get mine back, this was going to be a problem. I have big feet.

We took a right-hand turn, and I heard the crunch of gravel under the tires as we slowed down. I felt the other men in the van stirring. It sounded like we'd be getting out soon. I forced myself to stay relaxed, experimented with moving my arms and legs as much as I could to make sure they weren't asleep.

The van door slid open. My legs were cut loose, then my hands. My hands were still bound together, but I was no longer connected to the van. I was dragged out and thrown on the ground. A boot heel ground down on the Achilles tendon of my right leg and I involuntarily let out a yelp, then inwardly cursed myself for it. I clamped my jaws together and resolved not to make any more noises, no matter what they did.

"Get up," a man said. "If I have to carry you, I'm going to break your ankle."

I played along. They stood me up and I got my feet under me. I felt myself tensing up as they led me forward. There was a man on either side of me, each with a hand on one of my arms. I shivered, not just because of the cool evening breeze, but because of fear. I wondered if they were going to just shoot me in the back of the head and dump me.

I heard a door being pulled open, then I was pushed up a few stairs. I almost stumbled but managed to keep my balance.

They say blind people develop more acute senses to compensate for their lack of eyesight. I didn't know if the hood had been over my face long enough for that to happen, or if this place just stank. It smelled like old fried food, garbage that needed to be taken out, and sweaty funk. The carpet under my feet felt kind of greasy, and despite all my other concerns, I found myself not wanting to touch it.

They led me a few feet. I got the impression we were in a cramped hallway, mostly from having one guy's hip jammed into my bare ass, and the other guy's hip jammed into my bare privates. Then they shoved me through a doorway.

"Sit." I was shoved down on to a chair. My hands were still zip-tied together, behind my back, and it hurt to sit on them. I sat there as somebody ran another set of zip ties around my bound hands to the chair. Then I heard the "zip" as another set of the plastic ties snugged up around my ankles, binding me to the legs of the chair.

Then I sat. From the occasional rustling noise, I got the impression that someone was in there with me, but I wasn't sure. From farther away in the building I heard male voices. I was pretty sure one of them was Todd, and there were at least two others. I couldn't make out words, just the sound of them talking.

I wasn't sure how long I was there, but it was long enough for my arms and legs to start to ache. My left arm, the one that had been cut the year before, was the worst. The pins and needles started in my hand almost right away. I tried shifting to get comfortable but I was locked down to the chair, and couldn't move. The chair itself felt flimsy. It was made of wood and creaked under my weight every time I shifted. I had just a little bit of wiggle room with my hands. Zip ties actually made poor restraints. They could be broken open with raw strength, as long as you didn't mind some cuts. I felt pretty sure I could pop them apart, but right now it would be stupid. I had no idea what was going on around me. There could be five guys standing within feet of me, each with a gun pointed at my head. Busting loose right now was a recipe to be either killed or immediately recaptured.

I had to pee, and considered just letting loose on the floor, but didn't want to sit in it.

I made myself bide my time. This was one of the hardest things I'd ever done. I was good at waiting, but I wasn't good at being helpless.

Outside, the screen door slammed. I heard a snatch of words I could make out. It was something about "load the others into the van" but I couldn't hear anything else.

I heard the tread of feet on the carpet.

"How's he doing?" I was pretty sure it was Todd.

"He's been pretty still," another man said. I jumped at how close he was. It seemed like he was only a foot or so away.

The hood was jerked off my head, and I found myself staring into Rickson Todd's eyes.

CHAPTER EIGHTEEN

"Hello, Dent." Todd sounded awfully chipper, but then again he wasn't the one zip-tied to a chair.

I took a second to respond, using the time to look around at my surroundings. I was in a cramped bedroom. A mattress lay on the floor beside me, with dirty tangled sheets on top. There was no other furniture. Clothes lay all over the floor, in piles that seemed to have no rhyme or reason to me. The walls were decorated with a Confederate flag, a picture of Hitler, and pictures of nude models torn out of magazines. I didn't even know people read magazines like that anymore. I thought it was all online. The centerpiece of the room was a little wooden rack, screwed crookedly to the wall, that held signed baseballs.

"I hoped to capture either you or Dalton. I figured it would be you. I knew you'd fall for that damsel in distress routine. I bet you were surprised when she kicked you in the balls."

I didn't say anything. I'd been sitting there, knowing this was coming and had resolved not to take any bait Todd offered. I'd gone to that cold emotionless place, where I was totally goal-oriented and devoid of feelings. All I wanted was an opening to exploit.

Instead of talking, I thought about my surroundings. The hall outside the bedroom door was barely wide enough for a broad-shouldered man. The far wall was covered in cheap paneling. I was pretty sure I was in a single wide trailer home. That actually helped me out quite a bit. Trailer homes had never been as popular in the north-west as they had been in Appalachia where I grew up. In large parts of Portland, they were prohibited by zoning ordinances. I doubted we were in a trailer park. We were most likely on a rural, or semi-rural piece of property in one of the neighboring counties.

"How about we cut through all the bullshit, Dent," Todd said. "You tell me everything you know about Bolle's operation, and I'll let you walk out of here." He smirked when he said it.

I weighed possible responses, ranging from the anatomically impossible to the succinct and obscene.

"You throw in a million dollars and a pony and you've got a deal," I said, flat and mechanical. Judging by the Confederate flag and picture of Adolf on the wall, this place belonged to one of the West County Hammerheads. So I was in Washington County, probably one of the little pockets of rural poverty that existed out here. The Hammerheads flourished in places like that like germs in a Petri dish.

Todd seemed disappointed that I wasn't rising to the bait. I don't know what he expected. I wasn't prone to tears and begging. I wished he'd just go ahead and do whatever it was he was going to do. Visions of having my fingernails pulled out, or electricity applied to my genitals rose up, and I squashed them down as quickly as I could.

"Why me?" I asked. I might as well fish for some information. "Why bother capturing me?"

"You were a target of opportunity. It suits my needs to have Bolle concerned with getting one of his pet dogs back, while I pursue other interests."

I was surprised he revealed that much to me. He was probably going to kill me.

"I think you may be overestimating my worth to Bolle," I said. That was actually true. I wasn't entirely sure I believed Bolle would alter his plans a bit because I'd been captured. I could easily see him writing me off as a combat loss and driving on.

"I think you underestimate your ability to be a pain in the ass," Todd said. "You've got a fairly undistinguished background, but you caused us no end of problems last year."

"You're sitting in a trailer home that smells like ass, surrounded by your wannabe Nazi friends, and you want to talk about my undistinguished background?" I said.

He laughed. There was no getting to this guy, so I didn't know why I was even trying. He reminded me of the jock guys in high school, the ones that scored big on the football field and thought they were entitled to the occasional date rape of a cheerleader. Their arrogance had caused them to underestimate me more than once. They couldn't conceive of being beaten by some trashy kid who lived in a trailer and wore the same clothes several days a week. They were always surprised when I kicked the shit out of them.

"In all seriousness, Miller, you have some insights we might find valuable. I know there's a lot of water under the bridge, but it's not too late to salvage this situation. We can do this the easy way or the hard way. The easy way involves some money, a change in your situation for the better. The hard way involves a plane ride to somewhere dry and sandy and lots of quality time with some of my guys who have spent the last ten years making Abdullah the bomb maker tell us all his secrets."

I realized he actually meant it. He actually thought there was some chance he could offer me something that would make me switch sides. That's when I got pissed. I'd managed to keep it together through being stripped, hooded, and zip-tied to a chair, but when he suggested there was some chance I could join him, that's when I started seeing red.

"Fuck you, you piece of shit," I said. "You were Special Forces, then Delta. You've got all the skills and access to help people. Those girls you sold? They're the people guys like you are supposed to protect. You wanna pull my balls off? Fine. You'll probably even get me to talk. But you think I'm going to join you? Fuck you."

I wished Al was here. He was so much more articulate than I had been. He would have certainly come up with something more articulate than two "fuck yous" in a row.

It didn't seem to faze him. He gave me a look like you'd give to an awkward teenager that didn't know manners. It was part irritation, part pity, and it pissed me off all the more.

"I don't know how a man of your age and background manages to maintain so much innocence about how the world really works. Do you really think you're on the side of justice? Bolle has his secrets, just like me."

"Bolle isn't planning on blowing up a water reservoir."

An expression flickered across Todd's face that I couldn't quite place. It wasn't quite a surprise that I knew about Powell Butte. There was something else there that I didn't understand.

"You need to grow up and make some choices, Miller. You're either a sheep or a predator. That's it. You don't get another choice. The sheep are here to serve the predators."

"Does it matter to you that the sheep you're planning on blowing up are Americans?"

He smirked again. "Sheep are sheep, Miller, it doesn't matter what flavor they are. The people in this country are fat dumb and happy right now, content to be comfortable and entertained. There's a whole world of hungry people out there that want what we have, and they are willing to take it from us. The American people need to wake up and harden up, and it's going to take a big statement to pry them away from their bread and circuses. It took Pearl Harbor to wake people up last time, maybe this time it won't have to be as big."

"It's the job of people like you and me to make sure people don't have to worry about stuff like that."

"Sounds like you've made your choice to be a sheep. You can be just another sacrifice for the greater good. When my work here is done, you can take that plane ride, and I'll introduce you to some friends."

With that, he turned on his heel and walked out of the room. I heard snatches of the conversation through the thin walls. I don't know if it was because I no longer had the hood over my head, or because they weren't trying as hard to keep their voices down, but I could hear them better now.

"Are the trucks loaded?" Todd asked.

"They are," another man answered. He sounded older. I wondered if it was Curtis. "Brody and Dolph are going to stay here with your prisoner."

"Good. Tell them to keep their distance. He's still dangerous. They need to stick together and remember, no guns around the prisoner. They need to lock them up."

"Dolph was an MP in the National Guard. He knows what to do."

"I'm sure."

I heard feet on the steps outside, then the crunch of gravel. Then several engines started up. At least one of them sounded like a big diesel truck. I listened as they turned around in the gravel outside, then drove off. I could hear the sound of the diesel for a long time.

I could hear two men still talking in what I guessed would be the living room, off to my right. They were being quieter than Todd and Curtis had been. I heard the clank of metal, and the sound of a heavy door closing. Maybe the safe?

My left hand was asleep. I shifted in the chair, trying to find a way to relieve the pressure on the joint and get some feeling back. I tugged experimentally at my bonds. I could break them, but if I was going to do it, I needed to do it soon, before I was numb in all my extremities. I arched my back and heard the chair creak. I had little doubt I could bust this chair in half if I needed to, leaving my arms and legs zip-tied to it. I just needed to find the right opportunity.

I heard the sound of feet on the carpet, so I quit screwing around with my bonds and the chair. Two guys appeared in the hallway outside the door. They were a regular Mutt and Jeff. The little guy was short, shaved head and all tatted up. He had bright little eyes like a weasel and carried a Taser in his hand. He was wearing the regulation Hammerhead uniform of jeans, a flannel shirt, and a green nylon flight jacket.

The other guy was big and doughy, and as soon as I saw his face, I had him pegged for a victim of Fetal Alcohol Syndrome. His nose was upturned and had a flat nasal bridge. His upper lip was so thin it was almost nonexistent, and the little divot most people have between their upper lip and nose, called the philtrum, wasn't there. He had a dull, vacant look I'd come to associate with people of low mental function. Unusual for most people with FAS, he was big, and there looked like there were some muscles underneath all that flab. He wore a pair of dirty-looking jeans, and his belly hung out of a t-shirt with a picture of a zombie on it. He was carrying a folding metal chair. He unfolded it clumsily and sat down.

The smaller guy pressed the Taser into his hand.

"Here, Brody. Just like Curtis said. You sit here with this in your hand and if he tries to escape you shoot him with this."

Since the big guy was Brody, the little guy must be Dolph. He seemed to enjoy being in charge. He gave me an evil little grin and walked out of my view, back towards the living room. I didn't like the looks of him. He was a type I recognized. I'd known way too many guys like him in the military. They were always supply clerks or motor pool guys, but they acted like they were commando throat slitters. I bet Dolph had a sizable gun collection and an affinity for big, cheap knives he bought at truck stops and gun shows. He probably told people that didn't know any better he had been some kind of Special Forces operator. He probably knew better than try that on Curtis and Todd, but I would have bet money even his claim of being an MP was an exaggeration.

Brody just sat there, slack-jawed, with the Taser pointed at me. His finger was on the trigger and I hoped he didn't discharge the damn thing by accident. I had been shocked with a Taser entirely too many times lately.

"What am I supposed to do, Dolph? Just sit here?" Brody asked.

"Yeah. Just keep an eye on him. I'll come relieve you after a while."

Dolph's voice came from the front of the trailer. It sounded like he was rummaging around the kitchen.

"But I can see his pecker!" Brody's voice was a plaintive whine. He sounded more like a little kid than an adult.

"You don't have to look at his pecker. You just have to shock him if he tries to escape." Dolph sounded exasperated. I wondered exactly what his relationship to Brody was.

I just sat there and stared at Brody. He added a whole new layer of complication to things. I wanted to escape and was planning on going out of my way to at least maim, if not cheerfully kill, anybody that got in my way. But Brody was a special case. He was pointing a Taser at me, but I was willing to bet he had a borderline IQ. I'd run into guys like him before, had even arrested more than a few for doing some pretty awful things. I wasn't exactly a bleeding heart liberal, especially compared to quite a few people in Portland, but I always wondered how much people like Brody were responsible for their actions.

"Stop looking at me. I don't want you to look at me," Brody said. He lifted the Taser up higher, and I actually saw his finger tighten a little on the trigger.

I dropped my gaze to the floor in front of me. It gave me an excuse to shift in my chair. My feet were tingling a little, but my right arm was fine. It was my left hand that was bothering me. I'd had intermittent circulation and nerve problems ever since I got cut, and right now it felt like a flipper hanging off the end of my arm.

"Sweet Jesus, there's no food in here fit for a man to eat!" Dolph yelled from the kitchen. "This bologna looks like it's ready to grow legs and walk off."

"Curtis ain't been around much," Brody said. "I've been hungry a lot. I'm hungry right now."

So Curtis and Brody both lived here? What were they? Brothers?

I heard the tread of Dolph's cowboy boots across the linoleum of the kitchen floor, then heard the sound change when he hit the hallway carpet. He appeared in the doorway and stood there with his hands in his pockets. I felt his beady little eyes on me but didn't lift my head to meet his gaze.

"He's a big son of a bitch, isn't he? Doesn't look so tough all tied to a chair like that though."

"I don't like him," Brody said. "I think you should shoot him like we did the other guy. Then we can get in your truck and go get a chicken bucket."

Dolph cuffed Brody on the back of the head, and I tensed, waiting for the Taser barbs to embed themselves in my skin. Somehow Brody managed not to pull the trigger.

"Shut your mouth, Brody. You know we ain't supposed to talk about that."

Dolph stepped into the room, partially blocking Brody's shot. I calculated whether I should make my move now. With any luck, Brody would shoot Dolph in the ass with the Taser, and simplify my problems a little bit.

"It's going to be hours before Mr. Todd's people get here to take this fellow off our hands. I don't much like the idea of sitting here starving while we wait. We can't shoot him, but I do like your idea of a chicken bucket. You sit here and keep an eye on him. I'm gonna take the truck and I'll be back in a few minutes."

"He scares me," Brody whined.

Dolph took a step forward. He was uncomfortably close. I kept my head down. I wanted to break out of the chair and wrap my hands around his scrawny little neck, but I held off. I couldn't believe what I was hearing. Was he really going to leave me alone here with Brody?

"Oh, I don't think you need to be scared. He's a big old man but he ain't gonna go nowhere. He's buck naked and barefoot. His shit is pretty weak."

There was something in his voice I didn't like, and involuntarily I looked up. Brody's eyes were dilated and he had a smile on his face that creeped me out.

"Me and you will have some fun when I get back, don't you worry. I can't shoot you like Brody wants, but I got some latitude about what shape you're in when we hand you over to Mr. Todd. I got plans for you."

I realized two things. One, that I was right at eye level with Dolph's belt buckle. Two, that evidence of his plans was evident right at about belt buckle level. Shit.

It was a struggle to not bust the chair and launch myself at him then, but instead, I just dropped my head and stared at the floor. Dolph took another step forward, and for just half a second, rubbed himself against the top of my head. I stifled a growl that built in the back of my throat. I could maybe take both of them now, but my odds were much better if I waited until Brody was alone.

Dolph gave a little giggle, then stepped back out into the hall.

"See, Brody, big guys like that think they're tough, but you can make them your bitch if you want."

With that, he all but skipped down the hall. I heard him whistling as he crunched his way across the pavement. Then a car door slammed and he drove off.

"How long does it take to go get a chicken bucket anyway?" I asked Brody. It was worth a shot.

"It's down by the gas station," Brody answered. "Hey. You ain't supposed to talk to me. Be quiet."

He shook the Taser for emphasis. That didn't exactly answer my question. I didn't know how much time I had, but I needed to err on the side of guessing Dolph would be back soon.

"You know that guy that you saw Curtis and Dolph shoot? He isn't really dead."

"Curtis and Dolph didn't shoot him. I did. Curtis tole me to do it. Let me use his favorite gun. The man's head went splat all over."

Jesus. They were using Brody as their executioner. If they ever did get caught, that would make a fine legal mess.

"You ain't supposed to talk to me. Shut up, I don't want to talk about that."

I let it ride for a minute. Brody was agitated. He was clearly scared to be alone here with me. I wanted to build on that fear just enough to occupy his mind, but not enough that he just went ahead and Tased me.

I started scraping a fingernail on my right hand against the chair.

"Stop that. I don't like that noise," Brody said.

I quit for a minute, waited for him to lower the Taser and watched his breathing slow down. Then I started scratching the chair again.

"I said stop it!"

"It isn't me Brody. That's the guy you killed."

"Nuh uh. He's dead. I saw his brains, and me and Dolph put him down in a hole."

"He clawed his way out of the earth, Brody. He's a zombie. He looks just like the one on your shirt."

He actually looked down at his shirt for half a second, and I almost went for it then, but his head and the Taser snapped back up like they were on puppet strings.

"You're lying. He ain't no zombie."

I was flexing and relaxing all my muscles, trying to limber up. I guessed I'd been in the chair for a couple of hours. My left arm was a lost cause, but everything else was as good as it was going to get. I made sure the locking bar on the zip ties around my wrists was as close to the center as I could get it. They were on pretty tight, but I still managed to roll them around on my wrists until I had the locking bar where I wanted it.

I started to scratch the chair again.

"Stop it!"

I shook my head. I wanted him used to me moving.

"It isn't me, Brody. It's the zombie. That's him scratching at the front door now."

This was it. Brody looked involuntarily to his left. I stood, popping my arms up towards my shoulders, keeping my wrists close together as I did. The zip ties bit into my skin and broke. I lunged towards Brody.

I didn't manage to break the chair or break the zip ties around my ankles. I flopped forward right as he triggered the Taser and the probes flew over my head. I landed half in Brody's lap with my elbows on his knees. He looked down, confused.

I reached up, grabbed the back of his neck with my right hand, and rolled, peeling him out of the chair. We both landed on the floor, side by side. I drove my right thumb into his eye and he squealed. His hands flew to his face, and I managed to roll over onto my stomach, fighting against the chair that was still zip-tied to my lower legs.

My left hand was still numb, and I had no fine motor control, but I could still slap it like a big flipper into Brody's groin. He shrieked and grabbed his crotch. I used that as an opportunity to roll him so he was facing away from me, then snaked my right hand between his neck and the carpet, so I could wrap my forearm around his neck.

It was the world's sloppiest choke. If he'd had the slightest bit of skill he could have dropped his chin and rolled out of it. I had my right arm tight against his neck, but my grip on the back of his head with my left was weak, and I couldn't wrap my legs around him because they were still zip-tied to the chair. He made the mistake of an untrained person: he tried to pull my arm away from his neck with both hands. He wouldn't have won that contest on a good day, and it didn't help that my arms were slick with my own blood from busting the zip ties. Also, my fear of being corn holed by Dolph when he returned was fueling my adrenaline rush.

I increased the pressure on his carotid arteries. The harder he fought, the quicker he was depriving his brain of oxygen. He made one last effort, digging his fingernails into my arms, then his heels drummed on the floor and he was still. I held the choke on for a few seconds more. I wanted to make sure he was out, but I didn't want to kill him. I'd made that mistake before. I'd held a choke on a man for too long and killed him by accident. As messed up as Brody was, most of this wasn't his fault, and I wanted to give him a shot at living.

I let go of him and fought to sit up. The zip tie holding my right leg came off easy. I fought with the one on my left, twisting, and turning and giving myself a nasty gash before it finally came loose.

On wobbly legs, I managed to stand. I took stock. My left hand had gone from being numb to feeling like it was being jabbed with a thousand little needles, but I could use it. My right wrist and left leg were bleeding, from where the zip ties had dug into my skin, but I'd live. Brody was on the floor, snoring, he wouldn't be out for much longer. I needed to find something to secure him with.

I heard the crunch of feet on gravel, then the front screen door banged.

Shit.

I'd been so focused on Brody, I hadn't even heard the truck pull up. It was called auditory exclusion. It happened under stress, and it was no one's friend.

"Brody? What the fuck!" I heard Dolph yell. Dolph was no doubt looking at Brody's overturned chair in the hallway, but not seeing Brody.

I looked around for the Taser. It was probably somewhere in the piles of clothes and stacks of comic books, but I couldn't see it.

"Brody? You better not be fucking around."

Dolph was getting closer. Popping out into the narrow hallway and charging him wasn't a bright idea. I assumed he had a gun. He could close his eyes and jerk the trigger and still hit me in the confined space.

I looked for some kind of weapon. The room was too small to swing the busted chair.

The door opened in and to the right. The bed would be on Dolph's left.

There was a narrow space behind the open door. I slid back there, looking about for a weapon. I grabbed one of the baseballs off the wall rack. It was better than nothing.

"Brody? I'm gonna kick your ass." Dolph was right outside the door.

Brody gave a little groan and stirred. Great. He was waking up. It looked like I was going to snatch defeat from the jaws of victory here.

A moment of inspiration struck. I pulled the Confederate flag off the wall and dropped the baseball in the center. I gathered up the four corners and now I had an improvised flail.

If Dolph really had been an MP, he forgot the part of his training about how to enter a room. Instead of nutting up and bursting in, clearing the fatal funnel of the doorway as quickly as possible, he hesitated, creeping in and sticking his gun out in front of him. As he minced forward, I saw a big shiny magnum revolver. The hammer was cocked and his finger was on the trigger.

I swung the flail down as hard as I could. The baseball hit the top of his wrist, right behind his thumb. The gun discharged, abominably loud in this tight space, and flew out of his hand.

I stepped out from behind the door and got a glimpse of Dolph's beady little eyes before I swung the flail for all I was worth. The ball hit him square between the eyes and he stumbled backward into the hallway. I swung back to hit him again, but the cloth of the flag gave, and the ball bounced out of a big hole torn in the center. I succeeded only in smacking him in the face with the rolled up flag.

Dolph swatted at me like he couldn't make up his mind if he wanted to punch me or grab me. It was pretty clear that his whole plan revolved around having a gun in his hand, and without it, he didn't know whether to shit or go blind. I blasted a front kick into his groin and he bent over double against the wall of the hallway, clutching his balls and moaning.

I hadn't consciously decided to kill Dolph, but unlike Brody, I hadn't consciously decided not to either. All the fear and rage I'd been bottling up while I was zip-tied to the chair came to the surface like a geyser. I slammed Dolph to the ground and wrapped the rolled up flag around his neck. I crossed my hands and pulled. At first, he bucked wildly, then I felt his trachea collapse, like a beer can crushed in a fist. The back of his bald head turned bright red, and then he was still.

For a long moment, I couldn't make myself let go of the flag. All I could think about was that moment where he'd brushed up against me. Then, finally, my arms couldn't maintain the pressure anymore. They felt rubbery, and I was a little light-headed. I let go of the flag and Dolph slumped to the floor.

Mindful of my previous mistake, I made myself look and listen. I looked down the hallway to the living room and saw nobody. My ears were still ringing from the revolver's discharge in the tiny bedroom, but I didn't hear anything either. At this rate, I was going to be deaf before I turned fifty.

I stepped over Dolph and went to check on Brody. Hopefully, I could reason with him. I didn't feel up to another fight.

Brody was still. His brains were all over the floor of the bedroom. When I'd smacked Dolph's wrist with the flail, the bullet from the revolver had hit him in the back of the head as neatly as if it had been carefully aimed.

"Well shit," I said. "I tried."

CHAPTER NINETEEN

I wanted a phone and clothes, not necessarily in that order. I was tired of being naked and feeling vulnerable. Dolph's clothes weren't going to fit. I looked around the bedroom. Everything was covered with flecks of blood or brain matter, including, I realized, my lower legs. I almost vomited when I saw the pink and white chunks on my calves, but managed to hold it back.

"Fuck it," I said. "And drive on."

I scooped Dolph's big revolver off the floor. It was ridiculous, nearly as long as my arm, and polished like a mirror to boot. These skinhead assholes had a thing for hand cannons. I didn't need an advanced degree to guess they were compensating for something.

I left the horror show in the bedroom and walked deeper into the trailer to the master bedroom at the end. I guessed this was Curtis's room. It was a little neater and featured an honest-to-God waterbed with a mirror mounted on the ceiling, a big screen TV and a large collection of pornographic DVDs. The only clothes I could find that didn't smell ripe were a pair of stone washed jeans and a Lynrd Skynrd t-shirt. Beggars can't be choosers.

I stuck the horse pistol in the back of my pants. The best thing I could say for it was the heavy, double action trigger pull wouldn't fire by accident and blast my ass off. I went through Dolph's pockets and came up with a wallet, car keys, a handful of extra rounds for the gun, a sales receipt and some condoms. I read the receipt and saw he'd just purchased the condoms a few minutes ago, which I didn't want to think about too much.

"No phone," I said out loud. I took the keys and finally found what I wanted on the table in the living room. Next to the chicken bucket lay a cell phone.

It wasn't locked so I dialed the watch officer phone number.

Casey answered on the second ring.

"Casey, it's Dent."

"Dent! Oh man! We thought they took you. Where are you?"

"I'm not sure. They did take me. I think I'm somewhere in Washington County. I'm in a crappy single-wide trailer."

I craned my neck and looked out the dirty, fly-specked windows. There were piles of junk, construction debris and half-disassembled cars everywhere. I could see several outbuildings, but thankfully, no one moving around.

"It's on some property, at least a couple acres, with a trailer home. This place is a shit hole."

My eyes fell on the chicken bucket and my stomach rumbled. I couldn't remember the last time I'd eaten.

"Oh, and it's super close to a place that sells fried chicken."

"Uh. Ok. Keep the phone on. I'm tracking you down."

I heard her tapping away at a keyboard, then talking to somebody in the background.

My stomach growled again. The chicken smelled wonderful.

I popped the lid off the bucket. There were biscuits. I loved biscuits. The inside of the trailer was gross though. Apparently fried chicken was a staple food here because there were discarded greasy buckets and plates of old bones everywhere. The smell of rotting food wafted from the refrigerator and overflowing trash can.

Holding the phone between my shoulder and ear, I grabbed the chicken bucket and pushed my way out the door. The cool, early evening air smelled much better.

"Dent?" Now it was Bolle's voice on the phone. "Casey is narrowing down your location. Is there a place we can land the helo?"

Through the sagging chain link fence at the front of the property, I could see a field across the road. An underfed-looking horse stared back at me glumly.

"Yeah," I said around a mouthful of biscuit. "Across the street."

"Tell me what happened."

Between bites on a chicken leg, I outlined the basic story to him.

"Ok. Sit tight," Bolle said. "We're on our way."

"Whatever Todd is planning, I think it's tonight. He took some of the Hammerheads, and I think some other people with him."

"I want to investigate this compound you're at. Jack is landing in the parking lot right now, then we'll be there. Are you hurt?"

"Not that you'd notice. I could use some shoes though. They took mine."

"I'll see what I can do. Casey has your location fixed. You're in far Washington county, but it won't take long by air. Sit tight until we get there."

He clicked off, and it was just me, the chicken bucket, and the two dead guys. I ate a little more. It seemed weird to be standing there eating fried chicken with two men I'd just killed inside, but I felt tons better with some food in my belly. You had to take care of yourself.

I made myself go back in the trailer, for a more thorough search. Neither Dolph nor Brodie had gone anywhere. I was hoping to find my shoes or weapons, but they were nowhere to be found. I also didn't find a pair of shoes that would fit me. The general funk in the trailer was now overlaid by the meaty smell of blood and brains from Brody's shattered head, and the odor of Dolph's bowels letting go. I stepped back out on to the porch.

The property would have been a nice place if it hadn't been for the trash and debris strewn everywhere. There was a chicken coop, and some mature fruit trees. Over near the fence line, I could see a big plot that had probably once been a productive garden. Now it grew only weeds. Growing up in Appalachia, I'd seen this story acted out dozens of times. I bet an older couple had lived here, paid cash for everything, and done as much for themselves as they could. It was usually the next generation that let things go to hell, usually because they got into drugs or something similarly stupid.

Sooner than I expected, I heard the rattle of helicopter rotors. I gingerly walked down the gravel driveway on my bare feet, vowing that I would go barefoot more often and toughen up my soles, and then vowed that the real solution would be to not let myself get ambushed and my shoes taken. I posted myself by a broken down pickup truck near the gate.

The Little Bird was flying heavy. Jack had installed the benches on the outside, and they were full. Two people rode on each side of the little helicopter's fuselage with helmets and goggles down. Apparently, Bolle was no longer concerned about keeping a low profile. Landing the Little Bird in a field attracted attention. Flying it around with people sitting on the benches with rifles slung around their necks was probably going to get us on every conspiracy theory website on the Internet.

The Little Bird settled on its skids and four figures wearing armor jumped off. They each took a heavy backpack from the back compartment of the Little Bird and started jogging across the street. Freed of its cargo, the Little Bird all but sprang into the air. Jack started circling the compound. He'd taken the doors off the helicopter to save a paltry amount of weight and was flying low enough that I could see him working the controls. I held up my empty hands and he nodded his recognition. I saw him key his radio mic.

The first pair through the gate were Eddie and Dalton. They took turns covering the compound while the other doffed the heavy black nylon backpacks. Eddie had a pair of combat boots around his neck, tied together by the laces.

"Present for you, man," he said. "Socks are inside."

"I could kiss you," I said, sitting down on the tailgate of the truck and grabbing a boot.

"She might not like that," Eddie said and pointed a thumb at the pair bringing up the rear.

I realized it was Bolle and Alex. She was wearing a bulky tactical vest, a black helmet and a pair of goggles, but at the moment she was the most beautiful thing I'd ever seen.

Bolle dumped his ruck, then looked at me.

"You and Alex stay here while we do a quick clear up to the trailer home. Jack is making another run. As soon as he gets back with some more people, we're going to tear this place apart."

I nodded. Part of me wanted to insist that I should go clear the compound with them, but my common sense prevailed. I was wearing borrowed jeans, a t-shirt, and had a giant revolver stuffed in the back of my pants. Besides, I could talk to Alex.

The three of them moved forward, guns at the ready.

I looked at Alex.

"Hey," I said.

"Hey," she said as she pulled her earplugs out of her ears.

Then she hugged me. It felt good, even with a ceramic rifle plate between us, and with the edge of her helmet pressed against my cheek.

"I thought you were gone," she said.

"It wasn't a good day." I stood there holding her. I felt like I should let go, maybe keep an eye on the compound, but I just didn't want to let her go. The reality that I had almost been murdered and buried in an unmarked grave kept popping up in the back of my head, and I kept smashing it back down. What was bugging me the most was that I was alive only because my enemies had been stupid. If Todd had left me with someone halfway competent, I'd still be tied to the chair, and soon on my way somewhere dark in the belly of a Cascade Aviation plane.

"You smell like fried chicken, and that horrible body spray teenage boys wear," Alex said.

"I found these clothes inside. They stripped me naked. Best I could do."

"And the chicken?"

"There was no sense letting it go to waste," I said defensively.

She pulled back, looked at my wrist.

"You're bleeding."

"It's no big deal."

She insisted on bandaging me up, and I didn't mind letting her. Then I pulled on the boots Eddie had brought. They were actually a little big but I wasn't going to complain.

I heard the screen door to the trailer bang shut, and Eddie trotted back down the driveway towards us.

"Did you really just strangle a white supremacist with a Confederate flag? That's bad ass."

"It was what came to hand," I said.

"Then you ate his chicken bucket? That gets you style points, man. You should have your own action figure."

Next Dalton came down the driveway.

"Jack is on his way back with more people and the rest of the crime scene gear," he said. "But first Bolle wants all of you up here. He's found something pretty crazy in one of the outbuildings and wants you all to take a look."

I slid off the tailgate of the truck.

"Hang on a second," Alex said. "You just got kidnapped and held captive. You should be on leave or something."

She had a point. In any normal operation, I'd be put on paid administrative leave, rushed to the hospital, probably even assigned a personal counselor or something.

"I guess the rules are different here," I said and headed toward the shop to see what fresh madness Bolle had found.

CHAPTER TWENTY

The shop was one of those pre-fabricated sheet metal structures, maybe twenty feet by thirty. I'd noticed a tractor, a tiller, and all sorts of other equipment lined up outside the walls of the shed. It was all stuff that seemed like it should have been inside, under cover, and made me wonder what was actually in there instead.

Inside, it stank of human waste, sweat and old food. The floor was dirt. Cardboard had been laid over part of the floor, and it was littered with dirty blankets and trash. A long steel cable was strung across the floor, anchored at either end to the heavy metal posts that supported the ceiling. Other cables were hooked to it. I counted half a dozen, and each one ended in what looked very much like a leg shackle. I figured you could hook a person up to one of the shackles and they could hobble around, back and forth from the sleeping area on the cardboard, to the crude toilet that had been set up with an overflowing bucket underneath.

If there had been six people all shackled up in here, they must have spent most of their time getting untangled from one another.

Stacks of ramen noodles and bottled water occupied one corner. The weirdest thing was the giant television screen mounted on one wall, above a locked metal cabinet. A laptop computer was hooked up to the TV, and Casey was hunched over it, with Bolle and Dalton peering over her shoulder. As I watched, she stuck a thumb drive into one of the laptop's USB ports. The screen came to life and spit out a bunch of gobbledygook, and then we were looking at a series of folders.

"Ok. I'm in," she said. She moused around through the various folders.

"Wow. There's nothing on here but a bare-bones Linux operating system, a video player, and a bunch of video files. Like thousands of them."

She clicked on a file. It showed a guy with a sword beheading a bound man with a hood over his head. She stopped it and started another. This one was a woman being stoned to death someplace dry and dusty. The next one was a guy screaming in Arabic as he was executed by a firing squad.

She opened a dozen more. They were all violent: more beheadings, firing squads, bombings, firefights.

"Are these real?" Casey asked.

"Yeah," Dalton said. "People love to put atrocity videos on the Internet. There are hundreds of them out there."

"Wow," Casey said. "It looks like they've just been playing constantly, for days."

Casey looked over at the shackles. "So they've had some guys tied up in here, watching this stuff on a continuous loop? That's some serious Clockwork Orange bullshit, right there."

That reference sort of made sense to me. I'd have to Google it later.

"What's in the cabinet?" I asked, nodding at the metal box.

"Let's find out," Dalton said. He pulled a pair of bolt cutters out of one of the duffel bags and cut off the heavy padlock. Inside the cabinet was a cardboard box full of glass vials full of a clear liquid. Dalton set the bolt cutters aside and picked up one of the vials to read the label.

"Phencyclidine?" he said.

"Don't open that," Alex said from behind me. I hadn't realized she was behind me. "That's PCP. You know, angel dust."

"Oh," Dalton said. He gingerly set the vial back in the box.

Alex stepped forward.

"Oh my God. I've never seen that much before. It's only used in veterinary medicine these days."

"Why would you chain a bunch of people up, give them PCP, and then make them watch violent videos all day?" Casey asked.

Alex crossed her arms over her chest. "If you want them to do something heinous, that might be a way to do it. Nobody has ever run an experiment like that. No ethics committee would ever approve it. I don't know what the results of that might be. "

"Nothing good," I said.

Eddie walked in, carrying a shovel.

"You guys need to see this."

Past the shop building were more piles of junk and tangles of blackberry vines that had been allowed to grow out of control. We walked past a rusted out Dodge Dart with moss growing on it, and the smell hit me. Struecker, the fresh-faced kid from back east, was on his knees and digging with a pair of gloved hands. He was uncovering the outline of a dead man.

"I took some pictures before we started digging," Struecker said, and nodded at the camera sitting in the dirt beside him. Like the rest of us, he was taking shallow breaths through his mouth.

Alex pulled a vial of Vick's Vapor Rub from her bag. She rubbed some under her nose and passed it around. It helped. Some.

"I'm going to go back and copy that laptop," Casey said.

Bolle nodded, and she turned to go. She found an out of the way place to be noisily sick in the bushes, then wiped off her mouth and went back into the shop. It only smelled marginally better in there.

Alex donned gloves and helped clear the rest of the dirt away from the dead man.

"Gunshot wound to the head looks like," she said.

She was right. There was a hole the size of a silver dollar in his left cheek. By the way the skin was torn and the shards of bone were jutting out, it was most likely the exit wound. We'd likely find a smaller entrance wound on the top of the right side of his head. His left eye looked deflated.

"Probably shot while kneeling," Alex said after she lifted his head up.

His hands were bound in front. He was wearing paper coveralls and no shoes.

"Could be Middle Eastern, but it'll take a while to confirm that," Alex said. She pushed up the sleeves of the coveralls. "Look at his wrists."

He had big jagged wounds on the inside of his left wrist.

"Shine a light on here?" she asked.

Dalton pulled a penlight out of his pocket and shined it on the man's wrist. Alex bent close, flexed his hand back and forth. She had a powerful stomach apparently. I was doing ok with the smell, but I was several feet farther away and doing my best to not look and smell at the same time.

"Do you think he tried to cut his wrist?" I asked.

"Nope." She dropped the man's wrist and stood up. "Looks like he chewed on them."

Everybody was silent, as that sort of hung in the air between us for a little while. Towards the front of the property, I heard the sound of tires on gravel and doors slamming. The rest of Bolle's team announced that they had arrived over the radio, along with a couple of local deputies to help with traffic control.

"So, uh, you think he tried to chew through his own wrist?" Dalton asked. Even the seasoned Delta vet looked a little disturbed at that one.

Alex took a deep breath and looked away from the body. Everybody had their limits, and I was guessing she was pretty close to hers.

"I need to do a full autopsy to be sure, but it looks that way. I've never seen it before, but I've read about it, in mental patients, even some folks in POW camps and concentration camps, that sort of thing."

"Wow," I said. It was out of my mouth before I realized it.

"Let's run him through the SEEK," Bolle said.

SEEK was short for Security Electronic Enrollment Kit. It was a tablet-sized electronic device that was used for taking fingerprints and retinal scans. They'd become widespread during the war in Iraq and Afghanistan. Nobody carried driver's licenses or ID cards there, and our guys often had trouble figuring out if somebody was an insurgent or not. If the same guy got fingerprinted a couple of times near something like an IED blast, it was a clue that maybe we needed to keep an eye on him.

Dalton pulled out the SEEK. "Can somebody rinse his hands off?"

"We're messing with some evidence if we do that," Alex said.

Bolle shook his head. "It's more important to me to figure out who he is. We need to figure out what's going on."

Alex shrugged and pulled out a bottle of water. She squatted again to help Dalton clean off the corpse's fingers and take the prints. Dalton worked the controls, and then looked up.

"Ok, he's uploaded. Might be a couple of hours before we get a response. It'll go through AFIS, and the DOD."

AFIS was the Automated Fingerprint Identification System, run by the FBI. It was a huge database for people who had been fingerprinted for committing crimes, or because they'd joined the military or held numerous government positions. The DOD maintained a separate, classified database full of people US forces had fingerprinted all over the world, mostly in Iraq and Afghanistan.

We spent the next hour carefully getting the guy out of the hole, and into a bag. We documented each step. Finally, we had him in the bag and carried him to a waiting Washington County Medical Examiner van. Alex knew the guy from the county ME office and they compared notes quickly.

She walked back to me and Bolle.

"They've got a table waiting for me. I'll do the autopsy as quick as I can."

Bolle nodded. "Thank you, Doctor Pace."

She turned to me, and Bolle abruptly found something else to occupy his attention. She stood an arm's length from me, her arms folded across her chest.

"Well. I'm really glad you're not dead."

"Me too." I shuffled my feet on the gravel. I suddenly felt like an awkward high school kid who didn't know what to say to the attractive girl that was finally paying attention to him. I thought maybe after Alex and I spent enough time together, this would go away.

She took a step towards me.

"I guess I shouldn't grab you and kiss you right now, in front of all these people, huh?"

"I guess probably not," I said. "I mean, I want too. I just..."

She smiled at me then. I liked it when she smiled because when she did she smiled without reservation, self-consciousness, or pretense. Alex never gave a fake smile. If she smiled at me it was because something I did truly made me happy.

"Yeah. You're wearing a Lynrd Skynrd shirt, and I have a dead body to cut up. I guess we should save it."

"I guess so."

I expected her to go then, but she didn't. She just looked at me without saying anything, while over by the shed, Dalton and Bolle were conferring over a tablet. Drogan and Byrd were setting up tarps over the eight-foot chain link fence at the front of the property to keep out prying eyes. The guy over by the ME's van opened up the back door as Eddie and Struecker carried another body bag out of the trailer. I wondered who was inside, Dolph or Brody. I was standing there gazing into the eyes of the woman I loved, as the body of a man I'd killed was being loaded into the back of a van. I had a weird life.

"We figured out you were gone. We found your phone by the side of the street. There was no trace of you, and I realized something."

"What's that?" I asked, trying to focus on what she was saying as Eddie and Stuecker went back in the trailer, probably for the second body.

Then she stepped towards me and wrapped her arms around me. I didn't care who was watching, I hugged her back.

"I realized I loved you," she said.

"I love you too," I said. I didn't hesitate for an instant.

"I want to get Marshall," she said. "But don't you get killed. My dad is gone and you're all I have left. Promise me."

"I promise," I said and as soon as I did, I wondered if it was a mistake. I thought about those moments in the van when I expected I'd be hauled out and shot. It wasn't all up to me.

"After Marshall, I want to be done with this," she said. "I don't care what we do. I'm a doctor. I can make a living. I don't know what you can do, but I can't handle this."

"I want out," I said, and I realized I meant it. I'd had plenty of time to get used to not being a cop anymore. Even though I was on Bolle's team now, I didn't feel like I was a cop again.

"Maybe I could open a guitar store," I said. That actually sounded like a good idea.

"That sounds nice."

She kissed me, right there in front of everybody, and I didn't care. I kissed her back and didn't want it to end.

Finally, she pulled back.

"I have to go," she said.

"I know." She gave my hand a little squeeze, then walked over to the van. Eddie and Struecker were loading another bag into the back. It looked heavy. That one was definitely Brody.

She climbed into the passenger seat and shut the door. Everybody was very studiously not looking at me, which I appreciated.

I walked back to the shop, and the horrors it contained. I tried to shove Alex out of my head, best I was able.

It was time to go to work.

CHAPTER TWENTY-ONE

I walked over to Bolle and Dalton. They were looking intently at a tablet.

"We got a hit on the prints," Bolle said.

"That was quick," I said.

Bolle handed me a tablet. I was looking at an Army report from two years ago on a Abdel Lafif Farah. He'd be about seventeen years old right now, give or take. He'd been fingerprinted by an Army patrol after they found him hiding in a ditch a quarter mile from where an IED had detonated, wounding two US soldiers. He'd sustained minor injuries from shrapnel, and three of the goats he'd been herding had been killed.

"That's it?" I asked.

"That's it," Dalton said. "No other intel reports. We have access to most of them."

"This kid is an Afghan goat herder," I said.

"Looks like it. Either that, or he is a very deep cover, seventeen-year-old operative."

"And now he's dead in a backyard in Oregon."

"Yep," Dalton said. "There's no record of this guy entering the country. Nothing with ICE, DHS, nobody. It's like he was teleported from the middle of Afghanistan to here."

"Or he rode in on a Cascade Aviation cargo plane," I said.

"Kind of makes you wonder, doesn't it?"

"But if you're going to go to the trouble of smuggling in a bunch of dudes for some kind of an attack, why not find some real badasses? Surely there are some people who would love to come over here and deliver a little death to America that aren't teenage goat herders," I said. I was thinking out loud, trying to get all the pieces fit together in my mind.

Bolle pointed at the shop. "If you keep somebody in there long enough and fill them up with PCP and violent images, does it matter how they started out?"

"Huh," I said. He had a point.

Casey walked up with a tablet in her hand.

"It's really getting off the hook downtown."

She showed us the screen. We were seeing a jerky live feed from downtown. A pall of tear gas hung in the air, while a line of armored riot cops wearing gas masks and helmets marched down the street. It seemed like the skinheads and black masked anarchists were having a contest to see who could do the most property damage while being pelted with rubber bullets.

"That's the worst I've ever seen," I said. Protests were virtually the official sport of Portland, and I'd worked more than my share while I was a cop. They got out of hand sometimes, but I'd never seen anything like this.

The feed cut away to a news anchor sitting behind a desk. I recognized him from one of the local networks or the other. I could never keep them straight. They had all done something that pissed me off over the years.

"Those are the dramatic live pictures from downtown Portland, where the unrest has been going on since this morning. Portland Police report they've made dozens of arrests, and have activated mutual aid agreements with outside agencies. Local authorities appear to have been caught by surprise by the level of violence in what was supposed to be a peaceful protest. Senate Candidate Henderson Marshall had this to say."

"Marshall has a controlling interest in the station through several shell companies," Bolle murmured.

The shot cut away to Marshall, who was sitting in a chair next to an American flag.

"It's clear the current leaders in the city of Portland have been far too lax on this so-called peaceful demonstration. We need law and order, and we need it now. Clearly, the only real solution is to call up the National Guard and do it soon. This is an embarrassment, a national disgrace. One of my first acts as a US Senator will be to introduce legislation that transfers control of acts of civil unrest like this to the Department of Homeland Security. This is an act of sedition and needs to be treated as such. Portland, Oregon is part of the United

States, not some breakaway socialist republic, and it needs to start acting like it."

The shot cut back to the news anchor.

"What do you think viewers? Have city officials been too lax in handling the rioting downtown? Take our online poll!"

Casey turned off the tablet at that.

"Wow," she said.

"Indeed," Bolle said.

Struecker walked up. He looked a few years older than when I first met him a couple of days ago.

"We found a few things you should see," he said.

It was going to take days to thoroughly search the compound. I guessed it was two or three acres. There were at least a half a dozen abandoned vehicles, a dozen piles of junk, and a couple of smaller sheds in addition to the big metal shop. As Struecker led us over to a pile of trash bags, I wondered if there were more bodies buried here, and if so, if I wanted to be one of the people who helped find them. The dead guy we'd dug up was gone, but it seemed like the smell was stuck in my clothes and the inside of my nose.

The conversation I'd had with Alex was dangerous. My mind was starting to wander towards a life where I didn't have to ever see a dead person again, and I would wake up next to Alex every morning. I shoved all to the back of my mind again. I had a job to do first.

Struecker's find wasn't as dramatic. "I cut open this bag here," he said, holding up a black trash bag. "And found this."

At first, it looked like a random collection of trash. There were five soiled paper coveralls, just like the ones the dead guy had been wearing. There were also five empty shoe boxes. I didn't recognize the brand, but they were for black work shoes. There were also a bunch of plastic bags with barcodes and inventory tags on them.

"Five sets of discarded coveralls. Five sets of shoes. Five sets of work pants and work shirts," Struecker said.

"Somebody got some new threads," I said.

Casey was typing away on her tablet.

"That's a really popular uniform company," she said. "According to the stock numbers, they're black pants and white shirts."

She showed us the screen.

"It looks like a waiter's outfit," Bolle said.

"So six guys were chained up in the shop," I said. "One of them is dead. The other five are dressed in uniforms with new shoes. What the hell good does that do for us?"

"Seems like an odd choice for the water reservoir," Dalton said.

"I've got some calls to make," Bolle said and stepped away with his phone stuck to his ear.

"Hey, what's that?" Dalton said. He pulled an olive drab nylon bag out of the pile of trash. It had a broken shoulder strap.

"Look familiar?" Dalton asked.

It did, but it took me a second to place it. I had to go all the way back to my Army days.

"It's an ammo bag for a belt-fed machine gun. An M-60 or an M-240, one of those," I said.

"Your age is showing. They got rid of the M-60 a long time ago." Dalton unsnapped the bag and upended it. Some bent pieces of metal fell out. I recognized those right away. They were the links that held an ammunition belt together.

"The plot thickens," I said.

Bolle walked back to us.

"I just got off the phone with Lubbock. The extra Portland Police patrols at the reservoirs have been canceled due to the unrest, and he's telling me he's been directed to send his available staff to sights near the downtown core area. Apparently, he hasn't been authorized to pay overtime to bring more people in."

I stood up from where I'd been squatted down to look at the bag.

"That's convenient," I said."We wouldn't want to upset the budget."

"Jack is on his way," Bolle said. "Dalton, I want you Dent, Eddie and Struecker, to head out to Powell Butte on the Little Bird. You'll be on foot until I can get some other assets there with vehicles, but I want boots on the ground there now."

"What if it's all a misdirection?" I asked.

"What if it's not?" Bolle asked.

He had a point. We could think ourselves in circles with this shit.

"Ok," I said. I looked down at the t-shirt and stone washed jeans I was wearing.

"Jack has a set of body armor and weapons for you in the Little Bird," Bolle said. It probably wasn't that hard to read my mind.

The four of us jogged across the road and hopped the fence into the pasture. The horse looked at us with mild interest, then went back to chewing on grass.

I looked at Dalton.

"I've got an asset in place out by Powell Butte," I said.

"Let me guess. Bolle doesn't know about this asset."

I shook my head, then briefly explained who Dale Williams was.

"He's a good man," I said. "I'd like to bring him in. We just need to make sure we all recognize each other, so there are no misunderstandings."

He thought about it for a minute, then nodded. He handed me his phone.

I dialed Dale's number. He picked up on the first ring.

"I ain't got no guitars left, pink or otherwise." He sounded irritated.

"It's Dent," I said.

"How's it hanging?"

"Low and slow," I said. "Dale, I think it might be showtime soon."

"I wondered if all that business downtown was just a distraction. I'm actually leaving my hotel room to go for a little nature hike, as we speak."

I told him everything we thought we knew.

"A bunch of skinheads running around with a bunch of Ay-rabs dressed as waiters?" he asked. "I reckon they are doing their part to keep Portland weird. I'll keep a sharp eye."

The horse's ears perked up, and a few seconds later I heard the beating of the helicopter rotors.

"There's one more thing, Dale. These guys might have a belt fed weapon."

He gave a low whistle. "Well, that does make things more interesting. Be careful flying around in that little egg beater chopper of yours. They tend to attract bullets."

If he said anything else, it was lost in the roar of the helicopter's engine and rotors. I handed the phone back to Dalton as Jack landed a little ways off.

Dalton, Eddie, and Struecker each took a seat on the benches. Jack waved at me and pointed to a pile of gear strapped to the co-pilot seat next to him. I pulled out a plate carrier with extra ammo strapped to it and a gun case. Jack waved at me and gestured at the rotor blades whirling overhead.

I was glad he'd done it. My natural instinct to donning the carrier was to stick one arm up through the opening, which might well have put my hand into the rotor arc. Instead, I bent low and managed to wiggle into the vest. I pulled the rifle out of the case and slung it around my neck. Next came a helmet with an integrated microphone and headset.

I took a seat on the bench of the Little Bird, belted myself in, and gave Jack a thumbs up. He pulled up on the collective, and the little helicopter shot into the air, its engine screaming.

Riding strapped to the outside of a helicopter was a vastly different experience than riding on the inside. The last time I'd done this, it had been over Mogadishu, Somalia. I tried to push that thought out of my mind. That awful, bloody battle had technically been a victory, but I'd seen too many good men die or be maimed to celebrate it.

Jack gained altitude in an upwards spiral, then pointed the nose of the Little Bird to the east and poured on the gas. The Portland skyline grew bigger as we flew. Powell Butte lay on the other side.

I pushed thoughts of Mogadishu out of my head and told myself things would be different this time.

CHAPTER TWENTY-TWO

Although it was a warm June day, the ride across the city was cold. Even overloaded, the Little Bird was probably barreling through the sky at pretty close to a hundred miles an hour. We swung north of downtown, to avoid the tall buildings, but we were still close enough to see some plumes of smoke. Apparently, somebody had set some fires. That reminded me of the thick black columns of smoke hanging over Mogadishu, from piles of burning tires, and once again I shoved those memories out of my mind.

"What's the plan, boys?" Jack said over our radios.

"Let's do some orbits of the park," Dalton said. "If we don't see anything suspicious, we'll establish two observation posts on some high ground. Hopefully, we can get the city to get its shit together soon, and they'll post some of their security people or some cops out here. I don't want to get stuck pulling guard duty all day."

I could sense his frustration, and I shared it. This was likely to be a long, boring day standing in the sun wearing thirty pounds of body armor and getting gawked at by Portland hipsters out walking their dogs.

The butte came up quick. Goosebumps from the cold aside, I was enjoying all this flying around the city by helicopter. Portland wasn't huge, as cities went, but even on a good day, the traffic was bad. Driving from out in Washington county all the way across town to Powell Butte would have easily been an hour long slog, probably more with all the traffic being diverted out of downtown. We covered it in just a few minutes.

Jack did a couple of orbits of the park, each one at lower altitudes. It looked like business as usual. I saw groups of people walking their dogs, and taking in the views of the mountains. The parking lot was full, but it was mostly sedans with a smattering of SUVs and light trucks. I didn't see any sign of any moving trucks or similar large vehicles. They would have been unusual here on a normal day, but today they would have set off a giant red flag.

We hovered near the Mountain Finder, a place in the park where you could see all the mountains that surrounded Portland. It also overlooked big swaths of the park. Jack brought the skids to within a few inches of the ground and a couple of Portlanders watched, mouths agape, as Struecker and Eddie hopped off. Of course one of them whipped her cell phone and started taking video. Great.

Jack then moved the helo east, flying slow with the skids only a hundred or so feet above the ground. The Little Bird was unbalanced because Dalton and I were both sitting on one side. He took us to the ground over the reservoir itself, where we could keep an eye on the infrastructure. We were only a few hundred yards from the parking lot, so we'd be able to see that too. I anticipated a long day in the hot sun, guarding millions of gallons of water with nothing to drink.

As we headed towards the reservoir, I saw three vehicles moving up the access road to the parking lot. Two were pickup trucks with a pair of men riding in each bed. The other was a rental moving truck.

I keyed my radio microphone. "Dalton? The trucks?"

"I see them. Jack, get us on the ground."

I opened my mouth to argue. We would be vulnerable as the Little Bird made it's approach to the ground. Better to pull pitch and get us up in the air.

Before I could speak, one of the pickups jerked to a halt. A man stood up in the bed. Even from almost a quarter mile away, I recognized the gun he picked up. It was an M240B belt-fed machine gun. I'd carried one often enough in the Rangers to know it well.

At first, the red tracer rounds seemed to be floating lazily towards us, but the closer they got, the faster they seemed to move. Something hit the side of the helicopter next to my head with a thud loud enough that I could hear it over the engines. A tracer actually passed between my lower legs and I froze for a second, mesmerized by the faint red will'o wisps headed my way. Part of my brain was trying to do the math. For every tracer round I saw, there were four more plain old bullets I couldn't see.

I hit the latch on my safety belt and jumped off while the Little Bird's skids were still head high above the ground. Apparently, Dalton had the same plan. In my peripheral vision, I saw him drop off the bench too.

Thanks to the extra weight of my gear, I hit hard. I kept my legs loose and did a classic airborne ranger parachute landing fall, so I didn't break anything, but it was still no picnic. This stuff was easier when I was nineteen. I felt the air whoosh out of my lungs, and that familiar panicky feeling of not being able to breathe from having the wind knocked out of me.

I wound up on my back, with the sun in my eyes and gasping for breath. For a second I thought the Little Bird was going to land on me. It was banked over hard left, so far I thought the rotor blades were going to clip the ground, then the engine screamed as Jack poured on the power. Freed of the weight of me and Dalton, the helicopter shot into the sky with a flock of tracers chasing it. One of them hit the left side skid and bounced off, then the Little Bird was gone, hauling away from us as fast as Jack could make it go.

For a second there was quiet. I rolled over onto my stomach in the almost foot high grass and weeds. I managed to catch my breath, then saw Dalton about twenty feet from me. Our eyes met and we started crawling towards each other.

I heard the ripping, cracking sound of bullets passing overhead, followed an instant later by the sound of the gun going off down the hill from us. I pressed myself into the dirt, trying to become one with the earth.

I turned my head and could see geysers of dirt erupting from the hillside fifty yards or so uphill. It had been a while since somebody had shot a machine gun at me. After a few bursts, I started to get used to it again. I realized we were in a depression about a foot and a half deep. The gunner below us could rake the ground above and below us on the slope, but for the moment at least, we were safe.

I crawled up to Dalton, who was trying to see what was going down below without getting the top of his head blown off.

"We're in dead ground here," he said.

"Yeah, but we can't move," I said as another burst tore overhead. I could tell Dalton was looking at me to see how I was handling myself now that the shit was flying for real. I was glad I'd had a couple of seconds to compose myself.

Dalton reported to Bolle on the radio while the rounds tore overhead. While he talked I tried to simultaneously look around and not get shot at the same time. The pace of fire was slacking off. Belt fed machine guns had a voracious appetite for ammunition, and it was hard to keep up sustained fire for very long without running out.

There had been some hikers gawking at the helicopter right before the shooting started. I didn't see them now, hopefully because they'd had the sense to run away, and not because they were lying in the grass bleeding out.

I parted some of the grass and rose up a few inches. I could see the parking lot a little better. One pickup was parked nose towards us, with the gunner standing in back. It looked like they'd created some kind of makeshift pintle mount in the bed of the truck. The second pickup was blocking the access road to the park. There was a second gunner in the back of that one, with a field of fire that would shred anybody that tried to drive in. As I watched, a Subaru drove up the access road, and the gunner put a burst through the windshield.

"Two gunners," I said to Dalton. "Both belt-fed. They're shooting at people trying to drive in."

Dalton relayed that. I got a glimpse of a couple guys rolling up the back door of the moving van, then the gunner covering our position opened up. I buried myself into the ground as dirt sprayed a few feet in front of me, then I heard rounds passing overhead.

"We'll get there as soon as we can," Bolle said after Dalton finished describing the situation.

"If they come charging up that road, they're gonna get cut to pieces," I said.

Before Dalton could reply, I heard the popping sound of rifle fire off to our right.

"Dent? Dalton?" Eddie's voice came over the radio. "We can see you. We're sending some rounds their way, but they are a long way off." Over his mike, I could hear the shots even louder. Struecker must have been the one firing. I did the math in my head. Eddie and Struecker were right at the limit of the effective range of the weapons we were carrying. The stubby ten-inch barrels made them perfect for maneuvering inside cramped spaces, but they robbed the bullets of velocity they needed to engage out past a couple of hundred yards.

The machine gun below us opened up again, but this time no rounds landed near us. They must have been shooting at Eddie and Struecker.

"We're kinda hosed here. We've got nothing but open ground between us and that gun," Dalton said.

"Dalton?" Jack's voice crackled over our radio earpieces.

"You still up there?" Dalton asked.

"Yeah, I'm standing off a way. I took some rounds but I'm still flying. You've got two assholes with belt feds in the back of a pair of pickups, and some more assholes monkeying around in the back of a moving truck. All I've got is a pistol."

Jack sounded frustrated. He wasn't telling us anything we didn't already know, but it was still nice to know he was up there.

"Give me your phone," I said to Dalton.

"What? You want to dial 911 or something?"

"Just give it to me. I'm going to get a sniper in the air."

He handed me the phone and I dialed Dale.

"It's hanging low, I don't have time to fuck around," I said when he answered.

"What the hell have you gotten into over there? It sounds like the Tet Offensive all over again."

"Where are you, and do you have your rifle with you?"

"I'm at my car a few blocks from the park entrance. The rifle is right here in the trunk."

"You ever do any sniping from an airborne helicopter?"

"Not this century, but I reckon it's like riding a bicycle."

Between me talking to Dale on the phone, and Dalton talking to Jack on the radio, we managed to coordinate a place for them to meet. There was a church parking lot a half mile from us where Jack could land. As we talked, Eddie and Struecker drew some of the heat from us. They worked their way into a position a couple of hundred yards to our east and would pop up and shoot at the guys in the parking lot. They had a little more room to fire and maneuver, but it was only a matter of time before somebody caught a bullet.

"Bad news Dent," Eddie said over the radio. "There are cops coming up the access road."

"Shit," I said. "There's always somebody that doesn't get the memo."

"I've been looking at the ground between them and us," Dalton said, in level tones. "There's plenty of little depressions between us and them. Let's spread out. You throw a bang and then we'll alternate rushes. I'll go first."

What Dalton was proposing was likely suicide, but I wasn't about to let a bunch of Portland cops get chewed up by machine gun fire. In between bursts of gunfire, I heard the sound of sirens echoing all around the city. There were likely to be hundreds of cops here in the next few minutes, and I was guessing dozens of them would be dead if we didn't silence those guns.

I nodded and we wiggled to opposite ends of our little swale. As Dalton crawled he keyed his mic.

"Eddie, we're going to assault the parking lot by bounding overwatch."

"Huh?" was Eddie's reply.

It was my turn to key the mic. "Just shoot at the assholes in the parking lot, Eddie."

Eddie was a good guy to have in a fight, but I got the impression that his experience ran more towards the street brawl variety, and that he hadn't had any military training.

Dalton gave me a thumbs up. I pulled a flashbang off my vest, pulled the pin, let the lever go and hurled as far up and out as I could while lying on my side.

"Bang out!" I yelled. It was sort of unnecessary, but that's how we did it in the Rangers and I didn't want this Delta guy to show me up.

I knew the bang was coming, but I still flinched when it went off. Dalton took off down the hill like a jackrabbit, somehow managing to run down the slope without falling. I rolled up to my knees and took the safety off my carbine. For the last few minutes, my world had narrowed to a small claustrophobic space in the weeds. Now I had the whole slope in front of me.

The guy in the pickup closest to us was trying to track Dalton as he rushed down the hill. He was getting excited and instead of laying down short bursts, he just mashed down the trigger and tried to hose the hillside. His buddy was busy trying to link another belt to the one rapidly disappearing into the hungry maw of the gun. On the far side of the parking lot, I saw the other gunner open up on the approaching police cars.

My rifle had a simple, electronic red dot sight with no magnification, perfect for close quarters battle but the wrong tool for this job. At this range, the red dot floating in the center of the scope tube almost covered the whole cab of the pickup. I placed the dot over the machine gunner and started squeezing the trigger. I was firing on semi-automatic, so I only got one bullet with each trigger press, but I was pulling it pretty quick.

In my peripheral vision, I saw Dalton drop into a little depression in the ground, and start shooting.

Then it was my turn to run into the machine gun fire.

CHAPTER TWENTY-THREE

At some point, the US Army determined that a man could run for three to five seconds, and as long as dropped and found cover before that time was up, he had a reasonable chance of not getting shot. Thus, one of the basic skills drilled into every infantryman was the three to five-second rush. I'd done thousands of them during my time in the Army, and as I got up and charged down the hill, I counted in my head.

One one thousand. I felt horribly exposed and wanted nothing but to just lie right back down and hug the ground again. Dalton was prone on the ground, pulling the trigger for all he was worth, while the ground erupted with bullet strikes around him, so I couldn't abandon him. I zigzagged down the uneven slope. It was half run, half stumble. I tried to plan where I was going to plant my feet. The last thing I needed was a broken ankle right now.

Two one thousand. The gunner finally realized he was hitting high, far up the hillside behind Dalton, and let up on the trigger. My movement must have caught his assistant's eye because he slapped the gunner on the shoulder and pointed in my direction. Given a choice between the target he'd chewed up a hillside trying to hit, and a new target running straight at him, the gunner apparently decided I was the better choice.

Three one thousand. The muzzle of the gun swung towards me. Dalton squeezed the trigger even faster, and even from this distance, I could see the windshield of the truck craze and spiderweb from his rounds hitting it. He was hitting low, because of the range. I probably had been too. I started looking for a place to land. There was a little depression in the ground, something I wouldn't have even noticed on a normal day, but right now it looked like safety.

Four one thousand. I dove for the little depression in the ground like a crazed baseball player going head first into home plate. I hit the ground just as the gunner opened up and a swarm of bullets passed overhead.

I gulped some air and looked for Dalton. He slapped a fresh magazine into his rifle, then rose to a crouch. I slithered a few feet away from where I'd disappeared from the gunner's view, then popped up and started shooting. I remembered to hold high this time. I floated the dot half way over the gunner's head.

There's a knack to shooting a belt-fed machine gun at a moving target, and this guy didn't have it. When he first started shooting, he'd been exercising some discipline and shooting short bursts, but now he was treating the gun like a giant bullet hose. You had to lead your target and fire short, controlled bursts. This guy saw Dalton pop up and mashed down on the trigger and swept the muzzle across the hillside. I wondered if he realized there were two of us. There was only a dozen or so feet between me and Dalton, and in the dust noise and confusion, two dudes wearing body armor looked pretty much the same.

I fired off half a dozen rounds fast, barely allowing the dot to settle between shots, then I paused. I saw the machine gunner's buddy sprawled half in, half out of the truck.

"Fuck you!" I yelled in triumph. Later it would seem like a stupid thing to do, but just then I felt a savage surge of joy that I hadn't felt since that bad day in Somalia. I'd been on the receiving end of a shit storm of bullets, and it felt good to give one back that counted.

I hammered away, shooting at the gunner until my rifle ran dry. Dalton finished his sprint. He dropped to the ground and started shooting. I stood up and started my bound, managing to stuff a fresh magazine in my rifle as I ran. Dalton had been zigging to his left during his bound, and now I zagged to my right, opening up the distance between us, and giving the gunner more visual territory he had to cover by himself now that his assistant gunner was dead.

Occupied with trying to reload my rifle and not break an ankle, I let my rush go too long. The ground around me exploded in flying dirt and rocks, and instead of picking a spot, I just flopped down to the ground in the first little depression I saw. It was like being inside a tornado. The bullets cracked inches over my head and around me, thudding into the ground and throwing dry grass and dirt in my eyes. Something whanged off my head, probably a rock and not a bullet since I stayed conscious, but it still made my teeth click together. I tried to press myself deeper into the ground and felt the sick fear that I'd screwed up, that the position I was occupying didn't afford enough cover and my guts were about to get strewn all over the hillside.

Then there was silence. I heard the sound of the gunshots echoing around the butte for a few seconds, then a long pause with no noise. I dared to raise my head above the grass and saw the gunner messing with the gun. The feed cover was up and he was messing around with the gun.

"He's empty!" Dalton yelled. "Go!"

I stood up on shaky legs and charged. Instead of zig-zagging back and forth we both ran straight towards the pickup. Another gun started shooting. I flinched and almost dropped to the ground. I realized the gunner in the back of the pickup down by the entrance was the one shooting. He was lighting up the cops that were trying to make their way up the road. I heard a few answering pops in return. Those poor bastards were trying to assault a machine gun just like us, only from low ground.

As we ran, I saw a guy crawl out of the back of the moving van, shut the door and run to the cab of the truck. I'd been so focused on the gun truck, I'd forgotten about those guys. Over the sound of the machine, my poor abused ears could make out the thrum of rotor blades. I belatedly realized a voice had been talking in my radio earpiece, but I had no idea what it had said. More auditory exclusion. Hopefully, it had been Jack telling me he was on his way back with Dale.

Dalton outpaced me. The guy was like a damn gazelle. Despite my effort to run faster, he pulled away, taking long leaping strides down the hill. We were closing the distance quickly, but the guy down below was working like mad to get the machine gun back in action. I could see him jerking back and forth on the charging handle frantically. I couldn't tell at this distance, but my guess was he'd jammed the gun up and was trying to clear it.

Finally, he stopped monkeying with the gun and bent over to pick up the end of the ammo belt. We were still a hundred yards away. I started looking for a place to go to ground.

Dalton went from running full tilt to kneeling in one fluid movement. He raised his rifle, took aim and squeezed the trigger. The gunner dropped like he'd been hit with an ax.

"Nice shot!" I yelled as I drew abreast of him.

He flashed me a grin. "Let's go take that gun," he said, and we charged down the hill.

The Little Bird roared overhead, so low I ducked. I saw Dale strapped to the side, wearing a radio headset, triple denim, and a backward trucker cap. Jack flared the Little Bird out and brought it to a hover almost directly overhead.

I keyed my microphone. "Kill that asshole that's shooting at the cops!"

The tail of the Little Bird gave a prim little wiggle as Jack finessed the pedals to pivot the bird and give Dale a clear shot. He raised the long barrel of the bolt action M40. I never heard the shot over the sound of the helicopter, but the machine gun stopped firing immediately. Dale worked the bolt feverishly, and put more rounds into the driver of the pickup, and the assistant gunner in the bed.

I was sucking for air as we made it to the pickup but I still managed to catch up to Dalton.

"Drive or shoot?" he yelled over the sound of the rotors.

I looked at the truck. The hood was riddled with bullet holes and the windshield was a crazed mess of cracks and bullet holes, but all four tires were holding air. The machine gun was tilted down on its makeshift mount, and where the barrel touched the roof of the cab it was actually smoking it was so hot.

"Shoot!" I yelled. I wanted to put some bullets in people.

Dalton jerked the driver's side door open. The dead driver spilled out like a sack of meat. He was missing most of his lower jaw and had sprayed the inside of the cab with a fire hose of blood from his severed carotid. Dalton swept out the worst of the broken glass with his gloved hand and climbed into the mess.

The bed of the truck wasn't much better. The machine gunner had caught rounds in the chest and the face. I climbed up and managed not to slip in the blood and hundreds of spent shell casings.

Fueled by adrenaline, I managed to hoist the dead guy out of the bed of the truck and dropped him to the pavement with a splat. Then I turned my attention to the gun. The M-240B fed from a long, heavy belt of cartridges held together by metal links. If the belt dragged, or worse, became twisted, it would jam the gun up in an instant. It was the assistant gunner's job to help feed the cartridges into the gun smoothly, and if he was good at his job, he could link a new ammo belt onto the old one and make sure the gunner never ran out of ammo.

I had disposed of the assistant gunner, so now the ammo belt was dangling all the way down to an ammo can that could slide around loose on the floor of the truck. If I wasn't careful I would twist the belt if I rotated the gun around on its makeshift mount.

I hefted the belt. I could support it with my left hand, and since the weight of the gun was held up by the mount, aim and fire with my right. It wouldn't be perfect but I could make it work.

The moving truck was trundling down the reservoir access road. The Little Bird hovered over it and I saw Dale firing rounds into the cab. Over the ringing in my ears, I heard Dalton rev the engine of the pickup.

I pushed the button on my radio. "I'm ready. You ready?"

"We've got half a tank of gas, a leaking radiator, a shot out power steering pump and I'm sitting in a guy's brains."

"Hit it," I said.

CHAPTER TWENTY-FOUR

The pickup jerked backward, and I held onto the gun and mount for dear life as Dalton did a herky-jerky three-point turn, then we sped off after the moving truck. Our pickup lurched each time the transmission shifted gears, and I smelled burnt hydraulic fluid.

"Tranny's not so hot either," Dalton said over the radio.

The little carbine bullets we were shooting didn't do much damage to a vehicle individually, but we'd sure shot a bunch of them. We were still gaining on the moving truck. The Little Bird was alongside, about a hundred yards off, and Dale was pumping rounds into the cab. Jack was maintaining some altitude so he wouldn't plow into the rolling hills, and Dale was shooting down at an acute angle, working the bolt on the gun feverishly. I saw him stop shooting to shove more rounds into the loading port of the gun, and I wondered how much ammo he was carrying.

The moving truck was a crew cab. I saw a gun muzzle poke out of the back driver's side door and a lick of flame from a muzzle flash as somebody fired a burst at the helo. Jack peeled off. I couldn't tell if they'd been hit, but it didn't look like they were going to crash. Jack started a fast circle to get back on target.

We went around a bend in the road, and there was nothing past the moving truck but hillside, so I put the machine gun's butt against my shoulder, sighted on the back of the truck, and squeezed the trigger. I started firing five and six round bursts into the back. Depending on what was inside, the slugs might actually penetrate through the sheet metal of the truck into the cab.

"You know," Dalton said over the radio. "That thing is probably full of explosives."

I stopped shooting for a second to clear the gun's belt and keyed my mic.

"Ideas?" I asked, then went back to shooting. I wasn't particularly keen to die if the truck exploded, but I didn't want these assholes to get away with their little plan either.

"Hold on, I'm gonna see if the four wheel drive works, and try to get alongside."

I was grateful for the warning. I put the gun on safe and held onto the pintle with both hands as he floored it. The pickup fishtailed back and forth with one set of wheels on the gravel road, and the other on the grass. I thought for sure we were going to spin out or roll more than once, but Dalton managed to maintain control. Right as we drew even with the truck's rear bumper, the driver swerved over in front of us, putting his own wheels in the grass. We missed colliding by a handbreadth, and Dalton backed off a little.

The Little Bird was back. Jack zoomed in right over us, then matched speed. I looked up and saw the tail rotor was not very far over my head. Dale had the rifle hanging around his neck and was blazing away with a pistol. As I watched, the slide locked back on an empty magazine and he punched it out, letting it fall to the ground.

"I'm out of ammo for the rifle," Dale said over his radio. He sounded both calm and apologetic.

"I'm going to switch sides," Dalton said. "Try the tires."

He pulled over left like he was going to try to overtake the moving van on that side again, and as soon as the driver reacted to block him, cut the wheel back over to the right and stomped on the gas. The scant warning he'd given me was just enough to traverse the gun back over and move the ammo can with my foot.

Dalton pulled past the rear bumper of the truck, and I had a clear shot at the tires. I fired a long burst.

Despite what you see in the movies, it's actually hard to shoot out a moving tire, especially with a handgun. The sidewalls were thick on the truck tires, and the speed of rotation actually helped deflect the bullets.

All that was on my mind as I mashed down the trigger. I fired one burst and the muzzle climbed off target with no effect. I fought it down, took a half breath and fired again. Apparently, the rules were different when you shot a tire with a dozen .30 caliber machine gun bullets.

The tire disintegrated and a big chunk of rubber bounced off my helmet. The metal wheel dug into the gravel road. The truck slewed to the right, and for a second I thought it was going to roll over. The driver wisely got off the gas and fought to maintain control as it bounced across the grass. The moving truck slid to a halt, and Dalton gunned the engine of our pickup, pulling past the cargo area of the truck.

Now the cab was in my line of fire. I saw a man sitting in the passenger seat, slack-jawed with surprise. I lined up the front sight on the door and mashed on the trigger, letting twenty rounds go in one long, yammering burst before the muzzle climbed above the roof line and I was spraying the sky. I was off the trigger for a fraction of a second, just long enough to bring the muzzle back down, then I started hammering the cab of the truck with quick bursts of five and six rounds. All the glass was gone in the first couple of seconds, and the doors started to have more holes than metal. The thought of showing any mercy never occurred to me. I just kept shooting. In the Army we'd called this a "mad minute," a way to release pent up frustration and aggression via gunfire. Usually, an officer would start screaming at us to cease fire, and the sergeants would go around kicking asses until the shooting stopped.

Today I was limited only by my ammunition. I felt the tail end of the ammo belt pass through my left hand a fraction of a second before the gun clicked dry. All I could hear was a roaring that was something like the sound of the ocean and static from a radio combined.

"Coming out," Dalton yelled. I barely heard him. He'd wisely decided to stay in the cab of the truck while I hosed down the moving truck, rather than exit right under the muzzle of the machine gun. Even now he slid across the truck seat and came out of the passenger side.

I reached down and rooted through the empty ammo boxes until I found a full one. I opened it and pulled the end of a fresh belt of ammo.

"That's probably enough," Dalton said. "Somebody isn't getting their deposit back. Let's go check out the truck."

I took a few deep breaths to clear my head. Dalton was standing behind the front of the pickup, his rifle half raised. He was mostly looking at the moving truck, but he was giving me the occasional brief glance. Even though we'd just been engaged in a gunfight with fully automatic weapons, charged a mobile machine gun nest, and chased down a truck full of explosives, Dalton looked as relaxed as if he were out on a nature hike. I realized he was checking in on my mental state, to see how I was bearing up after the stress of the last few minutes.

That's when the shakes hit. I felt queasy like I might throw up, and the muscles in my jaw were quivering. It was hard to focus on anything but the cab of the truck. I realized I'd unloaded well over a hundred rounds into the truck, and I started remembering about all the lessons we'd learned about excessive force back in the police academy. I'd been reacting like I was still in the Army, but the body armor I was wearing had the word "Police" embroidered on the patches.

"Take a second and check your stuff. Then we'll clear the truck," Dalton said. My hearing was starting to come back. It sounded like there were hundreds of sirens coming towards us. "I want to get their phones and get them to Casey and Henry before your buddies on the police bureau get their hands on them."

Back when I'd been in the Army, Delta guys had a reputation for being arrogant. In some ways, it was deserved, but in others, they really did live in a different world. During the fight in Mogadishu, I'd seen some men act bravely. I'd seen others lose their shit. Sometimes it was the quiet, reserved guys that turned out to have balls made of pure brass, and the big boasting muscleheads that collapsed into a fetal position and shit their pants.

But the Delta guys had impressed me with their ruthless calm. They had acted like the whole thing had been some sort of training mission, instead of a desperate, bloody firefight. Dalton was displaying that calm now. He was focused on gathering intelligence for the next step in the fight, and making sure that I had my act together. Right now he was holding his rifle in one hand, and using the other to key his radio and give Bolle an update.

I focused on making sure I was ready. That was always a good, concrete step. First, I checked myself for any new bullet holes. People had been known to get shot and not realize it until it was too late. Part of me wanted to detach the M240B and haul it around like a big rifle, or maybe like a security blanket, but rationally, I knew that was a bad idea. Instead, I checked my carbine. The scope was undamaged and turned on. I had a round in the chamber.

I forced my self to take three big slow breaths and focus on what was happening around me. Jack was doing slow orbits around the park, with Dale still on the bench. I realized I hadn't heard from Eddie or Struecker for a while, then realized with a start that they were running down the road behind us. Struecker didn't look like he was even breathing hard, despite the sixty pounds of gear he was carrying, but Eddie was huffing and puffing.

Struecker slowed down when he saw me looking at him. He clearly wanted to make sure I recognized him before he charged up behind us. I waved him forward and he started jogging up.

"Struecker and Eddie are coming up from behind," I yelled to Dalton.

I let my carbine hang from its sling, in preparation to jump out of the truck, when a burst of gunfire broke the silence. Struecker hit the ground.

CHAPTER TWENTY-FIVE

At first, I had no idea where the fire was coming from. Puffs of dust kicked up around Struecker where he lay limp in the gravel.

"He's under the truck! He's under the truck!" Dalton screamed.

I couldn't see from where I was standing in the bed of the truck. I clambered over the side, slipping on a shell casing as I did so and unceremoniously falling over bed rail of the truck.

I landed hard on my right side. This was getting old. A round hit the side of the truck above my head with a sound like a beer can being crushed by a hammer. That's when I saw Curtis, lying on his side and shooting a rifle at us. Another shot hit in front of me, spraying dirt and gravel into my face.

I was half blind from the dirt in my eyes, and it wasn't the best position to shoot from, but I made it work. This sort of close range, furious violence was where the little carbines we carried shined. I placed the red dot of my scope in the middle of the fuzzy blob with the rifle and squeezed the trigger twice.

Curtis rolled behind the rear tire and the incoming fire stopped immediately. I sent another pair of rounds his way, just to be sure.

"I think you got him," Dalton said.

"Go help Struecker," I said.

I'd seen my share of gunshot victims, but Dalton's training was far superior. That left me and Eddie to deal with Curtis. Eddie was running up to Steucker, oblivious to any more threats from the truck. That left me. I blinked my eyes until I could see better, and stood.

I went wide around the back of the truck, with my carbine, ready to shoot. Curtis was still alive somehow. As I eased around the corner of the truck with my rifle in front of me, he took in a long ratcheting breath. When he breathed out it was accompanied by a fine spray of blood droplets. A bullet had passed clean through his chest, high up on the right side. His lung was probably collapsing and filling with blood. One ankle had been obliterated and his foot hung by a shred of flesh. Judging from the trail of blood, the foot wound had happened first, when I'd lit up the truck cab, then he'd dragged himself to his position here by the back of the truck.

I picked up the AK-47 that lay near him and saw one of my rifle bullets had gone clean through the stamped metal receiver. I tossed it over in the weeds. I pulled a pistol out of his belt and tossed it too. As I dug through his pockets for his phone, he coughed, spraying more blood.

"Killed my boys," he breathed.

"Yep," I said. I pulled the phone out. There was a folding pouch attached to my vest just for things like this. I pulled it out and dropped the phone inside.

"Can't breathe," he said.

"That's because you've got a big hole in your lung, asshole," I said.

I walked up to the cab of the truck and made myself look inside. What I saw would replay in my head every time I closed my eyes for a long time to come. Judging from the number of parts, there'd been three other men in the cab besides Curtis. I guessed he'd been sitting behind the driver, and the guy next to him had shielded him from some bullets.

Making myself sort through the mess, I came up with two more phones, one of which had a bullet hole through it. I stowed them both away and trotted back to the rear of the truck. Up the road, I saw Portland Police cruisers making their way towards us slowly, with officers with rifles walking alongside. They weren't quite pointed at us, but they weren't quite pointed away either.

Eddie ran up just then, huffing and puffing like a steam engine. His face was covered with droplets of blood, but he seemed uninjured.

"How's Struecker?" I asked.

"Dead," Eddie said. "Round went through his neck."

I decided to just not think about that at the moment.

"Will you and Dalton load him in the pickup? I want to see what's in the back of the truck."

He nodded and ran off.

I undid the latch on the back of the moving truck door and rolled it up a foot or so. I saw blue plastic barrels with strings of det-cord running between them. Some of the barrels were leaking white granular powder from the bullet holes I'd poked through them. The inside of the truck reeked of diesel fuel.

I walked back over to Curtis. "Is that ANFO in the truck?"

ANFO was short for ammonium nitrate and fuel oil. The ammonium nitrate came from fertilizer and mixed with the fuel oil, it made a bulky but powerful explosive.

Curtis coughed. "Yeah. ANFO."

"When does it go off?"

He shook his head.

"Not set yet. 30-minute delay."

"Thanks," I said and turned to go.

He reached out a bloody hand. "You have to help me."

He coughed again, and what looked like a chunk of lung flew off his lips and landed on the ground in front of him.

"The ambulances are that way." I jerked a thumb over towards the entrance to the park and walked over to where Eddie was carrying Struecker like a baby in his arms. I put down the tailgate of the truck. I hated to lay Struecker on all the blood and grue in the bed, but this way we didn't have to fold him up and put him in the cab.

Eddie put Struecker down. Dalton and I climbed in next to him.

"Drive us towards the cops real slow," I said.

Eddie nodded and climbed behind the wheel. I slung my rifle behind my back and pulled the pin that held the M240B in its makeshift mount. I set the big gun down on the floor of the pickup bed, where it wouldn't be pointed at anybody, and looked back at Dalton, who was staring down at Struecker's pale face.

"I never imagined I'd be shooting it out on American soil."

I didn't know what to say to that. I pushed my radio mic.

"Bolle? It's Dent. We're coming out. If you could make sure the Portland cops don't shoot us, that would be great."

He must have been standing right next to some vehicles running sirens because I could barely hear his reply.

"I'm working on it. I'm at the PPB command post now."

Up ahead, I saw the Little Bird come to a landing next to the parking lot. Dale unbuckled his belt and held his hands up in front of him for the benefit of the cops standing around there.

"Tell them not to shoot Dale Williams and Jack too."

The posture of the cops blocking the road ahead of us changed. They all relaxed a little, and one of the cruisers pulled aside to make a gap.

"Ok, Eddie," I said. "Speed it up a little."

The truck wasn't capable of going much faster than a good run. There were some terminal-sounding grinding noises coming from the transmission. I kept my hands flat on the roof of the truck as we passed among the cops. I recognized a couple of them, and I wondered if they recognized me.

There was a burly lieutenant getting things organized in the parking lot. They had big sections roped off with crime scene tape where I'd thrown the bodies out of the pickup, and around the other gun truck.

We ground to a halt and the engine died with a final-sounding sputter. The place was packed with cops, but they gave us a wide berth as we climbed out of the back of the bloody, shot up truck.

"Shoulda brought more ammo," a voice said in my ear.

It was Dale Williams. He had an unlit Marlboro hanging out of the corner of his mouth and his rifle slung over his shoulder. He was damn near seventy and should have been at home next to the fire reading a book. Instead, he'd spent the day strapped to the side of a helicopter shooting at people, and was apparently beating himself up for not bringing an extra box of rounds.

A car rolled up and Bolle got out. He had a phone glued to his ear.

He walked up and grabbed my arm, then motioned Eddie over.

"There's a Cascade Aviation jet at Portland International being rolled out of a hangar. There's no flight plan, but it looks like it's getting ready to take off. Get on the Little Bird, and go stop it."

I had about a million questions, but there was no time.

"Ok," I said.

I started towards the Little Bird. Jack was still in the cockpit and I heard the engine note change as he brought the power up.

"Is that 7.62 in those ammo boxes in the back of that truck?" Dale asked.

I nodded and Dale reached through the crush of people and snagged the ammo box. He pulled the belt apart and came up with about 30 rounds still linked together.

"That'll do for close range," he said and started for the Little Bird. He could pull the individual cartridges off the metal links and use them in his rifle.

"You're coming?" I asked.

"Son, this is the most fun I've had since the 70s. I wouldn't miss it for the world."

CHAPTER TWENTY-SIX

On the flight over the city, I had nothing to do but check my weapons and listen to the chatter on the radio. Jack was multitasking like a madman. In addition to flying at rooftop level over a major city, he was trying to coordinate with the tower at Portland International to enter their airspace.

"Negative, Black Jack One," the exasperated air traffic controller said. "Stay clear of the airspace."

"I'm trying to tell you," Jack said as he climbed to avoid an overpass in front of us. An eighteen wheeler passed half a dozen feet below my dangling boot soles. "I'm already in your airspace, I'm just so low you can't see me. I'm not asking you. I'm telling you. I'm headed for the commercial aviation terminal. You should be getting an order to cease all flight ops immediately from the FAA."

"I'm not aware of any such order, Black Jack One. Stay clear."

They went back and forth, then Bolle broke in.

"Dent, Jack, I'm trying to get the airport police moving. This is a cluster fuck and I think you're going to have to deal with it on your own."

"Business as usual," I said as I checked my carbine for the third time. It gave me something to do besides look at all the stuff whizzing by uncomfortably close as we flew over the traffic on Airport Way. Beside me on the bench, Dale was busy delinking the machine gun ammo and stuffing it in his pockets. He was totally focused on what he was doing. He looked like he was sitting at home in front of the elaborate array of equipment he used to hand load long range rifle cartridges, instead of sitting on the side of a helicopter that was in danger of running into an electrical line at any moment.

We were approaching the south-east corner of the airport, where all the privately owned business jets were kept.

"We're looking for a Gulfstream with tail number N379P," Jack said over the intercom.

I looked down below. I saw lots of pointy little business jets, all of them painted white.

"Uh… What's a Gulfstream look like?" I asked.

"Never mind, I see it."

I saw one plane, a little bigger than the rest, pulling away from the hangars. Jack goosed the throttle and we headed towards it.

"Tower, Black Jack One. You've got a Gulfstream number three seven niner P headed out for a departure," Jack said over the radio.

"Negative. I have no such departure." The controller was starting to sound more pissed.

"Well, you better tell him that."

I was no pilot, but it seemed like the jet was traveling way too fast. The nose was bouncing up and down and as it made a hard left turn to go out onto the taxiway, one wing tipped so far I thought it might strike the ground.

"Are we sure Marshall or Todd are on this thing?" I asked over the radio.

There was a long pause as I looked at the plane through my rifle scope. I wasn't sure what the little .300 Blackout rounds would do to a business jet, but I was willing to find out. Beside me, Dale held his rifle at the ready.

"We're not," Bolle finally said. "They rolled out of a closed hangar while my sources watched. We don't know who is on it."

On the taxiway, an airliner slammed on its brakes as the Gulfstream cut it off. I tried to get a bead on the quick moving little jet, but Jack was flying sideways, trying to keep the jet in view, without flying out over the runway.

I finally got the red dot centered on the cockpit of the plane, but an Alaska Air airliner on its takeoff run passed behind it, then I lost it again. The Gulfstream only had a few hundred feet to go before it could turn onto the runway proper.

"Oh shit," Jack said. I looked up. Another airliner was coming in on its final approach. It was probably a mile or two off, but it would gobble up that distance in seconds.

"United Air 737 on final at PDX 28R. Wave off. Wave off. Obstruction on the runway," Jack said.

Even over all the other noise, I heard the scream of the 737's engines as it fought to gain altitude. I thought for a second its landing gear would touch the top of the Gulfstream, then it clawed its way back into the sky. The Gulfstream stopped at the end of the runway, then gunned its engines.

Jack killed the helo's forward momentum and brought us into a low hover.

"I'm not doing this anymore," he said. "If an airliner full of people crashes, it's not gonna be because of me."

As I watched the Gulfstream screamed down the runway. The rest of the airport was in chaos. There were airliners sitting everywhere, their pilots having decided the best thing to do while things got sorted out was to stop moving. Down at the other end of the airport, I saw several vehicles with flashing red and blue lights approaching. Too little too late.

The Gulfstream took off, leveled out, and flew straight west, only a few hundred feet above the ground.

Jack whistled over the radio. "At that speed, he's gonna be over the Pacific in ten minutes."

Bolle came over the radio. "Pack it in, Jack. Head back to base."

"Will do." He pivoted the Little Bird until it's nose faced east and we started moving at a much more sedate speed.

"You did the right thing," I said.

"I know," Jack replied.

I craned my neck and watched the Gulfstream until it vanished. I wondered who was on board. I didn't know how far the little jet could fly, but I was guessing it would be out of our reach in no time.

I knew I should have been happy with our victory at the reservoir, but it was hollow. I wanted Todd, and I wanted Marshall.

CHAPTER TWENTY-SEVEN

Casey met us in the loading bay after Jack dropped us off. I trudged toward the big roll-up doors of the old factory feeling like I was a million years old. I hurt all over, and everything still sounded muffled and far away.

"Jesus, Dent. You're covered in blood."

I looked down. The knees of the jeans I was wearing had big bloody splotches on them. My boots stuck to the concrete floor as I walked. I smelled like an abattoir. I swayed a little on my feet and my eyes felt gritty like they were full of sand.

Seeing Casey triggered a memory. I dug in the dump pouch attached to my vest and pulled out the phones.

"Here," I said. "I pulled these off the guys at the reservoir."

She hesitated to take them from my sticky hands, but she did.

"I'll run them as soon as I can."

I nodded. "Can you help settle Dale? I think he's gonna stay with us for a while."

"Sure." She kept looking at me funny like there was something wrong with me. I felt like there was something more I should say, but I didn't know what it was.

"I'm gonna take a shower," I said.

"That's a good idea." She pointed over to a corner of the cavernous factory floor. "We got your Explorer towed over there."

She gave me one last look, then led Dale towards the operations center. Eddie followed. I'd never seen him this subdued before. Again, I felt like I should say something to him, but it just wouldn't come, so I wound up just walking over to my Explorer and digging a duffel bag out of the back. I walked to the door of my trailer and, after a glance to make sure nobody was around, stripped naked, leaving the bloody clothes in a big pile. Inside I scrubbed myself raw, going over every inch of my body with soap three times, but I was still convinced I could smell blood. Every time I closed my eyes, I saw the inside of the moving van cab. Every time I opened my eyes, the moment that Strueucker was shot replayed in my head. Had I screwed up and gotten him shot? I'd been closer to the back end of the moving van, it should have been my sector to cover. Was it just one of those things that happened? Sometimes no matter how good you were, the other side got a shot in.

Finally, I gave up and got out. I knew I needed sleep, but I also knew if I tried to lie down right now, I would just lie in bed with my mind racing. I toweled off and dressed. I had a spare 10mm in the bag, along with duplicates of my knives and such. When I walked back out of the trailer, I almost felt normal, and that seemed wrong.

I'd felt this way several times in my life. The first was after the fight in Mogadishu. Then after that, it had happened when I was a cop, and I'd killed two men, and even more after the events of last fall when I'd lost my job and gotten tangled up with Marshall and Todd. There was this feeling that my life had taken a profound shift, that I'd been involved in something exceptional and life-altering, then realizing that I still needed to eat, sleep, and go to the bathroom, just like before. Humans were animals that were always seeking to go back to their baseline and no matter how much your head told you things were different, your body was just glad to be alive and was wondering where your next meal was coming from.

Dale was standing in the doorway of the shop, smoking a cigarette and staring meditatively off into space. He still had his bolt gun slung over his shoulder, and I made a mental note to see if there was more ammo for it in the armory. I had half a mind not to disturb him but walked over anyway.

He looked at me as I walked up and blew smoke out of his nostrils.

"Well, that was different," he said.

"Yeah. I appreciate your help today."

"Least I could do." He shook his head. "Fucking skinhead Nazis. Who would have guessed it? I've half a mind to start driving to the retirement homes and handing out surplus Garand rifles. There are some boys in their nineties that know how to take care of Nazis."

I laughed. "That's what we were missing today. A bunch of old geezers with M1's. I shoulda thought of that."

He gave me a sharp glance. I don't know if it was something in my tone, or my body language or what, but he homed in on it.

"I'd say you boys did a pretty good job on your own today, Dent. Something eating you about it?"

"I think I got Struecker killed. I keep wondering if it was my fault."

"Tell me about it."

So I did. I recounted the last couple minutes of that frantic, wild ride in the pickup truck. I didn't leave anything out. I told him just like I remembered it, focusing on details of where I was, what I could see, even what my mental state had been. I tried to be as clinical as possible. We'd done this in the Rangers, examining each minute of an operation, looking for deficiencies in our tactics, techniques, and procedures. The after action reviews could be coldly brutal. Nobody was out to hurt your feelings, but nobody was going to go out of their way to spare them if you screwed up either. I'd tried to bring that same work ethic to my work at the Police Bureau and had found most people weren't interested. They just wanted to exaggerate their successes and gloss over their mistakes. Over the years, I'd known of at least officer who had died because of that, and more who had gotten hurt. I'd learned to accept it, and, whenever I could, tried to surround myself with people who were willing to do the same kind of rigorous self-assessment.

After I was done talking, Dale lit another cigarette and took a few drags while he stared off into space. I could practically hear the wheels turning in his mind. Finally, he exhaled another cloud of smoke and shook his head.

"I don't think anybody fucked up, least of all you. It's just one of those things that happened. Big boy games, big boy rules. Struecker knew the risks. Sometimes the other side gets a punch in."

A knot of tension I'd barely been aware of left my body. Deep down, I knew that if Dale thought I'd screwed up, he would have told me, directly and matter-of-factly, not so I would beat myself up and wallow in guilt but so I wouldn't screw up that way again.

"You know what your problem is?" Dale asked as he ground out his cigarette on his boot heel. "You take responsibility for too much. You've been beating yourself up for what happened to Mandy, and if you ain't careful you're going to beat yourself up for what happened to Struecker."

He looked around for a place to dump his cigarette butt, didn't see one, and slipped it in a pocket. It was an old soldier's habit.

"My daughter was a big girl and knew what she was getting into.

The fault lies with those men that beat her. Same goes for Struecker. I swear the world's full of two kinds of people, the ones who shit all over the floor and act like somebody else did it, and guys like you that see somebody else shit on the floor, and think it's their fault."

He hitched his rifle sling up a little higher on his shoulder and walked towards the command center.

"Enough of this navel-gazing. I'm hungry. Can a man get a sandwich around here?"

I laughed a little, at both him and me. I followed him into the break room and we both assembled obscenely large plates of food, then carried them into the command center. Henry was nodded off over in a corner, surrounded by empty energy drink cans and fast food wrappers. Casey looked bleary-eyed but she was still functional. She had the phones I'd given her hooked up to a desktop computer, and numbers and letters were scrolling up a display faster than I could decipher them. Over in the corner, several screens were tuned to the local news. The sound was off, but I could tell the attack at the reservoir was the top story. Two channels were showing a reporter standing in front of what now looked like hundreds of police and fire vehicles on the access road to the reservoir. The third showed an aerial view of the moving van from a news helicopter. It was surrounded by tape, and as I watched, some unlucky bastard in a bomb suit was approaching the back of the truck. I winced as one of the channels cut away to shaky cell phone video of the Little Bird flying down Airport Way. I saw myself strapped to the bench on the side.

"I was just getting ready to page you," Casey said. "Bolle is on his way back here with Drogan and Byrd. He's about twenty minutes out. He wants everybody ready for a briefing when he gets here."

"Ok," I said around a bite of sandwich. "We should probably wake Henry up. Anybody know where Alex is?"

"Here," a voice said behind me.

I turned, and there she was. I surprised myself at how quickly I set the sandwich down and gathered her up in my arms. This time I was unselfconscious about the fact that other people were in the room.

"Hey," I said.

"Hey yourself," she hugged me tightly for a long moment then let me go.

"Rough day at work," she said.

"Yeah," I said. "Rough day."

She pulled back, looked around the room for a minute, a little self-conscious, but she still held onto my hand. She opened her mouth to say something else, but something grabbed her attention.

"Isn't that the guy we're looking for?" she asked and pointed at one of the TV screens.

CHAPTER TWENTY-EIGHT

Henderson Marshall was on one of the screens, talking into the camera. Casey scrambled to find the right remote and turn the sound on.

"… unconscionable attack is further proof of the degeneracy of our society. It's clear that despite stealing over a third of what every hard-working American makes, our corrupt politicians and lazy public servants are incapable of protecting us."

As he droned on, I studied Marshall and the background. He was wearing a khaki shirt with epaulets, the sort of almost military looking thing I associated with men who went on safaris or sat around gun clubs talking about how immigrants were ruining the country. The background behind him was a featureless white wall. He sat in a metal folding chair, and propped up next to him was an AR-15 rifle.

Marshall picked up the rifle and showed it to the camera. "I've fought for this country my entire life. I've been prepared to fight in the halls of the US Senate, but lately I've been wondering if it's time for me to fight in a different way. It's moments like these that I think of the Minutemen of Lexington and Concord, and the brave men who fought for states rights during the Civil War. If it comes down to it, I'm willing to fight and to die for this country."

I noticed he had his finger on the trigger of the rifle. That was bad form at all times, but I thought it would be especially ironic if he cranked off a round by accident while delivering his little manifesto.

"I'm calling on all the true patriots out there, the real men of action in this country to stand up and do what's right. It's time to take this country back, and if our so-called leaders aren't willing to do the right thing, the rest of us need to be. Good night and God bless you."

The video ended and the broadcast cut away to a vapidly pretty local news anchor that I vaguely recognized. Casey cut the sound again.

"Wow," she said. "You know that asshole was in the Army for like a year and a half, and he never left the United States?"

Dale shook his head, and muttered something under his breath about "chicken hawks."

Casey got up and shook Henry awake. Alex caught my eye and cocked her head towards the door. I followed her out into the hallway and then into a vacant office.

She hugged me again, and as an added bonus laid a proper kiss on me. I was instantly horny, not just because it was Alex, but because of that good old-fashioned adrenaline afterglow.

Alex broke away and laughed. "At ease, soldier. I don't think we have time for that."

I wished we did but pushed it out of my mind.

"How are you?"

"I've been in a safe, well-lit place performing an autopsy. It's you that I'm worried about. It looked like things got a little crazy at the reservoir."

I looked down at myself. "I keep checking myself for extra holes and not finding any. Struecker's dead though"

"Yeah, I heard."

That hung in the air between us for a moment. The unspoken truth was that it just as easily could have been me. I wondered how many more times I could roll the dice and not come up snake eyes.

"Todd wasn't at the reservoir?" she asked.

"No," I said.

"Then it's not even close to being over."

"I don't know." It was the most honest answer I could give. "I haven't had a chance to even think about the next step."

"I'm tired of being on the sidelines," she said. "I'm tired of playing your girl Friday that patches you up when you get hurt, and investigates things while you're out saving the world. I want in."

I had a vision of her lying bloody and pale in the bed of that pickup truck, instead of Struecker, when I heard Bolle's voice down the hallway. Our little respite was over, and it was time to go back to work.

"Let's see what Bolle has to say, and go from there," I said.

She nodded, clearly not happy. She gave me the barest peck on the lips and walked out of the office.

The mood around the table was solemn. Drogan and Byrd kept

looking at the chair where Struecker would have sat. The rest of us didn't. I'd dealt with this before. Right now wasn't the time to mourn our dead and injured.

Bolle normally looked like he'd stepped out of the pages of GQ, but now he was rumpled and unshaven. His eyes were a little bloodshot. He was talking to Dale over in a corner when we walked in, and I was surprised to see them both nod and shake hands before Dale walked over and took a place at the table. Apparently, he was in.

Bolle looked around the room, as if he was counting heads, and coming up a little short.

"I want to thank all of you for your hard work these last few days. You've all taken great risks, and undergone sacrifices. Thanks to you, the water system for the city of Portland is safe, and some very bad people are no longer a threat."

He stood up, paced in front of the monitors mounted on the wall.

"The local FBI field office has agreed to take care of arrangements for Special Agent Struecker, notifying his family, and all that."

Bolle trailed off, stared into the corner for a few seconds. I looked around the table, everybody looked glum and defeated, like dogs with their tails between their legs. These people needed a pep talk. If this had been the military, Bolle would have been the aloof, cerebral officer, and it would have been the job of a senior sergeant to rally the troops. The problem was, Al had been Bolle's sergeant, but now Al was dead and there was no one to fill that role.

The silence started to weigh heavy in the room. I tried to think of something to say, but this wasn't my strong suit. I'd always felt that one of the weaknesses of Bolle's unit was it didn't feel like a team. It was an ad hoc collection of people thrown together on the fly. We didn't train together, hadn't gotten to know each other. We just went out and made it up as we went along. So far that had worked out, but it was times like this that really tested units.

Dale cleared his throat.

"I just want to thank you folks for all you've done," he said. "These bastards hurt my daughter pretty bad, and for six months I've been waiting for somebody to hold them accountable. I know you all haven't caught the people directly responsible for it yet, but I appreciate you trying. The Portland police just wanted to sweep the whole thing under the rug. If nothing else, we took some of those skinhead assholes out of circulation. My dad didn't fight his way across Europe so Nazi assholes could blow up people's drinking water right here in Oregon."

Bolle relaxed a little after that. I realized he'd recognized the need to rally the troops, and hadn't had the slightest idea how to do it. There were a few people around the table nodding their heads.

"We appreciate your help too, Mr. Williams," Bolle said. "I've just returned from the reservoir. The Portland Police Bureau and the FBI are still processing the scene. All of the men found at the scene were known members of the West County Hammerheads. They were all dead at the scene except for one, Curtis."

My eyebrows lifted. The last time I'd seen Curtis, he hadn't been in very good shape. I was surprised to find he was still alive.

"Curtis is in custody, in the hospital being treated for gunshot wounds. He's expected to survive, but as of right now we can't question him. The FBI is following all the obvious leads: digital profiles, who rented the truck, that sort of thing. Right now we've got nothing concrete to link them to Todd, Marshall, or Cascade Aviation, other than the obvious fact that Dent saw them all together at their compound."

Casey spoke up. "Dent took some phones off those guys. I've got them hooked up now so I can brute force decrypt them. Hopefully, I'll have some results soon."

Apparently, that was news to Bolle. He looked pleased.

"Excellent. I was hoping Henry could give us an update on the aircraft that left Portland International immediately after the attack."

Henry cleared his throat. "It was a Gulfstream 650ER, with a range of over 7,000 nautical miles. The jet turned off its transponder and headed straight out to sea, where it fell off radar. They could be on their way to Asia or Central America. Right now the FAA has launched an investigation into the unauthorized departure from PDX and the subsequent danger it posed to all those airliners. They'll probably be done in six months or so…"

Henry and Bolle rolled their eyes simultaneously. One of the reasons Bolle was so effective was his unit was lean. The rest of the Federal government would have to have a dozen meetings with PowerPoint presentations before they even got moving.

"We've got feelers out all over the world," Bolle said. "I'd really like to know if Marshall or Todd was on that plane, or if it was a red herring. If they've fled the country, we need to be ready to take this operation international."

My eyebrows shot up again. I didn't know Bolle had the ability to do that. That was an interesting twist. I wondered if we might wind up in some foreign garden spot like Afghanistan or Pakistan. Cascade Aviation didn't tend to operate in nice countries where you'd want to go on vacation.

"Did you learn anything from the autopsy, Dr. Pace?" Bolle asked.

Alex shifted in her seat. "I did a complete autopsy on the man we identified as Abdel Lafif Farah. He was borderline malnourished. He'd been beaten, more than once, as there were bruises all over his body in multiple stages of healing. It's no surprise that the cause of death was a close-range gunshot wound to the head from a large caliber handgun, but on autopsy, I found that his liver had been lacerated from a blow to the thorax, most likely a couple hours before he was shot. That would have killed him eventually if he hadn't received medical attention."

She stared at a spot on the wall. "The toxicology reports will take a few days to complete, so we don't know with any certainty that he was exposed to the PCP we found at the compound, but as I suspected, it appears that the wounds on his wrist were self-inflicted."

"He tried to chew his own wrist open?" Drogan said. He was a little pale.

Alex nodded. The room was quiet for a bit as everyone absorbed that little fact.

"Right now, we're at a standstill," Bolle said. "Based on Dent's testimony alone, we have probable cause to arrest Rickson Todd. We just have to find him. I am concerned that we don't know what was going on in that compound. Were there more men there like this Farah? If so, where are they now? If they left on that airplane, in some ways that's a relief, as they are off US soil."

"But why bring them here?" I asked. "If you wanted to brainwash them you could do that somewhere else in the world, much easier than here. Why bring them here, then leave with them again?"

"That's why I don't think Todd was on that plane," Bolle said. "I think he's still here and I think those men are too."

I nodded. This wasn't over yet, not by a long shot.

"Right now, we have another concern," Bolle said. "Up until now, our investigation has been secret, under the radar of the local police, and even the local FBI field office. Due to the high visibility events at the reservoir, and the airport, we're out in the open now. Other agencies are clamoring for a part of the investigation and this is going to turn into a turf war if we aren't careful."

He looked up at one of the screens on the wall. The sound was muted, but it was easy to tell we were the subject of the news report since they were showing the footage of us flying over Airport Way in the Little Bird again.

"Before the shootout at the reservoir, nobody wanted to touch this investigation. I found few friends when I wanted to pursue an indictment against a rich man like Henderson Marshall. Now everyone wants in. Some of them want in because they want to say they helped break open the conspiracy to attack the Portland water system. Careers can be made on far less."

Now Marshall's video was being replayed on the screen.

"Some of them though, are complicit, and they want to be part of manufacturing the narrative, controlling what evidence disappears. Some of them wear military uniforms, and some of them wear badges. You'll be tempted to trust them, but don't. The only people you can trust are in this room."

It was like the old Bolle had come back. He had that fire in his eyes that I remembered from last year. He reminded me of an old school tent revival preacher, drunk on damnation and hellfire. For me, this was revenge. That was part of it for him too, but he was on a crusade. Part of me felt like I should share his outrage at the corruption we'd uncovered, but I just couldn't. It was wrong, and I knew it, but my biggest concern was what had been done to the people I cared about.

"Right now we all need some rest," Bolle said. "We'll convene in the morning and plan our next move."

The meeting broke up. I caught Alex's eye and we both headed towards the door. The little trailer on the factory floor was the closest thing either of us had to a home at the moment, and spending some time there with her sounded pretty good right now.

Over on Casey's desk, something beeped. She walked over, wiggled a computer mouse and looked at the screen.

"Hey," she said. "I just cracked Curtis's phone."

Thoughts of domestic bliss temporarily forgotten, I walked over to stand behind Casey's chair.

"I'm dumping the contents now, and running an association matrix," she said.

Casey typed so fast I was surprised the keys weren't smoking. I couldn't follow what she was doing, but stayed anyway, hoping she could give us something to go on.

"Huh," she said, then kept typing. I held my tongue, fought the desire to ask her what was going on.

"Ok. He purged the phone relatively recently. I might be able to get some of that back, we'll see. There is one call in memory. Looks like he made it about an hour before things started at the reservoir."

On another screen, she called up a map of the city.

"The phone he called is still active, pinging cell towers."

The lines from four different cell towers crossed at a point in southeast Portland. As Casey zoomed in, I realized I recognized the neighborhood.

"Nice," Casey said. "We've got a good fix, down to a few houses. I'll see who the properties belong to."

"Don't bother," I said. "I know where we need to go."

She turned to look at me. I pointed at the screen.

"That house belongs to Steve Lubbock, my old boss."

I would have said the expression on my face was a smile, but apparently, I was wrong. Casey recoiled from me. She looked scared like she'd turned and seen a wild animal standing there instead of a man.

Maybe it was an apt analogy. I felt my nostrils flare, like a wolf scenting prey.

I was about to get something I wanted for a long time.

CHAPTER TWENTY-NINE

Eddie drove while I sat in the seat beside him, a shotgun held between my legs muzzle up. Dalton was in the back seat. In another vehicle behind us were Drogan and Byrd. The five of us were kitted out in tactical vests. The third vehicle in the convoy was a van carrying Casey and Alex. They were wearing vests too, but hopefully would only be processing evidence. Alex also had a medical kit, in case things really went to shit.

I'd wanted to leave the conference room and punch Lubbock's ticket right away, but Bolle put the brakes on. He actually wrote a search warrant and only moments ago had called us to tell us he'd had it signed by a Federal judge. Right now he was in the air, in the Little Bird. Jack would fly and Bolle would monitor things via the cameras mounted on the helo. We doubted Lubbock would try to run, but if he did, we would have eyes in the sky.

Part of me hoped Lubbock would try to run.

It was the middle of the night, and the streets were quiet around Lubbock's house. There was a light on in an upstairs bedroom. Our plan was pretty straightforward. Since this was terrorism-related, we'd gotten a no-knock warrant. We could just kick the door in. Drogan and Byrd parked their vehicle in front of Lubbock's garage, denying him the ability to escape in the car inside. They both bailed out and ran around to the back door in case Lubbock tried to flee that way. Eddie, Dalton and I ran up to the front door.

I wanted very badly for Dalton to blow up Lubbock's front door, but since we were in a residential neighborhood, and there was no evidence Lubbock had fortified the door, I was going to have to settle for the next best thing. I was carrying a stubby little sawed-off shotgun. Instead of the usual buckshot or slugs, it was loaded with special frangible "doorbuster" rounds. They were made of a compressed metal powder and would blow the lock to pieces, but not hurt anybody standing more than a couple of feet from the door on the other side.

Eddie held the screen door open, and I placed the muzzle of the shotgun against the door jamb at a forty-five-degree angle, right where the lock went into the frame. I triggered two quick shots, let the shotgun hang, then kicked the door. It flew open and bounced off the wall inside. I pulled my pistol and we were in, sweeping the living room and seeing no one.

From the back of the house, I heard breaking glass as Drogan and Byrd broke a window, so they could pull the drapes aside and cover a back room. Eddie, Dalton and I sprinted for the stairs. It was a calculated risk. We'd seen lights flicking on and off upstairs while we were waiting for the warrant, but no sign of anyone downstairs.

"Police! Search warrant!" I yelled as I ran up the stairs. At the top, I broke right, headed for the bedroom with the light on. I passed through the doorway and saw Lubbock standing beside the bed, which was covered with piles of clothes and suitcases. He was standing in profile to me, with his right hand reaching into a satchel.

"Put your hands up!" I yelled and holstered my pistol as I ran towards him. I wanted to put my hands on him so bad I could taste it.

It was a dumb mistake. I saw a flash of silver in his hand, and by the time I realized it was a little snub-nosed revolver, he shot me in the chest.

The impact of the slug into the hard armor plate barely registered. I crashed into him and slammed him against the wall. The gun was trapped between us and I heard it go off again. I got my right hand around his neck and drove his head into the wall. I had just enough time to see the dent in the drywall as we both tumbled to the floor in the narrow space between the bed and the wall.

I grabbed the revolver with my left hand and trapped it to his chest, squeezing hard in the hopes of stopping the cylinder from rotating. With my right, I blasted a hammer fist to the bridge of his nose and felt it pop and flatten. That seemed to work pretty well, so I let another one fly that hit him square in the teeth. He went limp and I twisted the little Smith and Wesson out of his grip.

Things got a little fuzzy after that. I remembered raising the little gun over my head and slamming it into Lubbock's face, more than once. Part of me was in a white-hot rage like nothing I'd ever felt before. Another part of me was detached, and noting the alarming number of blood droplets collecting on the wall, thought maybe I should stop because the whole point of this was to get Lubbock to talk.

I'll never know which one of those competing voices in my head would have won out because the decision was taken out of my hands. I felt myself being lifted up and dragged backward. I struggled for a second to free myself. There was a grab handle on the back of my vest, put there so we could drag a wounded teammate to safety. I realized Eddie was pulling me backward with one hand. With my gear on I probably weighed close to three hundred pounds, but in Eddie's grasp, I might as well have been a feather pillow.

"Need to cool it, Dent. You crack that guy's head open, he ain't gonna be able to tell us what we need to know." He said it in a tone that on the surface sounded like he was talking about the weather, but underneath was some steel. Beneath his affable, laid-back islander exterior, Eddie was a dangerous man. I wasn't sure who would win in a fight between us, but there was a big possibility both of us would lose.

Lubbock struggled to rise to his hands and knees. He was still alive then. I looked down at the little revolver in my hand. It was caked with blood and the trigger guard was bent into the trigger. I was lucky the thing hadn't gone off again when I hit him with it. Eddie still had a firm grip on the back of my vest. I made myself relax and stifle my anger.

"I'm good," I said. Eddie relaxed his grasp and I stood up.

Lubbock's face was pretty messed up. Dalton moved forward, pulling his first aid kit off his vest.

"They told me it would just be a pipe bomb, and nobody would get hurt," Lubbock said, and spit out part of a tooth.

Eddie and I looked at each other. That was a pretty significant admission. My cop brain kicked in. Lubbock hadn't been read his Miranda rights, but he'd said it spontaneously, without any prompting or questioning from us, thus his statement would be admissible in court. I automatically started writing my report in my head, which made me realize I hadn't written a single report since I joined Bolle's crew. Since some of the stuff I'd done could easily put me in prison, maybe that was a good thing.

"What the hell happened?" Bolle said from the doorway. I turned and saw him standing there with Alex behind him. She had her medical bag over her shoulder. There was a grassy field down the street just big enough for the Little Bird. Apparently, Jack had dropped Bolle off. I belatedly realized I could hear the helo's rotors overhead.

"He, uhhh… resisted arrest," Eddie said with a sidelong glance at me.

"Check him out," Bolle said with that little hand gesture of his that irritated me so much. It reminded me of a rich guy giving orders to his servant and made me wonder if that was how he saw us.

Alex's eyes flicked to me, then she pulled her bag off her shoulder and started towards Lubbock, who had that dazed, vacant look of somebody with a concussion.

"Uhh… Dent got shot," Eddie said.

Alex's head swiveled towards me and her eyebrows went up. "You got shot?"

"Oh yeah. I got shot." I fingered the hole in my vest. It was about the size of my pinky and could I could feel the slug in there on top of the armor plate of my vest.

"Come." Alex grabbed my wrist and tried to pull me towards the door.

"I really think my vest stopped it," I said.

Bolle looked at me. "Go," he said.

I let Alex lead me into the spare bedroom. The place had been ransacked. Drawers were opened and clothes were strewn all over the floor. She tapped the plate carrier.

"Off," she said and dug in her bag.

I was tempted to make a crack about her wanting to get my clothes off but had enough sense to tell she was in no mood. I pulled the carrier off, feeling instantly lighter by about 30 pounds and skinned out of my shirt. There was a little red mark in the "n" of my "Front Towards Enemy" tattoo.

"Sit down on the bed," Alex said. I complied and she stuck her stethoscope on my chest. I flinched at the cold metal.

"I think I'm fine," I said.

"Shut up and take deep breaths," she said.

I complied and she moved the stethoscope around, then palpated my chest, which despite everything else, actually felt kind of good.

"You know, if you hadn't been wearing your vest, you'd have a collapsed lung right now. Might have even hit your spine and put you in a wheelchair."

"Glad I was wearing the vest," I said.

"Let's work on not getting shot in the first place," she said. She wouldn't meet my eyes as she stowed her stuff back in the bag. I wanted to grab her hand and say I was sorry, even though I wasn't exactly sure for what, but I realized Bolle was standing in the doorway.

"Can you please tend to Lubbock, Dr. Pace?" Bolle asked. Alex nodded and walked out of the room without a word or a backward glance. I pulled my shirt on.

"Leave the plate carrier," Bolle said. "It's evidence."

I nodded and turned to walk out of the room, but Bolle blocked my way.

"You know, Dent, it's ok to fuck somebody up if they try to shoot you," he said. "But it's hard to justify it when you're using their own gun to beat them with."

It didn't take a forensic science genius to figure out what had happened in there. I just stood there, not sure what to say. Beating Lubbock had been wrong, in a strictly legal sense, but I was having a hard time feeling sorry about it.

"I'm closer than I've ever come," Bolle said. "I want Todd and Marshall, and Lubbock is a link in the chain that leads me to him. You've been useful to me, but don't jeopardize my work by losing control."

I didn't know what to say to that. Ethical issues aside, if Lubbock's brains were too scrambled to give a coherent statement, I'd lost a major opportunity for us to move forward in the case. I was starting to feel like a dumbass.

"Ok," I said finally.

Bolle's expression softened. "I don't know when you slept last. You've been kidnapped and in a couple of gunfights in the last few days. You're off the street. It isn't a punishment. I think you've gone too long with too little rest. Drogan is going to drive you back to Troutdale."

My eyes flicked towards the master bedroom, where Alex was working on Lubbock.

"After she patches up Lubbock, I'm going to need all the help I can get searching this place because I don't trust the locals," Bolle said. "We're not doing anything else operational. I won't let anything happen to her."

"Ok," I said again. I realized Bolle had a point. I felt spacey and disconnected from what was going on around me, courtesy of not enough sleep, and too much adrenaline. Everybody had a limit. My eyes felt like someone had taken sandpaper, to them and I had a pounding headache. My entire body hurt. I hadn't felt this wiped out since Ranger School when I was twenty years younger and much dumber.

"Thank you," Bolle said. He looked like he meant it. "I'm glad you weren't hurt."

Then he stepped aside and I walked out in the hall. Alex was wrapping gauze around Lubbock's head. She paused long enough to give me a look I couldn't quite read, then went back to work.

I shrugged, turned and walked out the door.

CHAPTER THIRTY

I remember getting in the car with Drogan and driving past a bored Portland police officer that was blocking the street for us. I must have fallen asleep because the next thing I knew I was waking up in a panic, unsure of where I was. I had my pistol half out of the holster before I realized we were right outside the roll-up door to the factory. Dale Williams was standing outside smoking a cigarette.

Drogan was giving me a look out of the corner of her eye. I slid my pistol back in the holster and got out without a word to her.

"Dent, your eyes look like two piss holes in a snow bank," Dale said.

"I'm a little tired," I said. My own voice sounded far away.

"How'd it go?"

"Lubbock shot me," I said. It felt strange to have those words come out of my mouth.

Dale looked me up and down.

"In the vest," I added.

He nodded. "Then what?"

"I beat the shit out of him."

Dale nodded as if that pleased him.

"It probably went a little too far," I said after a moment. "Lubbock pulled me off the street." I felt like I was admitting to doing something dirty when I said it. I think it reminded me too much of when I'd been fired from the Police Bureau.

Dale blew smoke out of his nostrils. "Lubbock still breathing?"

"Mostly."

"Well, that's a start. Why don't you tell it to me from the beginning?"

So I unloaded it all on him, from the minute I blew open the door to when Lubbock kicked me out of his crime scene. It felt good to tell somebody who maybe would have an inkling of what it was like. I realized then that there was an Al-sized hole in my life, and part of me really wanted Dale to step into it.

Dale stubbed out his smoke and dropped it into a coffee can half-filled with dirt he'd scrounged from somewhere.

"When was the last time you slept?"

"I don't really know."

"Back in Nam, we used to have these guys that would go out on a recon patrol, hide in the bush, for five, six days. They'd live in a hole in the ground and catch a cat nap here and there. They'd have Charlie all around them so they couldn't talk, had to eat fish and rice so Charlie wouldn't smell American food. Sometimes things would drop in the pot and they'd wind up shooting it out with Charlie. Some of those six-man teams killed a hundred or more VC before they got extracted."

By force of habit he tapped another smoke out of his pack, then caught himself and pushed it back in.

"Those guys would come back still all wired on adrenaline. They'd shit, shower, and shave and think they were ready to go out again. The times we let them, it was usually a disaster. A person can only take so much, no matter how hard they are. We'd keep them back at base and about twelve hours after the helo dropped 'em off they'd fall asleep for a whole day, then wake up and have the shakes for a day after that."

"You look just like one of those boy,s Dent. My advice is to go get something to eat and get some sleep. When that gal of yours comes back, see if she's up for a roll in the hay. That'll put you back on an even keel."

I wasn't sure if a roll in the hay with Alex was in the cards, but sleep and food sounded good. Dale and I walked through the roll-up door and he pressed the button to shut it behind us.

"I'm going to turn in myself. Henry set me up in one of those little trailers. I guess Bolle wants me to hang around a few days, get statements from me and such. I think he's trying to figure out how he's going to explain how a broke down old rancher wound up strapped to the side of his toy helicopter shooting it out with a bunch of skinhead assholes."

He gave me a wave and headed towards the trailers.

"Hey, Dale," I called after him. He looked over his shoulder.

"Thanks."

He gave me a thumbs up and kept on walking. Maybe after all this was over, I'd see if Dale needed a hired hand. I'd always wanted to be a cowboy when I was a kid.

The halls of the building were dark and deserted. It hadn't actually been bustling with people before, but now only me, Henry, and Dale were in the building. Henry was looking at half a dozen computer monitors and seemed to be doing several things at once. He was monitoring police radio traffic and monitoring the security cameras all over our building. He was also running some kind of simulation that involved figuring out the probability that the Cascade Aviation Gulfstream jet had landed at any particular airport in the world, based on a set of parameters that he was tweaking on the fly. Finally, on a laptop over in a corner, he was playing a computer game.

There were stacks of fast food wrappers and empty energy drink cans on the desk around him. Henry was engrossed in his work, so I left him to it. I didn't particularly feel like talking anyway so I went into the break room and ate two ridiculously large sandwiches.

I needed to go to sleep, but I found myself pacing around the little trailer, aimlessly opening and closing the various drawers and cupboards, looking for what, I didn't know. I found myself fingering the spot on my chest where the bullet had struck me. For some reason, I felt both sweaty and cold at the same time.

In the bathroom, I pulled off my shirt and looked in the mirror. There was still a little red mark, right there in the middle of my tattoo. I imagined a bullet hole there, and my lungs filling up with blood.

I found myself kneeling in front of the toilet, throwing up the food I'd just eaten. I retched long after my stomach was empty, and then lay there on the bathroom floor shaking and shivering. For several minutes I would have sworn I could smell the tires burning in the streets of Mogadishu. The last time I'd felt like this was after the fight that left eighteen of us dead. I was proud that I'd kept my shit together, but when we finally got back to the airport I'd puked up my chow just like this.

Finally, I rinsed out my mouth and dragged myself into the bed. The last thing I remembered was making sure my pistol was within arm's reach on the nightstand, and then I was asleep.

I dreamed. I dreamed about the shootout in the house in south-east Portland, only this time I got shot to pieces. I dreamed that back in the trailer when I hit Dolph in the head with the flail, he just turned around and laughed. I dreamed about Struecker getting shot, only this time it wasn't Curtis lying under the truck, it was Lubbock lying there with his little .38 and he shot me too.

Mostly, I relived that moment in the bedroom when Lubbock shot me. Each time it was worse. I wasn't wearing armor and I felt the bullet bore through my chest, and started coughing up blood. It was like watching a video over and over again, seen from outside my body. Each time I'd try to yell that I shouldn't go inside, but I went anyway. Each time Lubbock would shoot me again.

Then, like a bad edit in a movie, the scene shifted and I found myself beating the shit out of Lubbock. Only this time I didn't stop, and his head deflated. Then in that cruel twist that dreams so often take, Lubbock's curly black hair changed to be long and honey-colored, and I realized it was Alex's face under all that blood, and not Lubbock.

I woke up with my pistol in my hand. It was pitch-dark in the trailer. I had the safety off, my finger on the trigger, and the green glowing dots of the night sights lined up on the front door.

"Dent? God, it's dark in here." It was Alex's voice. I heard the front door creak shut.

My heart leaped into my throat. I gingerly took my finger off the trigger and pushed on the safety. I scrambled to put the gun back on the nightstand. I managed to get it there and pull my hand away before she found the light switch.

The trailer was flooded with light. I was sitting up in bed, my heart hammering in my throat, trying to shake the mental image of her lying on the floor of Lubbock's bedroom with blood all over her face.

"Did I startle you? I called out, but you didn't answer." She looked at me, a little concerned.

"Bad dream," I croaked.

She pulled some clothes out of a duffel bag and went into the bathroom to dress. Bad sign. She'd always dressed and undressed in front of me unselfconsciously before. I took some deep breaths and tried to get my heart rate to slow down. I tried to push how close I'd come to shooting her out of my mind. I took another look at the pistol to make sure the safety was on and got up for a drink of water. My throat felt parched and raw.

She came out of the bathroom wearing sweat pants and a t-shirt. She looked tired.

"How are you?" she asked.

I really didn't know how to answer that. The only thing that had kept her from a bullet wound at my hands was a four-pound trigger pull. I felt keyed up and ready to fight at a moment's notice like my nervous system was still jacked up and couldn't come down. At the moment I felt both so bone tired that I could barely move, but at the same time, I felt the urge to go run around the building. So I did what I usually did when women asked me that question.

"I'm fine," I said.

Her nose wrinkled a little like she didn't believe it, and I didn't blame her. I probably looked like an absolute mess sitting up in bed wild-eyed and shaking.

"You scare me sometimes, Dent," she said, without preamble.

"I'd never hurt you," I said, the words out of my mouth before I had a chance to think. I wondered if she'd noticed the gun after all.

She shook her head. "I know you'll never hurt me. It's everybody else I'm worried about."

Alex walked over to the sink, got her own drink of water, then looked at me over the rim of the glass.

"After my mom died, I was convinced I needed a dog. My dad wouldn't say no to me about anything after mom killed herself. He would have spent thousands for one from a breeder, but I was convinced I needed to rescue one from the pound. So we went to the animal shelter and came home with the biggest damn dog they had there. Ringo was probably part German Shepherd and part Rottweiler. He'd been found wandering the streets in Los Angeles, probably escaped from a dog fighting ring, and shipped up to Oregon by one of those rescue outfits."

She put her cup down and started brushing her hair. I always liked to watch her do that.

"Within days that dog bonded to me and would have taken a bullet for me. He was a teddy bear with me, but he was sure everybody else in the world was out to kill me. He barely tolerated my dad. He almost mauled the mailman and the cable guy."

"The final straw was one night when Mike Fisher, one of dad's guys from the police bureau, came by to get some paperwork signed. Ringo broke out of the bathroom and attacked him. I ran down into the living room to find Mike on his back with Ringo on top of him, biting his arm. Mike actually had his gun out and was getting ready to shoot Ringo when I called him off."

She put the hairbrush away and kept talking as she took out her contacts.

"After we got Mike patched up, Dad wouldn't even look me in the eye. He knew we couldn't keep that dog. He just didn't want to have to tell me. I was only a teenager, but I was smart enough to know it too. I'll never forget how relieved he looked when I finally said I knew Ringo had to go."

Alex pulled her glasses out of the bag and put them on.

"So I found an old guy up in the mountains who took Ringo. I'm sure after a while he was happy there, but I'll never forget the look he gave me the day I got in the car and left him there."

The trailer was silent for a minute while I processed all of that.

"Are you comparing me to a dog?" I asked finally.

She blinked, then winced.

"I'm sorry. I probably could have done that better."

"Yeah," I said. I realized the conversation we were having was significant, but I was way too tired to do a good job participating.

"What I'm trying to say is I'm worried about you. We've never really discussed what happened to Gibson Marshall, but I have some guesses."

If her guesses involved me shooting him down in cold blood, so his body could be dumped into a river, she was right.

"What you did tonight was wrong," she said. "You beat Lubbock after he wasn't a threat to you anymore. You gave him a concussion and he might lose an eye. I think you would have killed him if Eddie hadn't stopped you."

She was right and I knew it. At that moment, I would have beaten Lubbock until his skull caved in or until my arm got too tired to swing the pistol.

"I don't think my dad would have been ok with that," she said softly.

I realized she was right again. Al had done some sketchy stuff in the name of justice, most notably joining Bolle's little crusade. But he wouldn't have beaten Lubbock like that, and he wouldn't have let me do it either.

"What does this mean for us?" I asked. "Do you want me to leave?"

She shook her head. "No. I don't want to be separate from you, but I don't want to be all that close to you either. Can we just go to bed? We're both exhausted. Let's just get some sleep and we'll talk about this in the morning."

I nodded. We both crawled into bed. She lay on her side with her back facing me. I wanted to touch her, to kiss her, but that didn't seem like a good thing to try right now.

"Good night, Dent. I hope you sleep well," she said.

I didn't say anything back. Within minutes, her breathing was deep and regular. Despite my fatigue, I couldn't sleep. For one thing, I was afraid of more nightmares. I didn't want a repeat of the horror show I'd had in my head before she came in the trailer.

For another, I couldn't stop thinking about Alex. The foot of space between us on the bed felt like a thousand miles. I was bad at relationships. I'd had only a handful of girlfriends over the years. Some of those relationships had been doomed from the start. Many times I'd known that from the beginning, others I'd realized it only in retrospect.

A couple of those relationships probably had a chance though, and I'd fucked them up every time. Usually by retreating the second things got hard. I'd clung to this fervent hope that things would be different with Alex, but in the back of my mind, there had always been that little voice telling me that there was no way this was going to work out. I wasn't the type of guy who had happily ever after with women. I was just fooling myself to believe this was ever going to last.

A part of me resented her too. I resented how much of my own happiness depended on how she felt, and what she did. No matter how much I loved her, part of me would always chafe against how much she controlled my own mood. That part of me was telling me to cut and run right now. To accept the fact that Alex was going to be my next ex-girlfriend and stop betting on foolish hopes.

But I wanted her. I'd lost my job, my house, most of my money. Once my quest for revenge was over, I'd have nothing left to live for if she was gone.

I lay there for a long time, listening to her breathe. I wanted to wake her up, just to get her to talk to me, but I had no idea what I wanted to say.

Finally, I slept, and thankfully, didn't dream.

CHAPTER THIRTY-ONE

I woke up with my gun in my hand again. This time I managed to catch myself before I flicked off the safety and put my finger on the trigger, so I guess that was progress. In the pale light filtering through the curtains of the trailer, I could see Alex sitting up in bed, staring at me.

"Hey Dent, Alex," Eddie said and knocked again.

"We're up!" I yelled, then slid the pistol back in the holster on the nightstand.

"Meeting in ten," Eddie said, then I heard the sound of him walking off.

Alex got up, grabbed her duffel bag and went into the bathroom. I listened to her rustle around, getting ready. I debated saying something but didn't. Instead, I just got dressed. I brushed my teeth in the trailer's little sink and ran some wet fingers through my hair.

Alex stepped out of the bathroom and stood there with her arms folded across her chest.

I steeled myself. Here it comes, I thought.

"If you want me to sleep in the same bed with you, the gun needs to be unloaded, and out of reach. Put it in a drawer or something."

My palms got sweaty at the very thought. For most of my adult life, I'd had a gun close by. For the last six months, I'd had at least one either on my body or within arm's reach around the clock. Part of me wanted to tell her to go to hell, that I'd keep my gun wherever I damned well pleased. The more rational part of my mind realized that I was slipping a bit, that in the last several hours, I'd pointed guns at people that I cared about. Maybe she had a point.

I also felt a little pathetic at how relieved I'd been when she said she was willing to continue sharing a bed with me, even with conditions.

"Ok," I said.

"I'm worried about you," she said.

"I'm fine," I said automatically.

She actually rolled her eyes at that, reminding me that I'd known her when she was a teenager. Without another word she pivoted and walked out the door. I followed her. She was wearing a pair of khaki cargo pants, and I found myself reflecting on how great her ass looked in them as I followed her across the factory floor. For some reason that made me feel both guilty and glad to have something occupying my thoughts besides an endless loop of death and destruction.

We walked through the inner door and were greeted with the smell of coffee. I filled a mug full of my favorite drug, and piled a plate high with fruit and pastries, hoping I could avoid a repeat of last night's vomiting. I found a seat and felt a little thrill when Alex sat down next to me. I felt like I was back in high school, hoping to attract the attention of one of the girls.

Bolle had a spring in his step that I'd never seen before.

"We have a big day ahead of us. More on that in a minute. First, let's hear from Henry."

Henry had visible stubble on his chin, which meant he hadn't shaved in a week. He was wearing his favorite "I see the Fnords!" t-shirt. It occurred to me that every time I'd been in the command center, he had too. Beneath his dopey, slacker exterior, Henry was pretty hardcore.

"I've been crunching numbers non-stop since the Cascade Aviation jet took off," Henry said. "At first glance, there are thousands of potential landing places."

There was a map of the Pacific Ocean and Asia on the display behind him, with thousands of little red dots.

"At some of these, we have good intelligence, and are reasonably sure the plane hasn't landed."

Some of the dots winked out.

"Also, it turns out the plane couldn't have gone as far as we initially expected. That initial run to the coast at low altitude and high speed burned a tremendous amount of fuel. There was also some unstable weather moving across the Pacific in the hours after their departure which would have further decreased their range. With Jack's help, I was able to do some decent calculations and eliminate even more possibilities."

This time, a substantial number of dots winked out, leaving far fewer on the screen.

"As you can see, this eliminates all of Cascade Aviation's facilities in the Middle East. It's certainly possible they landed at one of the tiny airports still on the map, took on more fuel and proceeded somewhere else. We're working on gathering as much intelligence as we can to eliminate even more possibilities. But Jack brought up another interesting possibility."

This time, the map shifted, to cover a big chunk of the western United States. Instead of red dots, there was a red shaded half circle that took in most of the country as far east as the Rocky Mountains.

Jack set his coffee cup down and spoke up. "I'm wondering if that high-speed run to the west was a red herring. It would be pretty easy to bust radar coverage off the west coast, loiter at a low altitude for a while, then sneak your way back in."

He gestured to Henry, who zoomed in the US. Now the screen was full of an eye wateringly complicated array of circles, lines, and shaded terrain.

"For the most part, we rely on transponders to keep track of aircraft. They are a transmitter that tells the air traffic control system where airplanes are over the US. The Cascade Gulfstream turned off its transponder, so that means the only way to track it is with radar. We've got a pretty comprehensive system in this country, but there are plenty of gaps due to terrain, particularly if you are willing to fly low, which further decreases fuel efficiency."

Henry flipped to another graphic. This one showed a little icon of an airplane starting at a point over the ocean off Oregon, turning back east and weaving its way through the gaps in US air traffic radar coverage.

Now it was Henry's turn to talk. "We have the radar data from the hours immediately following the escape from PDX. There's plenty of aircraft on there that don't have transponders. Most small general aviation aircraft don't. But I can rule most of them out based on their flight characteristics and positions. So if we have a pretty good idea of where the Gulfstream wasn't, we can start modeling where it might be, based on different courses, speeds, and altitudes."

On the screen behind him, the computer started modeling different courses and destinations. Each time the little plane icon would start back at the point over the ocean, the place where the Cascade jet had disappeared off radar. Then it followed a course back over land, threading its way through gaps in radar coverage until it landed. Then the computer reset and tried it again, this time with a slightly different path. As I watched, the simulation sped up, walking through different scenarios at blinding speed.

"This is going to take a while," Henry said. "I'm refining the model as we go, but I think eventually this will give us a list of places to check for the plane."

It was easy to dismiss Henry as just another millennial slacker. I was a pretty good investigator, but nothing like this would have ever occurred to me. The movies always portrayed crimes being solved by a blinding flash of insight or a lucky break, but more often they were solved by hard work, grinding away at the possibilities until a solution was found.

"Excellent, Henry." Bolle beamed. I'd never seen him look genuinely happy before.

"Right now, I need all of you to get ready to go to Portland. We have a meeting with the US Attorney for Oregon in two hours, for depositions and a grand jury hearing. We're about to secure an indictment against Rickson Todd."

That was a major shift in gears. Until now, we'd been on the border of operating as a quasi-legal hit squad. Now we were getting ready to testify. I felt more than a little apprehension, wondering what to do if questions regarding certain dead bodies would come up.

The next couple of hours passed in a blur of activity. Eddie had procured decent clothes for me. I showered and shaved, and walked out of the trailer looking halfway respectable. The drape of my suit coat over my gun wasn't perfect, but you could only expect so much from off the rack.

I did a double take when I walked up to the knot of people milling around the roll-up doors at the back of the factory floor. There was a woman standing there I didn't recognize. She was short, with dark brown hair, and wearing a conservative gray pantsuit and carrying a leather briefcase. She smiled at me and I realized it was Casey.

She laughed. "Eddie helped me dye my hair. Don't get used to it, it's temporary."

"Huh," I said. "Eddie never surprises me with his talents."

Eddie buffed his fingernails on his stylish shark gray suit. Beside him, Dalton looked very much the Portland hipster, in a dark suit and skinny tie. We were turning out to be quite the mod squad.

There was a mood in the air that I couldn't quite put my finger on. Festive wasn't the right word, but there was a feeling of victory that felt familiar. I recognized it from my days working homicides. There was a feeling of accomplishment that you'd caught the guy, but you couldn't be too happy about it, because something had to happen to get you there.

I also realized we were starting to gel as a team. Together, we'd stopped a terrorist attack in a major American city. Dalton, Eddie, Casey, Alex, they'd all helped save my ass on one occasion or another, and I'd done things for them too.

Alex looked like a million bucks in a dark blue dress. She walked up, squeezed my hand for a second, then leaned in to whisper in my ear.

"I like that suit."

She let go of my hand and gave me a wink. I wondered how this evening would go.

We split up into a pair of Suburbans. Everyone was quiet in our vehicle, pouring over reports we'd written hastily that morning. I'd testified in court often enough to do it in my sleep, except I'd never had to delicately sidestep my way through so many issues before.

The Federal Courthouse was right across the street from Central Precinct. We drove past the place where Al had been shot, and within sight of the place where I'd been abducted. My balls actually hurt for a second remembering the kick to the groin. I remembered that time in the trailer, especially the way Dolph had rubbed himself against me, and my mind kind of skipped a beat for a second.

Now that I'd had some sleep, I was beginning to realize how far out on the ragged edge of fatigue I'd been. I still wasn't one hundred percent. I could have corked off for a long nap right here in the Suburban. I was clear-minded enough to realize Dale had been right. I needed a break.

We parked the Suburbans in the guarded parking garage under the courthouse and rode an elevator up to a bland waiting area. Bolle checked his phone and looked at his watch.

"They're about to interview Lubbock. If you think you can avoid breaking the door down and beating the shit out of him, you can watch."

I nodded and followed him through a warren of corridors. A plain-clothes US Marshall checked our ID, then led us into a cramped room full of audiovisual equipment. A bored-looking tech sat inside, making sure the equipment was working.

On the monitor, Lubbock sat passively, his face bandaged. One eye was swollen completely shut, and his face looked asymmetrical. The US Attorney for Oregon, Ana Burke walked in. I recognized her from when she'd been a Multnomah County deputy prosecutor. I knew her to be a competent, smart woman, who had somehow managed to secure a political appointment anyway. She took a seat, organized her notes, and tugged on her right earlobe.

That was apparently the signal. The tech pressed the record button, and on the wall behind Lubbock, a small light illuminated.

"Before we begin, Mr. Lubbock, I need you to confirm that this is being recorded, and you've waived your right to have an attorney present."

"Yes," Lubbock said. He had a slight lisp, thanks to the stitches in his lip.

"Yes to both of those Mr. Lubbock? That it's being recorded, and you've waived your right to an attorney?"

Burke was being extra careful. Henderson Marshall had millions at his disposal, and Burke knew if she was going to go after him, every step she took would be scrutinized by defense attorneys.

"Yes, to both," he said. "I know it's being recorded, and I don't want an attorney."

I couldn't believe what I was hearing. Lubbock had been a cop long before I was hired. Surely he knew better than to talk to Burke without an attorney. Prisons were full of people who thought they could lie their way out of a situation. I'd put quite a few of them there myself.

"Good," Burke said. "Now, let's start at the beginning when Mr. Todd first approached you."

Lubbock began to talk, halting at first, then with greater fluency. Reading between the lines, Todd's recruitment of Lubbock was a classic seduction, not of the body, but of the ego. Lubbock had always been the subject of subtle ridicule in the Bureau, and he knew it. He'd made his bones by ass kissing during the brief tenure of a police chief that had been brought in from the outside. For some reason, that chief liked the cut of Lubbock's jib. The chief's tenure had been brief. The only thing that united the various warring factions inside the department was the threat of an outsider sitting in the chief's chair. After his patron had been gone, Lubbock was still a lieutenant but would go no farther.

Being approached by a real deal operator, a former Delta Force and CIA guy had made Lubbock feel like one of the guys. By a twisting series of internecine bickering, he'd been placed in charge of the

Person Crimes department in the Detective Division, a job usually held by a Captain. We'd seen a fall off in clearance rates, and a couple of minor personnel scandals and none of the up and coming Captains had wanted to sit in the hot seat, so we'd wound up with Steve Lubbock.

At first, Todd had met Lubbock for the occasional lunch, where he'd share tidbits of information about Cascade Aviation, and dangle the idea of a retirement job in front of Lubbock. After a while, Todd's questions became more direct, asking for information about the Bureau's counterterrorism investigations, security at the reservoirs, that sort of thing. Henderson Marshall also ran a security company called Transnational Resolutions, and Lubbock assumed he'd been asking because he was fishing for a city consulting contract.

Then the gifts had started: opera tickets, a free vacation to Europe, things that Lubbock's soon to be ex-wife always wanted. The requests for information became much more specific, and also started to cover any active human trafficking investigations. At some point, Lubbock must have realized he'd compromised himself, but by then it was too late. It was a classic agent recruitment, the sort of thing intelligence officers were supposed to do in other countries. Officially, they weren't supposed to do it here, but if you believed that, you probably believed in Santa Claus too.

When Gibson Marshall was arrested, Todd had borne down with full force, becoming vaguely threatening, and demanding constant updates on the investigation. He'd even demanded a copy of the investigative file. Lubbock had thought about coming clean, but he'd chickened out and provided Todd with up to the minute updates on our status and location.

By the time Mandy had been beaten and almost killed, Lubbock was in so deep there was no way out. Todd owned him. So when Todd told him to pull all the security back from Powell Butte Reservoir at a certain time, Lubbock had desperately wanted to believe it was a ploy to detonate a small device, that wouldn't hurt anybody, but inspire the city to spend millions on upgraded security.

One of the things I noticed as he talked was it was all about him. He'd been complicit in Mandy being beaten almost to death, abetted human trafficking of teenage girls, and assisted in a terror attack on US soil, but as he talked his whole spiel was about how he'd been a hapless victim. The thought that maybe the badge he wore obligated him more than the average person never seemed to occur to him. He was so pathetic I couldn't even get worked up enough to be angry with him.

Burke circled back and started asking clarifying questions. Bolle looked at his watch.

"We need to head back. Your turn to be deposed is coming up."

I nodded and we slipped out. I followed Bolle to the elevator.

"What kind of plea are they giving Lubbock?" I asked.

Bolle didn't meet my eyes for a second. I felt a sinking feeling in my stomach that had nothing to do with the elevator.

"He's going into WitSec."

The Federal Witness Security program, colloquially named as "Witness Protection."

"So he's walking? He helped Mandy get beaten, facilitated a terror attack, and shot me in the chest and he's walking?"

Bolle still wouldn't look me in the eyes. I was too tired to be pissed. I guess at this point nothing surprised me anymore.

The elevator stopped at our floor.

"Sometimes to catch the big fish, you have to let the little one go," Bolle said. "This way we don't have to explain the multiple facial fractures, and the fact that he'll likely never see out of that eye again. Think about that the next time you arrest somebody."

With that, he got off the elevator and walked down the hall.

I almost let the door close so I could ride the elevator down to the ground floor and walk out. But Alex was still somewhere in here.

Besides, I needed to see this thing through. After that though, I was going to walk away from all this and never come back.

CHAPTER THIRTY-TWO

The rest of the day passed in a familiar pattern of sitting in a bland waiting room until it was my turn to be interviewed. First, I gave a deposition to one of the assistant US Attorneys for Oregon, a guy in his forties with a bad comb-over. There were no surprises here. He knew exactly what questions to ask, and more importantly, what not to ask. I knew the right answers, and the whole thing was over in about an hour.

The grand jury hearing wasn't much harder. This group of sixteen jurors were in the middle of their run, so they were still fresh enough to be interested, but they had been at it long enough that they didn't ask lots of questions about things that didn't matter. Over the years I'd had some grand jurors throw me some real curve balls, mostly because they watched too many cop shows on TV. These folks mostly sat quietly and listened in rapt attention as I described being kidnapped off the street in Portland, the search of the trailer and compound, the shootout at the reservoir, and finally the evidence that had led us to Lubbock. There were quite a few wide eyes when I described running into the machine gun fire at the reservoir, and I as I told it, I felt my stomach clench up. I had the story down pat by now, and it was over with quickly.

As I exited the jury room, Alex was on her way in, so I didn't get a chance to talk with her. In the waiting room, Casey was doing something on a laptop that I found indecipherable, Dalton was taking a cat nap, and Eddie was reading a thick Russian novel. I sat there for a while, lost in thought, relieving the moment that Struecker had been shot over and over in my head. I knew eventually I was going to have to let it go, but for right now I worried over it like a dog with a bone.

Finally, Alex was done, and Bolle led us into a conference room. He was full of nervous energy, like a kid on the first day of school. After a few minutes, Burke came in.

"The grand jury voted to indict Rickson Todd on over thirty felonies," she said without preamble. Everybody in the room relaxed. Maybe this had all been worth it after all.

"I could probably indict Henderson Marshall right now, but I couldn't convict him," she continued. "I need you to keep working. Marshall and Todd are the biggest threat to our national security since 9/11, and I want to put both of them in prison."

She paced the room in front of us.

"Marshall has millions. He also has powerful friends. This isn't going to be like forcing a plea bargain out of some low-level drug dealer. This case will probably go to trial, and every single facet is going to be scrutinized by the best attorneys Marshall's money can buy."

She looked at Bolle, then at me. "The slightest hint of prosecutorial or investigative misconduct will get picked apart and questioned. This thing could take years between trials and appeals. The case package you present to me has to be absolutely clean if I'm going to proceed."

That was a pretty loud and clear message. I wondered how much she knew about what had really happened. I didn't envy Burke. This case was a giant hot potato. There was no telling how many worms were in this can. Marshall was probably only one of many people involved. She was in her early fifties. She would be lucky if the whole thing was finished before she retired.

It was the sort of thing that would make or break a career. If she won, she'd be the prosecutor that took down a massive conspiracy to conduct a terror attack on US soil. If she lost, she'd be a laughing stock. Even if she won, she'd no doubt make some powerful enemies.

I wondered how much more of my life I wanted to devote to all this. I looked over at Alex. Her mouth was set in a hard little line and she was picking at an imaginary piece of lint on her dress.

I wondered if it would be easier if both Todd and Marshall caught a bullet in the head. It worked out pretty well for Marshall junior.

Burke excused herself, and Bolle stood up.

"You've all done outstanding work. As of a few minutes ago, Rickson Todd is a Federal fugitive. We're putting his name and description out quietly at first, to people in agencies we trust. But within a few days, there's a good chance you'll see him on the FBI's ten most wanted list."

"In the meantime, we're officially on stand down for two days. We all need a break. Tomorrow, Drogan, Byrd and I are going to escort Struecker's body home to the East coast. Tonight, we've got some activities planned for back at the base that will hopefully help everybody relax."

Some of us blinked at Bolle's mention of "activities." I hoped to God we weren't going to be doing a ropes course, or trust falls or something like that. I wasn't particularly in the mood to be social.

Bolle led us back down to the Suburbans in the parking garage. I realized that even inside the supposedly safe confines of the Federal building, my head was still on a swivel. I was checking doors and corners, looking at the hands and waistbands of everybody we encountered in the halls. Bolle was right. I needed a break.

The ride back to the factory was silent. Each of us was involved in our own thoughts, and fighting our inner battle with fatigue. Bolle did a bunch of texting on his phone on the drive back, which was unusual for him.

As we pulled into the parking lot, I smelled grilling meat. There was a pickup truck parked outside the garage door, and a big grill, which was the source of all the lovely smells. Dale was wearing an apron and flipping over steaks as we rolled up, and his son Robert was setting up folding chairs and tables.

Bolle gathered everyone around, then stepped back as Dale handed the grill tongs over to Robert and walked up.

"I've been wanting to find some way to thank you folks, and this was the best I could do. You've all put in some hard work, and put yourselves on the line, to put those men that hurt my daughter where they belong. I don't even have the words for what that means to me. No matter what happens, I owe each and every one of you a debt. You'll always have a friend in me and my family."

Behind him, Robert nodded. I realized Dale was on the verge of tears, and I was choking up a little myself.

It turned out it was just what we all needed. After a week of gunfights, kidnappings and digging dead men out of the dirt, everyone needed to relax and let off some steam. There was enough food for everyone to be full several times over, and just enough beer for everyone to have two, but not more. That was a shrewd choice. I rarely drank more than a couple of beers in a sitting, but tonight I could have easily given in to temptation and gotten blotto.

By accident or design, Dale was sliding into the role of the group's senior sergeant. Bolle sat uncomfortably in a chair, as if afraid he might have to make small talk with somebody. I wondered if he'd ever eaten off a paper plate before. Dale made the rounds, making sure everybody was fed, and initiating small talk. I got to see a different side of Dalton. He was a funny bastard, with an almost inexhaustible supply of stories and anecdotes from his world travels. Eddie was just as funny, and soon the two of them had us laughing so hard we forgot the events of the last few days.

Alex sat next to me, and as we sat there in the warm hazy glow of a food coma, her hand kind of naturally found mine. For a while, I could sit there and pretend we had a normal life together, that we were a couple at a social event with friends from work. I guess in a way that was true, but most jobs didn't involve dodging machine gun fire.

Dalton finished one long, complicated story involving a misunderstanding with an Afghani rug merchant. Henry seemed to have a kind of hero worship thing going for Dalton, and was oblivious to how close Casey was sitting next to him. I wondered if Alex and I weren't going to be the only two fraternizing co-workers. When the laughter died down, Alex squeezed my hand and cocked her head towards the trailer.

We made our farewells. Eddie gave me a knowing little grin, but nobody said anything crass.

I followed her into the trailer. I stopped in the little kitchen, took off my pistol, unloaded it, and put in a drawer. Alex stood there with her arms across her chest, and I just looked at her, not sure if I should say something, or hug her, or what.

"I don't know what to do," I finally said.

"Everything is just so complicated right now," she said. "I don't really want to talk. Just come here."

That was a relief in more ways than one. I just pulled her to me and smelled her hair, grateful that she was still willing to be there with me. After a while, she kissed me and then things progressed from there.

We made slow, quiet love. Afterwards I think she was crying a little bit, but she turned away from me and I wasn't sure.

CHAPTER THIRTY-THREE

I woke up surprised at how good I felt. The problem with the trailer being parked inside the factory was there was no way to tell what time it was if the garage doors were rolled shut. I padded around quietly so as not to wake Alex and finally found my watch.

Damn. It was almost noon. That's why I felt so good. Sixteen hours of sleep was a fix for numerous ills. I managed to dress without making too much noise. Alex rolled over and muttered in her sleep, then was still.

I felt naked walking out of the trailer without a gun, but I made myself do it anyway. I was afraid more rustling around in the trailer would wake Alex, and I'd resolved to start taking some steps towards being a normal human being again.

I followed the smell of coffee to the watch room. Henry had the duty apparently. He was rumpled-looking as ever but had a certain satisfied expression that I recognized. Good for him.

He was playing with his airplane modeling software when I walked in. He gave me a wave.

"Coffee is fresh," he said.

I grunted my thanks and filled a mug with pure liquid goodness. Henry was a coffee snob, and could always be relied on to have a good brew on hand. It was black as midnight, with a perfect, oily sheen on top. I'm not sure what beans he was using but he managed to make coffee as good as it smelled. It took a sip and instantly the fog lifted from my brain.

Henry must have sensed my suddenly enhanced cognitive abilities, and decided it was ok to try to communicate with me.

"Bolle, Drogan, and Byrd are on their way east with Struecker's body," Henry said. "They are going to escort the coffin to Boston, then

Drogan and Bolle are flying back. Byrd's staying for the funeral. Apparently, he knows Struecker's family."

I nodded. Thinking about Struecker's death brought me back to reality a little bit.

"Everybody else is still asleep. Jack is over at the hangar, sleeping with the helicopter. I guess it needed some kind of maintenance and he finished it up last night."

I nodded. I was trying to figure out how I was going to spend my day. I wondered if I could convince Alex to get out of town with me. My SUV was still parked in the garage bay. Maybe we could head up into the mountains for a night or two.

One of the desk phones rang and Henry answered it. He listened for a second, then held the receiver out for me.

"It's for you. Some guy named Zach?"

For a second, the name drew a complete blank, then I remembered the security guard at the water reservoir.

"Zach, how can I help you?" I wondered if he could give us some more information about Lubbock. On the way back from grand jury the day before, I'd been making a list in my mind of loose ends that needed to be tied up. It was time to start thinking like an investigator again, and not a door kicker.

"Hey, uh, Detective Miller. This is Zach, the security guy from the Water Bureau?" He sounded uncertain like he'd debated calling and fully expected to be blown off by the real cops.

"Good to hear from you, Zach. You gave us an awesome briefing that day, and it really helped us out when those assholes tried to blow up the reservoir." I needed to shore up this guy's confidence before he flaked on me.

"It did? Wow. Hey, you remember those pictures you showed me, the one of the bald guy?" It worked. I could hear the confidence in his voice.

"I do."

"Well, I'm at the zoo right now with my daughter and I just saw him."

My stomach went cold.

"Are you sure it's him?"

"Pretty sure. I've been studying it on my phone. He's with five guys dressed as waiters."

"Where in the zoo?" My mind was racing, trying to figure out what to do next.

"The amphitheater, down by the elephants. There's a free kids' concert starting in a few minutes."

"Oh shit," I said. It was out of my mouth before I had a chance to think.

"They all went inside the cafe here. You want me to go inside and see if I can get sight of them again?"

"No. Zach, I want you to take your daughter and get out of there now. Right now. This is going to be bad."

"Uh, ok. Well, call me back if you need anything."

I didn't even say anything to him. I just hung up and turned to Henry, who was typing away frantically.

"Kids' concert at the zoo today," he said pointing at a computer monitor. "There's free admission. It's a multicultural event, kids from all over the place invited."

"Shit," I said. ?My brain was vapor locked. Bolle was gone and nobody had been left in charge.

"It starts at noon," Henry said. He pointed at the time at the bottom of the computer screen. "Sixteen minutes from now."

Having a definite deadline snapped me out of my fugue.

"Call Jack. Tell him to get the Little Bird over here. Then call Portland Police and the zoo. Try to get them to evacuate. I'm going to start waking our people up."

"I can wake everyone up," Henry said and mashed down on a button on the console in front of him. I jumped when an alarm klaxon blared. He let it ring for thirty seconds or so then turned it off and picked up a phone. I ran out into the hallway, nearly colliding with a bleary-eyed Dalton who was wearing PT shorts, a t-shirt and a pair of running shoes. He had an empty coffee mug in his hands.

"What the hell?" he asked.

"Todd is at the Oregon Zoo. He's going to shoot up a bunch of kids. Jack is on the way with the Little Bird."

Dalton set the mug down on the floor. "I'll unlock the gun cage."

I ran out into the factory floor. Dale was dressed and standing by the garage door, an unlit cigarette dangling from his mouth. Eddie appeared barefoot in the doorway of his trailer, rubbing the sleep out of his eyes.

"We're rolling in five. Gear up in the gun locker."

Dale started towards me. Eddie disappeared inside the trailer and reappeared a few seconds later with a pair of boots in his hand.

I turned and ran back towards the gun cage. Dalton was throwing gear into the hallway. It was a good idea because there was no way for all of us to fit inside at once. I picked up a vest, already laden with ammo, flash bangs, and other gear and threw it over my head. Dalton handed me a spare Glock pistol, which I shoved in the holster attached to the front of the vest. Then he tossed me a carbine and a helmet.

Dale and Eddie ran down the hall. Dale had his long gun slung over his shoulder and Eddie was trying to pull a boot on and run at the same time. I kicked a vest towards each of them and turned to Dalton.

"There's a kids' concert at the zoo. Remember the security guard from the Water Bureau? He saw Todd there with five guys dressed as waiters."

"Shit," he said and handed me a radio. "Cops?"

I stuffed the radio in a pouch and plugged the earpiece into my ear, trying to keep all the various cords and straps on the vest from getting tangled.

"Henry's trying. The concert starts at noon."

"Shit," he said again and handed me two more radios.

I turned to hand the radios to Dale and Eddie. Alex was standing in the hallway, wearing sweatpants, a t-shirt, and her medical backpack.

"I'm coming," she said. She looked so much like her father at that moment it was uncanny.

I opened my mouth to argue, then shut it. Instead, I turned to Dalton.

"I need another vest, helmet and carbine."

He handed them out without comment. Alex shucked her backpack and I helped her into the vest. She grunted at the weight.

"Will you ride inside the cockpit with Jack? There's only room for four on the skids."

"Ok," she said, ducking her head, so I could put the carbine sling over it. "Helicopters scare the shit out of me anyway."

As I handed her the helmet, I realized then she was scared. Her hands were shaking and the corners of her mouth quivered a little bit. Nobody would have blamed her for staying here, but she was coming anyway.

"I love you," I said before I had time to think.

She kissed me quickly on the lips. "I love you too."

I shoved the kiss out of my mind and looked around. We were a pretty motley looking bunch, with the t-shirts, gym shorts and what not, but everybody had armor and a gun.

"Let's roll," I said.

We trotted towards the factory floor. I could hear the clatter of rotor blades as we went. Jack was flaring for a landing as we broke out into the sunlight. The doors were still off the bird, and the benches were still rigged. Perfect. We ducked under the rotor arc and I helped Alex shrug out of her backpack. I clipped it to the back seat with a carabiner, then turned to see that she was buckling herself in.

Dale and I took one side of the helo, Eddie and Dalton took the other. I strapped the belt across my lap and pulled a headset off from where it was hanging on a hook. It killed the rotor noise a little.

I keyed the mic. "Henry tell you what was up?"

"Yup. Oregon zoo. Are we ready on the left?"

Eddie and Dalton both stuck their thumbs out so Jack could see them in the little mirror stuck on the sides of the canopy bubble.

"Ready right?"

Dale and I gave a thumbs up and we were off, lumbering into the sky in a running takeoff. The Little Bird's engine screamed and we cleared the parking lot fence by only a couple of feet.

Jack gained altitude slowly and pointed the nose of the helo west. I tried to look out at the horizon and not at the ground rushing by beneath my boots. I tried to decide if I would feel better if the Little Bird was higher in the sky or not.

Henry's voice crackled over the radio. "I'm on the phone with a Portland Police watch commander. He's confused as fuck and it doesn't sound like he believes me."

"Jesus. Was he asleep when somebody tried to blow up the reservoir? How about the FBI?"

"I'm going to try them next. Casey is on the phone with Zoo security. That's not going real well either."

Now that we were maybe a thousand feet over the city, Jack leveled off and poured on the power. We were about fifteen miles as the crow, or the Little Bird, flew from the zoo. The Little Bird could go well over a hundred miles an hour, and it felt like Jack had the throttles nailed. My eyes burned and stung in the wind, and I belatedly remembered the goggles on top of my helmet.

We screamed over the river and Jack gained a little more altitude as we headed for the west hills. The Oregon Zoo was sixty acres shoehorned into the west hills of Portland adjacent to Forest Park. It was really a bad place for a major tourist attraction. The terrain limited how big the zoo could grow, and made access difficult. It had been years since I'd been to the zoo. People never got murdered there, so I'd not had any reason to go. The last time I'd been had been over a decade ago, with a woman I'd been dating.

"We need a plan," I said. "Dale needs to be the primary shooter. This place is going to be packed with innocent people and if we do any shooting it needs to be surgical. We'll reconnoiter by air, and see if we need to find a place for Jack to set us down."

"Concur," Dalton said.

Dale gave me a thumbs up. On the ride over, he'd already fed a handful of match grade rounds into the magazine of the bull barreled . 308 rifle he cradled in his lap. Now he flipped open the scope caps and looked through the lens. The rifle he was toting was old school, a bolt action when most people favored a semi-automatic, but it was a precision instrument. Out to several hundred meters, he could not only hit a head sized target but pick which eye the bullet would enter.

I found myself hoping Zach had been wrong, that this was all a false alarm and we were all going to look like a bunch of idiots hanging out in our helicopter over the zoo. This was a nightmare scenario. Trying to sort out and engage a bunch of hostile targets in the throngs of parents and children at the zoo was doomed to failure.

I pushed all doubts out of my mind. I checked my carbine to make sure a round was in the chamber and looked through the electronic sight to make sure the dot was showing. I let the stubby little rifle hang off the strap around my neck, and checked my pistol. Everything was good to go.

We flew over Highway 26, Jack gaining altitude to match the slope of the hill.

"We'll be over the zoo in 30 seconds. Should pop out over the elephant exhibit," Jack said over the intercom. Instead of following the highway as it turned south, Jack flew due west, taking us over some trees so low the rotor wash made the tops of the branches blow around. Then we were over a giant, sandy enclosure and I saw an elephant run under the skids.

Ahead of us was the amphitheater. On the big lawn in front of it were hundreds of kids with their parents, sitting on blankets with their picnic baskets. Every head in the place was pointed in our direction and I saw all sorts of cameras and cell phones pointed in our direction.

"People on the roof of the cafe," Alex said. She sounded calm.

Jack had settled into a hover over the elephant enclosure. All of the elephants had run over to the other end and had formed a line facing us. I leaned forward so I could see out past the nose of the helicopter. I could see people walking around on the roof of the cafe a hundred or so yards distant.

"Jack, can you do a pedal turn so Dale can get his scope on them."

It wouldn't do to blow away a bunch of maintenance guys working on the HVAC system. From this distance, I could see a handful of men with white shirts walking around. A couple of them had black bags.

Jack pivoted the helicopter to the left, so the side Dale and I were sitting on faced the cafe. Dale raised the rifle to his eye.

"Guy with an AK-47," Dale said over the intercom. "He's pointing it at the crowd."

I opened my mouth to tell him to shoot when he pulled the trigger. A figure on the roof dropped like a rag doll. Dale rode the recoil and worked the bolt to chamber a new round.

A saw a winking yellow light from the roof, a muzzle flash.

"Incoming," Jack said and juked the helicopter around. All hope that this was a false alarm had vanished.

At least they were shooting at us, and not the kids.

CHAPTER THIRTY-FOUR

The Little Bird lurched to the side as Jack threw the stick over. We lost a little altitude and for a second I thought we were going to plunge into the elephant enclosure, then Jack leveled out and we were actually flying sideways towards the cafe.

"Dale," Jack said over the intercom.

The cafe was now less than 100 yards away. That was a chip shot for Dale. We were close enough now that I could see the men scrambling off the roof, save one, who stood out in the open, cranking off rounds with his AK. Dale's bolt gun spoke again and the muzzle flash winked out.

"I don't have a shot on the rest," Dale said.

Dale was being judicious about pulling the trigger. Unlike a shooting range, where there was a nice dirt berm to catch bullets, if we missed here there was a good chance a stray bullet would find its way into an innocent person. Even if we hit a hostile, the bullet could pass through his body and hit somebody on the other side. This was like the mass shooting at the mall, only worse. That time I'd only had to deal with one shooter.

"Best place to put you guys down is going to be on the roof of the building," Jack said.

"Copy," I said. "Set us down there."

There was also an excellent chance that we would roll right in on some asshole shooting at us from a concealed position, but this might just be the day we all got to be dead heroes. I had a brief image of a bunch of rifle bullets tearing into Alex's body, then pushed it out of my mind.

"Want me to stay and provide top cover?" Dale asked, as mildly as if he were asking me if I wanted to play a round of golf.

"Yes," I said. His talents were best used from an elevated position. Even from the roof of the cafe, his line of sight would be limited compared to what it would be buzzing around in the Little Bird.

"Unbuckle my kit from the back seat," Alex said.

"What?" I said as I craned my neck forward, trying to see ahead of us.

"They're going to shoot people," Alex said. "I'm going to help."

The likelihood that we would kill all the shooters before they hurt innocent people was zero. Telling her to wait in the helo would be stupid, both because she could help people and because there was no way she would listen to me.

A guy in a white waiter's outfit popped out from a corner of a building, cranked a couple of rounds off at us, and popped back, quicker than I could react. I raised my carbine, but all that was under the red dot was a scared looking woman clutching a small child. I jerked the muzzle off of her and tried to look everywhere at once.

The roof of the cafe was a convoluted mess, with a couple of tall spires that were supposed to look like the thatched roof of a grass hut, and a big glass dome that was the top of an aviary. Jack threaded through all that and brought the helo to a stop with one skid on a big metal air handler unit. There was an outdoor seating area below us, and a couple of umbrellas blew over.

I reached back, unclipped Alex's medical kit, and then jumped off the skid. I forgot to take the headphones off first, and nearly fell when I hit the limit of the cord. I pulled them off and Dale reeled them in. I made sure the ear-piece for my handheld radio was still in place, then I took a knee and looked around.

The lawn below was bedlam. People were running in every direction, grabbing their kids and leaving behind coolers, picnic baskets, and strollers. As the Little Bird gained altitude, I heard a couple of gunshots.

"Can anyone see that?" I yelled. I was looking for a way down. If I shinnied over the edge and hung, I would be able to drop down onto the dining area, but I would be dreadfully exposed while I did it.

"Can't see it," Dalton yelled. He and Eddie were both trying to simultaneously look around and stay low while Alex struggled into the heavy backpack.

"We need to get off this roof. Cover me," I said.

Dalton nodded. He ran over and knelt on the edge of the roof next to me, rifle barrel pointing out. I swallowed hard and made myself dangle my legs over the edge, then hang from my fingers, expecting a bullet between the shoulder blades all the while. I dropped and landed semi-gracefully, considering the all the gear I was wearing.

I shook myself off and knelt behind an overturned table. It wouldn't stop a bullet but it would at least be concealment. I gave a thumbs up and heard Dalton yell "moving" before he landed behind me.

I heard the rhythmic thumping of Dale's bolt gun over the sound of the Little Bird's engines.

"There are two white guys in the service road behind the cafe trying to get into a truck," Dale said over the radio. "We didn't hit them, but they ran into the crowd. Pretty sure one of them was Todd."

Eddie came down next, landing with surprising grace for such a big guy. Alex was smart. She took off the bag she'd just struggled into, dropped it to Eddie, then came down herself.

A fusillade of shots sounded from around the corner, and there was more screaming.

"Let's go," I said.

I got up and ran for the stairs that would take us down to street level. There was no time to come up with any real plan other than follow the sound of gunfire and hope to get there before too many people died.

We charged down the stairs, trying to point guns and see in all directions. Alex was carrying the most brutal load. She didn't have flashbangs and other tactical gear on her vest, but the heavy medical kit more than made up for it. She'd also never trained in how to perform in an active shooter response cell, but apparently common sense went a long way. She moved with us and kept her stubby little carbine pointed in the directions nobody else was covering.

Most of the shooting seemed to come from near the snack bar to the north. We passed dull gray lacquered steel shell casings on the pavement. There was no organized evacuation. People were just running in random directions. Some were just standing in one spot and screaming. I was in the lead, Dalton was behind and to my left, with Alex behind and to my right. Eddie completed the diamond by covering our rear, somehow managing to trot while looking backward.

We ran by the primate exhibit, where one wise looking old orangutan sat watching us pass with wise eyes, unfazed by the noise. There was another burst of gunfire, this time much closer, to our right. Out of the corner of my eye, I saw a man holding a rifle. I pivoted, bringing my rifle up.

Alex shot first. She fired two rounds in rapid succession, while still moving forward, just like her dad had taught her. The shooter dropped, firing a shot from his AK in the air as he went down. He hit the ground and the rifle fell out of his hand. He lay there, wide-eyed, gasping for air with bloody froth on his lips.

Alex froze, her carbine not quite pointed at him.

"What do I do? Do I help him?"

"No," I said. I aimed carefully, putting the red dot of my sight right on the wounded man's ear and squeezed the trigger. The little carbine had negligible recoil, and as I looked through the sight, I saw the top of his head fly off.

Dalton and I ran forward, trying not to step in the mess but getting some on our boots anyway. Dalton grabbed the man's AK while I ran my hands over him. He had a spare magazine stuffed in his waistband but nothing else, not even a wallet. He was a virtual twin to the guy we'd dug up out at Curtis's compound. Early twenties, Middle Eastern. Dead.

"No bombs," I said.

"OK," Dalton said. He popped the dust cover off the AK and pulled out the bolt carrier. He dropped the now useless gun on the pavement and tucked the bolt inside his vest.

"Let's go find the next one," he said.

Ahead of us, an elderly man lay in a fan of blood, not moving. His broken eyeglasses lay on the ground next to him. Farther down, a crowd of people was gathered around a screaming little girl.

I looked back at Alex, who still stood frozen.

"Good work," I said. "Now go be a doctor."

I pointed where the girl lay on the ground and that seemed to break the spell. She put the carbine on safe, let it hang on the sling and ran to the girl.

"I'm a doctor," I heard her say just as there was another rattle of gunfire. Then the Little Bird was overhead, flying sideways. I heard the thump of Dale's rifle and a spent .308 case fell out of the sky and bounced off the pavement by my foot.

"Got one," Dale said. "Over by the carousel."

"Is that four?" I asked.

"Yeah," Dalton said. "One left."

"And Todd," I said.

"And Todd," he agreed. "And his buddy."

"One by the snack bar," Jack said. "Shit, he just ducked under cover."

"Where is that?" I said, trying to picture the zoo in my head.

"This way." Dalton seemed to know where he was going, so I let him be the point of the triangle. I took the right. Eddie took the left. Now the two of us would have to share responsibility for covering our backs.

Alex was kneeling over the girl, digging into her pack with gloved hands. I wanted to ask Eddie to stay behind to cover her while she worked, or do it myself, but it would be wrong.

I heard the pop of a gunshot from up ahead. It sounded like it was from a pistol. Then I heard the heavier knocking sound of the AK-47.

Ahead of us the Little Bird dipped down so low the skids were at almost head height. The rotor blades were dangerously close to a dozen different obstructions. Jack had somehow found a pocket exactly the right size to stick the helicopter into without shearing the blades off.

"Looks like you've got a civilian with a pistol duking it out with the active shooter," Jack said.

"Got it," Dalton said. We passed a woman in her twenties sitting on the ground crying. Her arm was laid open by a rifle round and several people were clustered around her pressing clothes and even cloth napkins against her wound. I saw a guy start to pull out his belt and hoped he knew how to apply a tourniquet.

Ahead of us, in the open-air seating area by the snack bar, we saw a woman with a pistol. She was young, maybe thirty. She had a nose ring and one of those emo haircuts that looked like it had been done with a bowl and a pair of shears. The pistol was tiny, maybe a little .380 or .32. The shooter ducked out of the hallway leading to the bathrooms and cranked off a couple rounds at her. One missed. The other dug a chunk out of the concrete flower planter she was hiding behind, throwing chunks of dirt and concrete in her face, but she was game. She fired a round at the guy. I couldn't tell if she hit him, but he popped back out of view.

"Hey," I yelled, not quite pointing my carbine at her.

She whirled and fortunately didn't point the gun at us. She blinked at the sight of us standing there in jeans and workout clothes, while wearing the big tactical vests with "POLICE" stenciled on the front, then very carefully pointed the gun at the ground.

"It's ok that I have this!" she yelled. "I have a concealed handgun license."

She started to dig into a pocket.

"It's ok," I yelled. "Just get out of here."

She hesitated. I jumped when Dalton fired two shots right next to my ear. That was apparently the impetus she needed to run off, gun still in her hand. I hoped she had the sense to put it away before she ran into a wall of Portland cops descending on the zoo. I could hear dozens of sirens in the distance.

"He poked his head out but I didn't get him," Dalton said. "What do you say we do two bangs, about a second apart, and then enter."

That was a really shitty plan. There was a long, narrow hallway that led back to the bathrooms. Flashbangs or no, we would be rushing into a fatal funnel, with a guy waiting on the other side with an AK-47. Normal law enforcement strategy would be to surround this guy and wait him out, maybe throw in some tear gas. But that could take hours that we didn't have. He was likely the last shooter, but we weren't sure, plus Todd was still somewhere in the vicinity.

"You guys bang. I'll be first through," Eddie said. He'd handled the flash bangs like a live rattlesnake. Apparently, he preferred being the first through the door to throwing one.

"I wish I had my demo kit," Dalton said as he pulled a bang out of his vest. I wished he did too. We could throw half a block of plastic explosives through the door, and settle this once and for all.

I pulled out a grenade too. "I'll bang second. Whenever you're ready."

Eddie covered the doorway as we both pulled the pins on our grenades. Dalton threw first, and as the grenade sailed through the air, the muzzle of an AK-47 poked around the corner and spit flame. The guy was firing blindly. The rounds came nowhere near us.

The grenade sailed into the opening. I looked away and closed my eyes when it detonated, but I could still see the bright flash through my closed eyelids and the sharp crack was like an icepick into my already abused eardrums. I opened my eyes and chucked my own grenade through the opening. I had enough time to see that the muzzle of the rifle had vanished and that the grenade was on target, then I shut my eyes again.

There was another bright flash, but this time, the blast didn't seem as loud. All I could hear was a high whine. My ears were shutting down. Eddie was already in motion as I opened my eyes. I followed his broad back towards the doorway. He turned towards the opening of the hallway and I heard muffled shots.

Eddie hit the ground right in front of me, and I almost tripped over him. He stuck his carbine out in front of him like a big pistol and blasted away one-handed. I leaned over so I could see into the hallway. The shooter was lying on his back, shooting wildly. There was a giant scorch mark on his shirt where at least one of the grenades had caught him, and his face was burned. It looked like he was shooting blind.

I let loose a barrage of fire, busting off a third of a magazine. Between me and Eddie, the guy practically came apart. I stopped shooting, flipped my safety on and looked down at Eddie. He was sitting on his butt, blinking.

"Ahhhh…" he said. Blood was running down his face. I saw a neat little white hole in the front of his helmet, near the top.

"Check the shooter," I yelled to Dalton.

Velcroed to the front of our vests, each of us had a nylon pouch called a "blow out kit." I ripped Eddie's off his vest and pulled out a trauma dressing. I unsnapped the chin strap of his helmet and then hesitated. Eddie had a far away, unfocused look in his eyes and I wondered if the helmet was the only thing holding his head together.

I took a deep breath and pulled the helmet off. There was a big gash on the crown of his head, and a copious amount of blood flowed through his dark curly hair, but his skull looked intact.

I looked at the inside of his helmet. The bullet had curved between the layers of bullet resistant material, and the tip was poking out of the inside of the helmet.

"You are one lucky bastard," I said.

He looked at me with unfocused eyes. "I don't feel lucky."

I started winding the bandage around his head.

"That really fucking hurts," Eddie said through gritted teeth.

"I bet," I replied, and checked the rest of him out. There were two holes in the nylon cover of his vest. I stuck a finger in both. The ceramic plates of his armor had stopped the rounds from penetrating. Either could have easily been a lethal wound.

"Does your chest hurt?" I asked.

He took a deep breath.

"Yeah," he said, and frowned as if he realized it hurt for the first time. Multiple injuries were like that. Sometimes you got so focused on one thing, you didn't realize all the other things hurt.

"Excuse me?"

Eddie and I both turned. Standing in the doorway was the woman who'd been shooting at the terrorist. She was pulling on a pair of bright purple nitrile gloves.

"I'm an emergency room nurse?"

"Outstanding," I said as I stood up. "Can you help him out? He's not as scary as he looks."

She knelt down beside Eddie.

"Hi," he said, looking a little confused, then gave her a big goofy grin. Shock did weird things to people.

Dalton walked out of the hallway, tucking another AK-47 bolt carrier into his vest. He took in the nurse kneeling by Eddie wordlessly.

"You guys sure shot the shit out of him. Now what?"

Over the whine in my ears, I listened. I could hear screaming, sirens, and the sound of the Little Bird's rotors, but no more shooting.

I keyed my radio.

"Jack, I think we dumped the last shooter by the snack bar. What do you have?"

"We haven't seen any more shooting," Jack said. "We've been flying orbits. I can't pick Todd out of the crowd. Dale shot the tires out of the truck they were trying to get into, so we shut down his escape route. Most of the crowd is headed toward the main exit. You've got a wall of cops headed your way."

I stood there for a minute thinking. There were thousands of people milling around. All Todd had to do was blend in and he could work his way out of the perimeter.

"Let's head for the entrance," Dalton said. "We've got nothing to lose."

I looked at Eddie.

"I'm good, bro. Go get 'em," he said.

I looked at Dalton.

"All right. Let's go hunting."

CHAPTER THIRTY-FIVE

I was exhausted, but we ran anyway. The path to the exit sloped uphill and I lowered my head and charged. Dalton took off at a ground eating pace that I found hard to match. We passed two more dead people, a man and a woman, but thankfully no children. We passed more people who were wounded, and I was glad to see that every one of them was being helped by someone. It was good to see ordinary people stepping up and helping out. Plus, selfishly, I was glad I didn't have to make the choice between looking for Todd and leaving somebody to bleed out alone.

I was breathing hard, and there was a stitch in my side. I was fighting the urge to ask Dalton to slow down, and on the verge of losing when he stopped so fast I nearly bowled him over.

"Look," he said. He pointed over towards a cotton candy stand. There was a golf cart there. He sprinted over to it and slid behind the wheel while I bent over with my hands on my knees and hyperventilated.

"It works!" he said, backing the cart up next to me.

With my armor on, I barely fit. My butt had no sooner touched the cushion than Dalton stomped on the accelerator and my head snapped back. Dalton weaved among the fleeing zoo attendees while I tried to catch my breath.

I caught my breath and keyed my mic.

"Alex? You there? You ok?"

"I'm fine," she snapped. "Busy."

Well, that was good to hear.

We weren't seeing any more wounded people. The shooters hadn't penetrated this far into the zoo. The crowd was now mostly older folks, and people trying to tote small kids up the hill. They all looked scared and confused. One woman saw my rifle and screamed.

"It's ok," I said. "We're cops."

The Little Bird passed overhead.

"You're about to run into a bunch of Portland Cops, by the mountain goat exhibit," Jack said on the radio.

Dalton let up on the accelerator a little and then we were confronted with a phalanx of a dozen Portland cops in groups of three or four. They weren't trying to stop anybody, just eyeballing everyone who was trying to leave, to make sure they weren't carrying weapons. Behind them groups of SWAT operators were forming up with Portland Fire and Rescue medics, forming teams to go in and look for the wounded.

"Federal Agents!" I yelled and kept my hands away from my rifle.

A bald sergeant nodded and waved us forward.

"Most of the wounded are down around the primate area and the concert lawn," Dalton said. "Where's your command post?"

"Mall security office," the sergeant said.

Dalton nodded and drove forward. It was the right move. The sergeant didn't try to stop us, and we didn't get bogged down trying to establish our bona-fides.

Soon the crush of people was too heavy and we abandoned the golf cart. The zoo exit was in sight.

"The command post is liable to be a cluster fuck," Dalton said. "Todd will be gone by the time we convince them to listen to us. We just need to John Wayne this."

I nodded in agreement. We forced our way forward through the crowd, and out the turnstiles. The parking lot in front of the zoo was a sea of flashing lights and people. A bunch of cops and zoo security people were trying to do their best to create some kind of order. I dashed into the parking lot and found a minivan. I climbed up the hood and onto the roof, trying to look through the sea of faces.

"Good idea," Dalton said. He ran over to a pickup a few rows over and climbed up on top of the cab.

This was hopeless. There were thousands of people in my view. The cops were telling everyone to run to the Children's Museum on the other side of the parking lot. Some people were obeying. Others had gotten into their cars and were trying to flee, only to add to the congestion in the parking lot. As I watched, two Subarus backed into each other with the thump and crunch of metal and plastic.

More people were thronging towards the elevators to the MAX

station. A tunnel for the city passenger rail system ran under the street level here, and people were lining up to take the ride down. Others were just walking towards the park.

Then I saw him. The crowd parted for an instant and I locked eyes with Rickson Todd. There was another, younger man next to him with a high and tight haircut. They both looked like sharks swimming in a sea of fish. They were both carrying laptop sized bags slung over their shoulders. I was willing to bet there was something other than computers in them though.

Our eyes locked for an instant, then he was gone, swallowed up by the crowd of people.

"I just saw him," I said on the radio as I climbed down off the mini-van. "He's headed north, towards the elevators."

Dalton caught up with me as I started running through the parking lot. We weaved between cars snarled in a traffic jam and people on foot milling around aimlessly. Jack hovered low overhead.

We managed to work our way through the parking lot, one row at a time. A woman in a Volvo nearly backed over me. I climbed on top of a Honda and the owner started yelling at me to get down.

"I see him. Over by the elevators," Dale said. "I don't have a shot."

I stood up on the roof of the Honda, ignoring the owner who was screaming at me that he was going to sue me. I didn't see Todd but I did see his buddy. He was standing in a clear space as if the fleeing civilians sensed he was bad news. I brought my gun up, but there were too many people passing behind him and between us for me to get a clear shot.

As I watched, he reached into the bag and pulled out a stubby little machine pistol. In one fluid motion, he extended the stock and shouldered the weapon, sighting in on the Little Bird.

"Jack..." was all I had time to say before he mashed down on the trigger. The gun spat fire as Jake banked the Little Bird to the left. For a second I was sure the rotor blades were going to hit some of the parked cars. Then Jacked saved it and pulled the collective up, gaining altitude.

"Caught some rounds," he said over the radio. He sounded shaky.

I scrambled down the hood of the Honda. The owner had wisely made himself scarce at the sound of the gunshots. Dalton and I ran.

In some ways, the gunfire had made this easier. People had scattered away from the elevators at the sound of the shots. I saw Todd's buddy running towards the elevators, stuffing a fresh magazine into the machine pistol as he ran. I stopped running, put the red dot of my sight between his shoulder blades and put my finger on the trigger, but a screaming woman ran between us. I jerked my finger off the trigger like it was burning hot, and swallowed hard. I'd very nearly shot her.

Dalton pulled ahead of me. The crowd between us and the elevators was gone, leaving just us, Todd and his buddy. Todd was standing with one arm holding the elevator doors open, the other hand held a machine pistol outstretched. He dumped the magazine at me and Dalton in short staccato bursts. We both dove to the pavement. I heard rounds crack overhead. Shooting full auto one-handed like that was a poor way to hit anything but I wasn't willing to tempt fate.

I risked a peek just in time to see the elevator doors slide closed. Dalton and I both got up and ran again. Out of the corner of my eye, I saw the Little Bird lurching in the air. It looked like Jack was looking for a place to land over by the Vietnam Veterans Memorial.

Dalton mashed down the elevator button and changed magazines in his carbine.

"Are we doing this?" I asked. "As soon as those doors open, they're going to unload on us."

"I have a plan," Dalton said. "How many bangs do you have left?"

I felt the pouches on the front of my vest. "Two."

"Perfect."

The elevator doors slid open and Dalton hopped inside. I followed before I realized he hadn't told me the plan yet.

The Washington Park MAX station was 259 feet under the parking lot. When the train line had been extended to the west, the transit company had bored a tunnel just under three miles long through the hill that was inconveniently in their way.

Dalton pulled a smoke grenade off his vest.

"I'm going to pop smoke as soon as the door opens," he said. "You bang right and left. Get a bang in your left hand, pull the pin but don't let up on the spoon. Then grab one in your right, and I'll pull the pin for you. When the doors open we'll button hook out the doors."

This was crazy, but I did it anyway. I pulled a flashbang out with my left hand and pulled the pin. I held the lever flush against the body of the grenade. As soon as I let it go, the three-second delay would start, and the grenade would go off, no matter what. I pulled the second grenade out with my right hand and Dalton pulled the pin. Then we posted on either side of the elevator door.

"It's been a pleasure serving with you," Dalton said. The elevator slowed and Dalton pulled the pin on the smoke grenade. It sputtered and sparked, then the elevator car started to fill with purple smoke. Dalton held onto it for as long as he could, then it got too hot and he dropped it on the floor.

The car stopped and the doors opened with a ding. Dalton kicked the smoke grenade out, then I let the two flashbangs fly, trying to expose as little of my body as I did so. I heard gunfire and the elevator wall opposite the door dimpled with impacts. The grenades cracked off within half a second of each other, and I was out of the elevator. I hooked around the opening, exiting on the same side I'd been standing on.

The purple smoke was so dense I couldn't see anything. I charged through the smoke, hearing more gunfire. The smoke started to get a little thinner and I could see light, and a vague figure with arms outstretched in front. I raised the carbine, getting the red dot on target, but holding my fire until I could take another couple of steps and positively identify my target.

The smoke cleared slightly and I realized it was Todd. We fired at the same time.

An impact drove the carbine back into my face. I felt like I'd been hit with a bat. I dropped to my butt. I couldn't see and experienced a moment of vertigo. I wiped something wet out of my eye. Things were still blurry.

I brought my carbine up and realized I couldn't see through the optical sight mounted on top. I dropped it, letting it hang on its sling, and pulled my pistol out just in time to see Todd vanish down the rail tunnel.

A big red spot of blood hit the ground in front of me and I realized I was bleeding. My head and neck hurt and I could barely see.

I reached up and even through my gloves could feel a flap of dangling skin right over the bridge of my nose. At least now the blood was running down my nose instead of into my eyes.

I checked my gear. The optical sight on my carbine was smashed. A bullet had hit it right in the base where it was mounted to the top of the gun's receiver and drove it back into my face.

The gun had backup metal sights, but they would only work if I ditched the optic. I pulled on the lever that would pop the optical sight off, but it was hopelessly jammed. Above us, the giant suction fans that kept the air flowing through the tunnel complex were starting to clear the purple smoke from the grenade.

"Need some help, Dent." I heard Dalton's voice from behind me.

I spun around on my butt, not trusting my balance. Dalton was propped against a set of elevator doors, sitting in a pool of blood. A dozen yards past him, I saw Todd's companion lying in a puddle of blood and skull fragments.

Dalton looked pale and was struggling to wrap a tourniquet around his right thigh. I fought to my feet and made myself stumble over. I felt woozy and off balance.

The bullet had entered Dalton's thigh midway between his hip and knee. The entrance was a neat little hole, but the exit was huge and ragged. I saw a splinter of bone poking out and grimaced. The blood flow was heavy, but not spurting out like an arterial hit. I helped him secure the tourniquet and wrapped a pair of combat dressings around it as tight as I could.

"Fuck," he said. "I did six tours and it's an asshole in my own country that aces me?"

"We need to get you to a medic," I said. I wondered if I could pick him up and put him in the elevator.

Dalton keyed his radio, then shook his head.

"I got nothing."

I knew it wouldn't work, but I tried mine too. I mashed down on the transmit button and was rewarded only with a harsh beeping sound that told me radio wasn't communicating with the network.

"Me either," I said.

"You need to get your ass down that tunnel and finish Todd," Dalton said.

"I can't leave you."

He pushed me in the chest.

"Go. The only thing that will make this worth it is if you smoke that asshole. He took everything from me, and now I can't even walk. Get your ass down there. There will be a bunch of cops down here in a few minutes. I'm not going to bleed to death in that time."

I looked at Dalton's leg. The bandages hadn't soaked through. He lay back and with a moan pushed his foot up against the wall, so his leg was elevated above his heart.

"Ok." I stood. I was less dizzy but I still felt unsteady. A big drop of blood fell off the tip off my nose and splatted on the ground, but it was nothing compared to Dalton's wound. I was having trouble breathing through my nose and realized it was probably broken. Again.

"Good hunting," he said, and then, feeling like I was doing

something wrong, I ran for the tunnel.

There were two parallel tunnels, one for the eastbound trains, one for the westbound. I went over to where Todd had vanished into the darkness. A narrow walkway ran along the side of each tunnel, vanishing into blackness. There was a pile of shell casings in front of the entrance, and a splash of blood.

Running down the tunnel, with the lights of the platform behind me, I'd be silhouetted, and an easy target for anyone lying in wait. I realized my fear of dying was gradually being replaced with a mild curiosity about how it was going to happen.

There was a paltry little waist-high gate blocking access to the walkway. The walkway along the side of the tunnel was a couple of feet wide. I wasn't going to have to worry about getting smashed by a train as it went by, but it was an awfully narrow space to be charging into gunfire.

At first, there was plenty of light spilling into the tunnel from the platform. As I moved forward I saw drops of blood about the size of a quarter every few feet. There was a dark shape on the concrete in the middle of the walkway and as I crept closer I saw it was a Heckler and Koch machine pistol. I examined it briefly and saw the bolt was locked back on an empty magazine. Apparently, Todd had emptied it, and lacking any more ammo, had abandoned it in the tunnel.

I didn't have any use for it, so I left it. I had my own pistol in my hand, and the useless carbine slung across my back. I realized, too late, that I should have taken Dalton's carbine. I didn't want to go back now.

The farther I got from the platform, the darker it became. So far there hadn't been anything on the walkway that would trip me, but I couldn't just stumble around in complete darkness. I couldn't remember the exact number, but I remembered the tunnel was something like three miles long, with the station more or less in the center, so I had a mile and a half of creeping around in the dark.

There was a powerful light clipped under my pistol, and another flashlight in a pocket of my vest, but turning either on would be a big invitation to getting shot. In the pocket of my jeans, I found my car keys. I hadn't driven my personal vehicle in what felt like forever, but I still habitually stuffed my keys in my pocket. Clipped on my key ring was a miniature red LED flashlight.

I held the gun in my right hand and my key ring in my left. As I crept forward, I squeezed the little light on in bursts and random intervals. The concrete underfoot was light colored so the drops of blood showed up black under the red light.

I saw a dim blue light up ahead. I crept up to it and realized I was looking into a video camera. There was a yellow box with "Emergency Phone" written on the side. There was a door here. I pulled on it. At first, it didn't want to open but I gave it a hard tug and it finally gave with a squeal of hinges. I blipped the light under my pistol for a fraction of a second and saw a narrow, empty passage with another door at the other end. Apparently, there were cross passages connecting the two tunnels. That made sense.

I shut the door and turned back to the train tunnel. I blipped the light under my pistol again, turning it on for only a fraction of a second, then sidestepping as far as I could without falling onto the track. I didn't see anybody or collect a bullet in the face, so apparently my quarry wasn't close.

Still, I felt like a sitting duck as I opened the call box and picked up the phone. There was a single button in the box, so I pressed it. I heard a long beeping tone in the earpiece, then silence. I was just about to give up when someone answered.

"Operations. You need to get out of our tunnel." He sounded like he was chewing on a sandwich as he talked.

"This is Special Agent Dent Miller of the Joint Interagency Task Force. I'm chasing an armed suspect in the east half of the tunnel."

He didn't say anything and except for the heavy breathing, I would have thought he'd hung up.

"Uhhhh... I have to talk to my supervisor. Stay on the line."

I left the phone dangling and moved on. I didn't have time for TriMet to get its shit in one sock. They'd probably had to hold a board meeting or something to decide what to do. Instead, I kept moving down the tunnel, balancing the need to hurry, with a need to not walk into a bullet.

I moved forward at a jog. My head throbbed in time to my feet pounding on the pavement. I passed two more of the side passages, with their cameras and call boxes.

The drops of blood on the concrete in front of me were getting bigger, and closer together. Now they were half the size of my palm and spaced less than a stride apart. I debated whether to slow down. With any luck, Todd would either die or pass out, and I'd find his body here on the platform. I could decide then whether to put a bullet in his limp form or not.

I felt the train coming before I heard it. At first, it was a gentle breeze, barely perceptible on my cheeks, then a real wind, enough to ruffle my hair. Probably, I should have heard it sooner, but my ears were ringing thanks to the gunfire and explosions. I finally heard it about the same time as I saw the light. The tunnel here had a very subtle curve to my left and the headlight played on the wall, then came straight at me.

My eyes, adapted to the dim light of the tunnel, shut down in the bright light. I squinted and hugged the wall as the train bore down on me. I knew as long as I stayed close to the wall of the tunnel, there was no way the train could hurt me, but as the bore of the tunnel quickly filled with hundreds of tons of metal going fifty miles an hour, my lizard brain was screaming I was about to get smashed.

The inside of the train was lit up. Most of the passengers didn't see me, but one woman did a double take as the train flashed past.

It was terribly loud, which was why I didn't hear the gunshots. My first clue I was being shot at was when a chunk of concrete flew off the wall and smacked into my shoulder. I thought something had flown off the train, then another one smacked me square in the center of the chest, like a hard punch, and I realized what was going on.

The train was past me, quick as it had come, and I dove off the platform and onto the tracks. I didn't have far to go. The platform was only at waist level above the tracks. I didn't exactly stick the landing. I was grateful for the hard plates in my vest as I hit the train track with my back.

I replayed what had happened. Apparently, Todd had been lying in wait for me, and when I was illuminated by the lights of the train had started shooting.

I fingered the hole in the front of my vest. If I'd been wearing a soft vest, like the one patrol cops wear under their uniforms, I would be hurting. The hard plates I was wearing were rated against rifle fire.

Damn, I thought. *That's twice.*

I rolled up onto my haunches but didn't stand up. I stayed there in a low squat, rather than stick my head out above the level of the platform.

Now what? I thought.

I didn't have to worry about getting electrocuted. The train drew its power from an overhead line, so I could step on the rails without worrying about getting fried. I supposed another train would come, but I would have enough warning to chin up onto the walkway if that happened. Besides they were usually at least fifteen minutes apart. This would be over one way or another by then.

I couldn't see much down there. I strained my ears to hear anything. I hoped for some noise, the scuff of a shoe, jangle of keys, something that would tell me where he was. Todd probably wasn't that stupid though. I felt a burst of fear that came from being outclassed. Todd was a former Delta guy, way out of my league, and I wondered if I was about to die.

He was also bleeding, and probably in some amount of pain. If there had been more blood on the walkway, I'd have been tempted to just try to wait him out, but there was a chance it would take him hours to bleed out, and he'd have plenty of time to reconfigure a bandage.

The shots had come from the east, towards the mouth of the tunnel. What had he done after shooting? Had he hauled ass and run? Had he stayed put? Or was he now creeping up the walkway towards me?

Slowly, and as quietly as possible, I moved over towards the walkway, and pressed up against it, still in my squat. My thighs were killing me, and I knew I couldn't hold this position for much longer. He'd have to be practically on top of me to see me. There was still a big purple splotch in the center of my vision thanks to the train headlight. Inwardly I cursed myself for making such a hambone mistake.

I tried to think of something clever. I was out of flashbangs, not that I would want to detonate one in the confined space of the tunnel. I had one smoke grenade left. That wouldn't do me any good. The goal was to see more, not less. I had several magazines for my smashed rifle, a couple for my pistol, some flex cuffs, a push dagger on my belt, and a folding knife in my pocket.

I had some chemical lights, little plastic tubes that would light up if I broke a vial inside and shook them to mix two chemicals together. I eased one out of its pouch, thinking maybe I could snap it and throw it up on the walkway, then move up the tracks before I got shot. If I could get a couple of them up there, I might be able to bracket him with light.

That plan sucked. I was acutely aware that sooner or later, my luck was going to run out if I kept pushing shitty plans.

Right as I was getting ready to snap the light and throw it, I heard a soft, scuffling sound. What was it? Was it a shoe sole on concrete? Or was it a rat? Did the tunnel even have rats?

I was pretty sure it wasn't my imagination. Sound was funny down here in the tunnel, and my abused ears didn't make it any easier, but I was fairly convinced I'd just heard the scuff of a shoe on the platform right over my head.

Now what? If he was on to me, all he'd have to do is lean over the platform and put a bullet in the top of my head. To further complicate things, I was still squatting, and my thighs burned. I needed to shift positions soon or I was going to fall flat on my ass. I was already worried that when I tried to stand my legs would give out.

I didn't snap the chemlight, but I threw it off in the dark, down the tracks. I heard another scuff from above, and the slightest intake of breath. He was right above me.

I pivoted as I stood, and turned on the light clipped to my pistol. There he was. In stark relief in the harsh brightness, I saw Todd. I had a scant half-second to take in the blood soaking the bottom part of his white shirt and the pistol in his hand before I started squeezing the trigger. He was looking down the tracks, his pistol pressed out in front of him when I planted the front sight on his side and let loose.

He pivoted towards me, bringing his gun around, as I triggered three fast rounds into him, pausing between shots only to get a glimpse of my front sight before pressing the trigger again. Pistol bullets rarely drop somebody instantly, which was why I was shooting fast, but I was surprised to see no reaction from him. In that peculiar slow motion of a gunfight, I clearly saw the muzzle of his gun swinging towards my head. I tripped off two more shots, quicker this time, not even stopping to find my sight after the first one.

People frequently get shot in the hand in gunfights. They have a weapon pressed out in front of them, and bullets tend to go where people look. As I recovered from recoil from the second shot, I saw the pistol drop from a hand hit by one of my bullets. Instead of giving up, he lowered his head and charged me.

I had time to crank off another shot or two as he launched himself at me, then he slammed into me like a cruise missile, driving me backward. I managed to tuck my chin, but still saw stars as my head slammed into the metal rail. My pistol went flying and the fight was on.

He was a beast. Wounded though he was, he was all over me. He'd managed to land straddling me, and inched his way up my chest, pinning me to the rails with his body weight. I tried the most basic of ground fighting maneuvers, bucking him off, but he was too high on my chest for that to work. He unleashed a rain of blows at my head. I covered my face with my forearms and tried to punch back blindly with my right.

That was almost a costly mistake. He grabbed my right arm and started to apply a joint lock, but I was able to slip out of his ruined right hand. It was slick with blood, and I felt a jagged edge of bone scrape against my hand as I pulled.

Todd was clearly more skilled on the ground. The only advantage I had was I hadn't been shot full of holes. In my free time after getting fired from the Bureau, I'd trained with a former Louisiana dope cope who specialized in exactly this type of fight. He called it a Fucked Up Tangle, and what I'd learned from him was about to save my life.

I fought that familiar panic that always came when I was pinned on the ground. I'd spent hours on the mat, just overcoming that panic before I could learn any actual skills. I tried to shrimp upwards, towards my shoulders, so I could get his weight lower down, towards my hips, and at the same time launched a sloppy attack upwards with my left hand.

My pistol was on the gravel, just out of arm's reach. The flashlight was still activated, and in the glow reflected off the sides of the tunnel, I saw him give me a predator's grin. He countered my moves easily, and actually managed to slide farther up on my chest, to the point his knees were in my armpits. That actually worked to my advantage, as it got him off my belt line. I reached past his body, where, strapped to my belt, just to the right of the buckle, was an odd little knife. The blade was about as long as my hand, and the handle was egg shaped. I grabbed it and the edge was oriented inward towards me, instead of out like most knives.

It had been designed for situations just like this. I'd tried all sorts of fancy martial arts shit when it came to knives. When my instructor told me "just jam it into him over and over like a monkey with a screwdriver," I knew I'd found my trainer.

I wrapped my left arm around Todd's waist and buried my head in his belly. My cheek was pressed against his bloody abdomen, and I almost retched at the taste of blood. It was hard for him to hit me in the head like that, but if I stayed that way there were all sorts of nasty things he could do to me. Hopefully, this wouldn't take long.

I jammed the knife in his back. I'd never stabbed somebody before. I was surprised at the amount of resistance to the blade, particularly when I tried to cut sideways. He gave a little grunt and doubled down on his efforts to punch me in the back of the head.

I pulled the knife out and tried again, lower this time. I felt the tip grate off the top of his hip bone, then sink into soft flesh. I realized he was wearing body armor. The first time I'd been stabbing him through Kevlar. I sunk the knife in as deep as it would go, then ripped sideways. That was why the edge was on the inside, I was stronger pulling than pushing.

He jumped like he'd been touched with a hot electrical wire. Hot blood ran over my hand. I pulled the knife out and stabbed again, this time reaching as far to my left as I could. I almost drove the point through my own left hand where I had him clinched, then adjusted. This time when I ripped to the right, I felt the blade grate against his spinal column.

Todd screamed an animal sound that I knew I would remember for many nights to come. He weakened and flinched away from the blade in his back. Even with him high up on my chest, I was able to roll, flipping him underneath me. I wound up on top of him, between his legs. In jujitsu terms, I was in his guard, and a skilled practitioner had plenty of options, but not when they were bleeding out from a knife wound.

Still, he tried. I was in a shitty position, with my shoulders right under his hips. He wrapped his legs around my head and neck and tried to put a lock on my outstretched left arm. I just kept stabbing into his lower abdomen, then managed to drive forward and up with my knees. I got his ass lifted up off the ground and started stabbing into his buttocks and perineum.

One blow sunk into his testicles. He screamed, and he broke. All thoughts of technique were gone. He simply writhed and tried to get away from the pain. His legs dropped and he tried to sit up. I drove forward with my legs and cracked him under the chin with the top of my helmet. Then I pushed his face into the ground with my left hand and slammed the Clinch Pick into his throat, then ripped out.

A hot spray of blood hit me in the face. I recoiled backward for a half-second, then stabbed again. His feet drummed against the floor, and then he was still. I rolled off of him, sweaty and hyperventilating. The taste of his blood was in my mouth. I tried to spit, but I was so dry nothing came out. I vomited instead and found I actually preferred that taste.

I got up on shaky legs, almost collapsed, then gained my footing. I was trembling all over, and my muscles burned. I managed to sheath the Clinch Pick with quivering hands and not stab myself in the process, then walked over to my pistol. I cleared a jammed shell casing and pointed it at Todd.

He was still and covered with blood, but I had this image of him rising up and trying to kill me again, like some monster from a horror movie. I took a step towards him, and without even making a conscious decision, put the sights on his forehead and squeezed the trigger.

The sound of the shot echoed up and down the tunnel for a long time.

"I probably didn't need to do that," I said out loud as I holstered the pistol. "But it made me feel better."

I took stock. I felt like I'd been dragged behind a truck, and I thought at least some of the blood on my face was from the re-opened cut on my head, and my chest hurt when I breathed but I didn't have any serious wounds.

With my last energy, I hauled Todd off the train tracks and onto the platform. I wasn't sure if hitting a body on the tracks would derail a train, but I didn't want to find out. I marked his body with a chemlight, then started walking back the way I'd come. I hadn't noticed the slight downward slope on the way out, but I sure noticed the uphill climb coming back. I gave some serious thought about just sitting down and waiting for someone to come to help me, but didn't want things to end like that.

I just trudged onward, thinking about nothing in particular other than the throbbing pain in my head, and the ringing in my ears. After a while, I perked up when I saw the light shining down from the station and started walking a little faster.

As I walked into the underground station, I ran into the Portland Police SWAT team and had about ten rifles not quite pointed at me. After a fun few moments establishing my identity, I found myself riding up in the elevator with a Sergeant and Lieutenant, both of whom stayed silent for the whole ride, but kept looking at me out of the corner of their eyes and standing as far away from me as they could to keep from getting any blood on them.

At the top, a paramedic bandaged my head, and then I climbed into the back of the Sergeant's car for a ride downtown. As we drove away, a light rain began to fall. There were still hundreds of people standing around outside the zoo, and through the rain-streaked windows, I looked at as many of them as I could, particularly the kids. I knew some people had gotten shot, but all these people were ok, and I was glad.

We pulled out past a cordon of police cars with their lights flashing, then with the smell of blood and gunpowder in my nostrils, I put my head against the door frame and fell asleep.

CHAPTER THIRTY-SIX

In the end, only four innocent people died at the zoo, none of them children. Many more had been shot. Quite a few of them had been saved by their fellow Portlanders who improvised bandages with t-shirts and whatever came to hand. I tried to tell myself that considering the number of shooters, we'd pulled off a miracle keeping the casualty count that low, but I knew those four deaths would weigh on me, just like the eighteen dead from the Pioneer Place mall haunted my dreams.

I managed to get cleaned up, and, after a massive jurisdictional fight between the Multnomah District Attorney and the US Attorney for Oregon, gave a deposition to both of them at once. They listened with rapt attention as I described the fight at the zoo and the long chase down the tunnel. I didn't pull any punches or leave anything out. Finally, I ran out of steam when I finished the story and the room was silent.

"Jesus. It sounds like something out of a movie," Burke said.

"Hell, I was there," I said. "And I hardly believe it myself."

I walked out into the waiting room to find Alex sitting there by herself. She looked up at me but didn't rise to greet me. She looked pale and somehow smaller, as if she'd shrunk into herself.

"Hey," I said. "You saved that girl."

"Yeah, I did."

She didn't say anything else, and I was kind of at a loss for words myself. The silence hung there between us.

"I shot that guy too," she said, finally.

"Yeah. You did good."

She nodded, didn't say anything for a little while.

"Then you shot him in the head, while he was lying there," she said.

"Yep," I said, and that was it. I could give a long laundry list of reasons why I'd done that. Every second we spent trying to secure a suspect was time his buddies could use to murder people. He could have had a bomb. I could go on for hours. But I didn't.

She rubbed her hands together as if washing them.

"Do you think my dad would have done that?" she asked.

"Yes," I said without hesitation. Al Pace had killed two men during his days at the Police Bureau, bad men, and never lost a moment of sleep over it. He would have shot that man without pausing for thought.

"I said I wanted in, didn't I?" she asked and gave a bitter little laugh.

I didn't know what to say to that. Violence had been a way of life for me for as long as I could remember. I was happy to get through a day without having to hurt somebody, but I didn't take it for granted. I guess even though she was a cop's kid, it just wasn't the same. I felt like there was a gulf between us that could never be crossed unless she saw and did the same things I'd had to do, which was the last thing I wanted for her. It seemed like I always wound up stuck in this place in my relationships.

The door to the conference room opened, and Burke stepped out.

"Dr. Pace, we're ready for you."

She stood and walked to the door, giving me a haunted look. I wanted to go to her, hug her, maybe kiss her, but she kept moving away from me and I didn't pursue her.

Downtown was quiet when I stepped out of the building. I saw Dale standing the regulation distance from the courthouse, puffing on a cigarette and talking on his cell phone. He nodded in my direction and I walked over.

"Well, I'm glad that's over," he said as he pocketed his phone.

"No kidding," I said. "Now what?"

I was asking myself that question as much as I was asking him. I had no idea what to do right now.

"If we were younger, I'd suggest we go get drunk and chase some women, but at our age that ain't likely to end well. What do you say we go see Dalton and Eddie up at the hospital?"

That seemed like as good an idea as any. Dale had the keys to a bland government sedan, and as we drove up the hill to Oregon Health Sciences University, we listened to radio coverage of the zoo attack. Much of what was being said was wild speculation, mixed with incorrect facts and the occasional bit of truth. In my experience, that was par for the course.

We parked in the garage and walked over to the hospital. The last time I'd been here, I'd found myself in a vicious fight for my life in one of the stairwells that ended with me ripping a guy's ear off and breaking his neck. He had been the third man I'd killed since leaving the army. Since then, I'd lost track.

Dalton and Eddie were sharing a room. Eddie was asleep over by the window, his head wrapped in a bandage. Dalton's bed was closest to the door. He was awake, with his leg propped up and encased in a complicated apparatus made of straps and rods that looked like it belonged in a museum for medieval torture devices. He was watching news coverage of the zoo attack with the sound turned almost all the way down.

Dale and I took seats and I handed Dalton the cup of coffee I'd picked up at the stand downstairs. He breathed in the smell like a starving man smelling a t-bone.

"My life is better, thank you." He was glassy-eyed and his speech was a little slurred. There was a myriad of gadgets hooked up to him by tubes and wires. One of them I recognized as a morphine pump. He was probably stewed to the eyeballs on opiates, and I didn't blame him.

"Femur's shattered," he said between sips of coffee. "This is gonna take a while. Probably get a titanium rod."

I winced. That was a horrible injury. He was lucky he wasn't getting his leg amputated.

Dalton shifted in his bed to get more comfortable, or maybe just less uncomfortable.

"Tell me what happened after you ran down the tunnel," he said.

I told him about the fight with Todd. It seemed like a bad dream to me. For hours after, right up until the time I went into the room to give my deposition, I'd been checking myself for wounds, to make sure I didn't have a hole in my somewhere that somebody had missed. Telling it for the second time seemed to make it feel like a more distant memory.

"You stabbed him in the junk? That's badass," Dalton said when I finished. "I can't believe that fucker's finally dead. I wish I could have been there."

"Me too," I said and meant it for multiple reasons. Someday I'd have to try to get Dalton to tell me his history with Todd, but today wasn't the day.

Dalton's attention was captured by the television. Henderson Marshall was on the screen. Apparently, he wasn't in Portland anymore. He was standing in front of a white sheet hung on a wall, with a rifle propped up next to him. I almost asked Dalton to turn up the sound, but then realized I didn't really want to hear Marshall's voice right now.

"One down, one to go," Dalton said, then mimed shooting the TV screen. He felt around on the arm of his bed for the button that would give him a hit of morphine from the pain pump.

"Oh, I'm sure there's more," Dale said as he stirred his coffee. "This shit never ends."

"No, it really doesn't," I said. At that moment my phone vibrated. I dug it out of a pocket and looked at the screen.

Need you back at ops. Strategy meeting with Bolle. Casey

I realized Dale was looking at his phone too. "No rest for the weary," he said as he stood to go.

Dalton was nodding off, so we slipped out quietly. As we walked out of the room, we nearly collided with a nurse who was pushing a cart laden with flowers, baked goods, and fruit baskets.

"Your friends in there are popular," the nurse said. "I guess word got out they were patients here and stuff has been showing up non stop."

Dale reached down and picked up a piece of bright orange construction paper with a child's drawing on it. It showed a bunch of stick people holding hands and an elephant. A very good likeness of the Little Bird hovered overhead. Scrawled below, I could just make out "Thanks for not letting me get shot at the zoo."

Dale was blinking, hard. I realized the old guy was trying not to cry in front of me, about the same time my own vision got a little blurry.

He put the card down on the cart.

"Make sure the guys in there get those, ok?" he said, then pulled a bandanna out of his back pocket and blew his nose.

The nurse nodded and squeezed him on the shoulder.

As we headed towards the elevator, our phones buzzed again.

"I was thinking about heading home," Dale said. "But I reckon I'll see this through."

"Yeah," I said. "I guess I will too."

Rose City Kill Zone, Dent Miller Thriller #3, is available now!

Did you enjoy Rose City Renegade? Please leave a review on Amazon!

Join the Dent Miller Army Mailing List and we'll send you a link to a free Dent Miller short story! We promise not to spam your inbox. We'll email you a few times a year, when there is a new DL Barbur book release, or we have something interesting to say.

Join by visiting www.dlbarbur.com

You can also check out the Dent Miller community on Facebook: www.facebook.com/dlbarbur

Made in the USA
Las Vegas, NV
11 February 2021